THE
BLIND
SPLIT

THE
BLIND
SPLIT

THE BLIND SPLIT

A Rosedale Investigation

LYN FARRELL

**CAMEL
PRESS**

Kenmore, WA

CAMEL PRESS

A Camel Press book published by Epicenter Press

Epicenter Press
6524 NE 181st St.
Suite 2
Kenmore, WA 98028

For more information go to:
www.Camelpress.com
www.Coffeetownpress.com
www.Epicenterpress.com
www.lynfarrell.com

This is a work of fiction. Names, characters, places, brands, media, and incidents are either the product of the author's imagination or are used fictitiously.

Cover design by Scott Book
Interior design by Melissa Vail Coffman

The Blind Split
Copyright © 2022 by Lyn Farrell

ISBN: 978-1-94207-873-9 (Trade Paper)
ISBN: 978-1-94207-874-6 (eBook)

Printed in the United States of America

For all the COVID-19 first line responders,
among whom I am proud to include:
My late sister, Susan Campione, R.N.,
My niece, Emily Durkin, M.D.,
My son-in-law, Bob Stuart, M.D. and
Will Schikorra, EMT.
They risk their lives for ours.

ACKNOWLEDGMENTS

I WISH TO ACKNOWLEDGE THREE INDIVIDUALS WHO shared their life stories with me. One discovered a brother she didn't know she had, one had an episode of transient amnesia after a fall and one whose daughter was comatose. She woke up when the family dog was brought to her bedside. Authors are magpies who pick up jewels whenever they see or hear them. I hope I did justice to your fictionalized story.

I also wish to acknowledge and thank Dr. Robert Stuart who always ensures the medical accuracy of the clinical details of a case. Any errors in medical matters are mine alone. Officer Robert Pfannes advises me on police procedure and has been very generous with his time. Tara Gavin, editor extraordinaire, used her keen eye and picked up several crucial oversights. The MSU Writing Group is my sounding board and always helpful. Thank you all.

Finally, I wish to thank the publication team at Camel Press, Jennifer McCord, Associate Publisher and Executive Editor, and Phil Garrett, President, Epicenter Press. Jennifer has been my writing coach on this one.

Without Jennifer, I would never have achieved my dream of being a published novelist.

ONE

Billy Jo Bradley was in the shower when she heard the phone ringing downstairs in the office of Rosedale Investigations. The Private Investigator business, headed by former Detective PD Pascoe, was located in a remodeled house just off the main square in the small town of Rosedale, Tennessee. Billy Jo's apartment was on the second floor of the building. She always kept the door to her apartment open, at least during business hours, so she could hear the phone.

It's probably Dory and she needs me to walk her dog, Billy Jo thought. Getting out of the shower, she donned a black bra and panties while mentally preparing to spend yet another day closeted in her apartment where she both lived and worked. She looked at herself in the full-length mirror, noticing she had gained a little weight in the last month. Trying to keep fit when all the gyms were closed hadn't been easy. Walking Dory's dog had been virtually her only form of exercise. She wiggled into a seriously tight pair of black jeans, put on a white blouse, and tugged a comb through her irritatingly long hair. Because the beauty salons were closed, due to the COVID-19 pandemic, it had been two months since she had been able to get a haircut.

Rosedale Investigations had been shuttered since the initial case of COVID-19 was reported in Tennessee during the first week in March. Although the Governor's Stay at Home order didn't go into effect until April, PD Pascoe closed their business immediately after hearing about a 44-year-old man who was positive for the virus and lived just outside the village of Rosedale. Having the epidemic land so close to home activated Billie Jo's latent germ phobia. She had been cleaning surfaces with bleach wipes in her upstairs apartment and the main floor office every day since.

The Governor's Stay at Home order sent shock waves through the community, already reeling from reports about the volume of COVID-19 cases in N.Y and other eastern states. As Billy Jo told her boss and adopted grandfather, PD Pascoe, while she usually prided herself on being a rebel, this time she planned to fully obey the social distancing and mask orders.

It hadn't been easy. It had been literally been two months since she had participated in any of her normal social activities. She missed the Romanov Club where she danced with Johnny, her invariably-stoned boyfriend. She was tired of her own cooking, too many pizzas, her out-of-control hair, and having to tell clients the office was closed. She walked downstairs and clicked "play" on the answering machine to listen to the message. It was Dory Clarkson's voice saying, "It's over, Billy Jo. The Governor lifted the Stay at Home order this morning."

She dialed her back immediately, smiling as she envisioned Miss Dory, an older African American woman who had joined the agency a year ago. Dory had taken Billy Jo under her motherly wing, providing guidance (often quite irksome) about her footwear and clothes. Not even waiting for Dory to say hello, Billy Jo said "Really? We're out?"

"We are, but the mask rule is still in effect for businesses in Rose County and we need to adhere to the social distancing guidelines. So what's on the docket?"

"Our two feuding couples, the Franklins and the Thompsons have decided to divorce. They no longer give a flip about the mutual adultery that was going on. Andrea Thompson will be marrying John Franklin and Barbara Franklin is engaged to George Thompson."

"A good result. I'll send both couples our bill, of course, but given the outcome, they may not pay the full amount. This stupid epidemic is costing us big time. If we haven't delivered a report to a client by the time they get a bill, they usually balk. Can you get a brief report written to go with the photos and the bill?" Dory asked.

"Of course."

"What else is happening?"

"You won't believe it, but Lexie Lovell, the client we saw last spring, has called again."

"Who? Sorry, Billy Jo, I can't remember the particulars," Dory said.

"She was the girl whose father died and left his estate to be split half and half between her and her brother. She hadn't known about the existence of this brother before her father's death and was quite justly pissed. She was extremely disappointed in him having a child with a woman who wasn't her mother. And now that he's dead, she can't tell him how she feels. Her father's accounting firm has finally been sold and his executor is ready to disburse the funds, pending our locating the brother."

"I remember now. Lexie was the one with the mother who was like the three monkeys with hands covering their eyes, ears, and mouth. When asked about the little brother, the woman had *seen nothing, heard nothing, and knew nothing.* It was all a pack of lies. Her husband has another *kid* and the wife knows nothing? Ridiculous. Women always know these things."

Billy Jo chuckled. "I believe you informed her in your most superior accent, 'Ma'am when you are ready to stop *prevaricating*, we will be happy to help.' Anyway, Lexie found some documents in her father's office that could help track down her brother. She is coming by later. Sorry, Dory, I've got another call coming in."

She quickly pushed the button to accept the incoming call from PD Pascoe, the founder of the PI business. PD had continued her paycheck during the shutdown with the explicit understanding that she would be present and working during business hours. If she missed his calls, he was not pleased. And he had avoided all her efforts to convince him to call her cell phone.

"Morning, Billy Jo. I presume you know the Governor lifted the Stay at Home order? I want to get the whole team together after lunch and go over our cases. What about that teen-aged boy, Richard Morelli, who went missing? Did you ever find out anything about him?"

"I did. Unfortunately, it was the kind of case that will only make us a pittance. The kid had argued with his mother and in a blazing feat of originality went to live with his father. The couple is divorced and the father forgot to inform the mother. What time is everyone coming in?"

"I told Wayne and Dory to show up for a staff meeting at one o'clock today. Better get the masks out. I presume you ordered them?"

"I did and I got one of those thermometers you use to take a person's temperature from a distance. I'll get everything ready and I'll wipe down the conference table and chairs," Billy Jo said cheerfully and hung up.

HUMMING TO HERSELF AS SHE CLEANED, Billy Jo was just about finished using bleach wipes on the conference room table when she heard the doorbell ring. In the past, they had left the front door unlocked, depending on a tinkling bell that hung from the doorknob to alert the team to anyone entering the building. She walked to the front door and peeked out. It had been raining since midnight and despite a fitful sun struggling to appear, the trees were still dripping. The blossoming shrub roses that lined the sidewalk leading to the front door were opening, lending a bright Paris pink to the wet walkway. Lexie Lovell was standing on the porch. She wore a dark red trench coat, high heels and carried a folder under her left arm. Opening the door just a slice, Billy Jo said, "Hello, Lexie. Sorry, I can't let you in at the moment."

"The Governor lifted the Stay at Home order today," Lexie said.

"I'm aware, and the Rosedale Investigations team will be here at 1:00. We're going to go over all our cases then. I'll call you as soon as the meeting ends and set up a time for you to come in and update us. Okay?"

"I guess," Lexie said, sounding frustrated and tapping her fingers on the black wrought-iron porch railing that was dotted with raindrops. "Maybe I should leave the folder with you."

"Sure. What's in it?" Billy Jo said, reaching through misty rain for the accordion-pleated file.

"As I told you on the phone, I finally got into my father's house. Stupid probate clerks wouldn't let me in until a couple of days ago. I searched his desk and his computer," she said.

Hearing the girl say she'd searched her dad's computer, Billy Jo, who was the computer guru for the business, thought it unlikely that Lexie had truly plumbed the depths of the machine. "Lucky you knew his password," she said, hoping the girl would inadvertently reveal it.

"It was my birthday, October eleventh. Anyway, I found the name of the woman who was shacked up with my father, a gold-digger of course, and the birth certificate for the kid, my so-called brother."

"That's great, Lexie. Really good work. Congratulations on your engagement, by the way. I saw your picture in the town paper," Billy Jo said.

Lexie held out her left hand with its modest diamond, her face pink with pride. "I'll wait to hear from you," she said, as she turned and walked down the shining sidewalk.

Closing the door, Billy Jo carried the damp folder to her desk and walked into the kitchen for coffee and another bleach wipe. She could hardly wait to delve into Lexie's case but it was still early and her brain worked better after a dose of caffeine. Luckily, she had started a pot of coffee before she took her shower. She had a feeling the case would be complex and if she was the one who solved it could be just the thing to push Detective Pascoe into finally making her a partner in the firm. From her admittedly biased perspective, he was running out of excuses.

RETURNING TO HER DESK, BILLY JO wiped the folder Lexie gave her with a bleach wipe and pulled out the entire set of documents. There was a photo of an attractive redhead. She was slim but looked about six months pregnant. There was a Pre-Nuptial Agreement, a tri-fold brochure of the islands in Greece, a card from a local florist reading, "You are more beautiful than Poppy," and the boy's birth certificate. Theodore Chase Lovell had been born in October. He would now be two and a half. The name of the father was Edward Lovell.

"He's just a toddler," Billy Jo murmured to herself. Quickly reading over the Pre-Nuptial document, Billy Jo scrutinized the name of the boy's mother. It was Pansy Jane Delaney. *This was going to be a piece of cake.*

Putting her fingers to her computer keyboard (she sprayed it with an anti-viral spray every morning) and hearing the machine spring to life, she felt a rise of satisfaction. "People are so predictable," she said aloud and clicked on the button for the facial recognition software. She laid the photo of Pansy Jane Delaney on the glass for the scanner and touched her mouse. Images flipped through rapidly. Then the computer stopped and the face of the woman looked back at her. On the screen, she had bruises on her lip and a black eye, but it was definitely the same woman. The name, however, was not Pansy Jane. It was Poppy Anne.

Maybe not quite so predictable after all, Billy Jo thought, frowning. She entered both names into the computer program PD had purloined from the Nashville Police when he retired from the force. The program had the arrest records and subsequent prosecutions of every criminal in the state. Pansy Jane didn't have a record, but Poppy Anne most definitely did. She had form for solicitation, grievous bodily harm, and theft.

"Well, well, well," Billy Jo said aloud to the silent room as she picked up her cooling coffee cup and took a sip.

TWO

IT WAS STILL RAINING WHEN INVESTIGATOR Dory Clarkson arrived at the office. She was beautifully dressed, as usual, wearing a purple raincoat over a red and violet patterned dress, amethyst earrings, and red high heels. She pulled a mask up to cover her mouth and nose as she entered the business. Billy Jo was unsurprised to see that the mask matched her outfit.

"Air hug," Dory greeted Billy Jo, holding her brown arms wide.

"Is this what we do now?" Billy Jo asked. "No real hugs?"

"Not yet, apparently," Dory looked closely at Billy Jo. Her eyes skimmed from her face to her toes. She was barefoot. "Best get your shoes on, Girl. Some clients could show up. And that black bra's showing through your white blouse."

"Yes ma'am," Billy Jo said. Running up the stairs she yelled, "Fashion Nazi!" over her shoulder and heard Dory chuckle. It had been so long since Dory nagged her about her clothes, she didn't even mind. In fact, she found it kind of endearing. It always struck her as funny that despite Dory being over sixty and a good thirty pounds overweight, everyone saw her as the glamor gal she believed herself to be.

When she came back downstairs, having donned shoes and a blue sweater, Dory gave her the stink-eye.

"What?" Billy Jo asked, raising her dark eyebrows, an expression of blameless innocence on her heart-shaped face.

"You know what, Missy. I know you don't have the office checkbook because I've had it at my place in the Flower Pot district this whole time. And I made sure to take the office credit card too. How did you buy all this?"

Dory gestured to a cluster of green potted plants that stood in the corner of the waiting room. The area now sported an Oriental rug, a couch, and new chairs. Billy Jo's former reception desk had been replaced with a sleek new model. Framed photographs of gleaming racehorses, the distinctive stacked stone walls of the area, pictures of tumbling waterfalls and lazy brown rivers hung on the walls.

"Come look at the storeroom," Billy Jo said happily. "It used to be stuffed with boxes, the vacuum cleaner, brooms, mops, and old cans of paint. I cleaned it all out and made it into an office for you and Wayne. I haven't had a thing to do for weeks and the office needed updating."

"Give, Girl. How did you pay for this?"

"Memorized the office credit card number," Billy Jo said in a quiet tone, looking down at her shoes.

"And the expiration date? And the security code?" Dory asked pointedly.

At that moment, the front door opened and Detective Wayne Nichols walked in. He was nearing sixty but very fit. He was a big-boned man with salt and pepper hair that went well with what he wore—a trench coat, dark slacks, and a striped shirt. Billy Jo had been slightly apprehensive when Wayne joined the firm, afraid he would dismiss her because she was young and hadn't any police training. To her surprise, despite the usual skepticism of long-time cops, Wayne Nichols had become her strongest supporter.

"It will be interesting to see how long it takes a couple of old-timers to notice the changes," Dory whispered.

"Good Morning Ladies," Wayne said, shaking the raindrops off his raincoat and hanging it on the hooks just inside the door. Looking around the entryway he added, "This was your work I take it, Billy Jo? Very nice."

"All my usual haunts were closed, Wayne. I couldn't go to the Romanov club, out to eat, or shop for clothes. I couldn't even get a haircut. Had to do something to keep from going stir crazy," Billy Jo said with a slightly shamefaced smile.

"Miss Industrious here made us an office, Wayne," Dory told him. "Don't know if you remember, but this house has three bedrooms on the main floor. One was enlarged to make into the conference room, one is PD's office, but the third was being used for old junk. Billy Jo cleaned it out and furnished it with back-to-back desks for us. She also got us each a laptop. Take a look."

"Good work," Wayne said, smiling as he looked into the new office. Both Dory and Wayne had previously used the conference room as an office or usurped Billy Jo's reception desk when they needed a computer. Their lack of office space had resulted in her having to work on her laptop while sitting on the bed in her upstairs apartment.

At that moment, they heard Detective Pascoe entering the office through the back door. "Greetings, everybody," he called out. "I got some sandwiches and fruit. Just putting the fruit in the refrigerator. Hold on. Billy Jo Bradley get your butt in here right now! What the heck is this smell?"

When she walked into the kitchen, Billy Jo was struck by how much older PD looked in just two months since she'd seen him in person. His hair had gone completely white and was so long it touched his shoulders. He was standing at the open refrigerator door and his clothes hung loose on his bony old body. She felt a sharp twinge of sorrow at his frailty. PD was her only family. Her mother had died of ovarian cancer when she was a teenager, her father had never been in the picture, and her maternal grandfather, Aaron, died a few years after her mother passed away. PD had been her grandfather's best friend. The two men had served in the Army together in Viet Nam. Her grandfather's dying request was for PD to be there for Billy Jo. He had kept his promise. When PD decided to remodel the house in Rosedale for his PI business, he tracked Billy Jo down and offered to let her live in the upstairs apartment in exchange for serving as a receptionist and IT person for the office. His generous offer had come at just the right time. Waiting table while going to night school had reduced her to living in her car.

"Sorry, PD. My germ phobia has gotten the best of me. I've been bleach-spraying the groceries," she said as Wayne and Dory joined them in the kitchen.

"Lucy does the same thing at our place," Wayne said, shaking his head. "Take a look in the storeroom, Partner. In our absence, Miss Billy Jo has been busy."

PD glanced into the former storeroom, raised his eyebrows at their youngest colleague, and said, "Guess it serves me right for not working you hard enough, Billy Jo. Can you give me a cost on all this later, Dory?"

She nodded.

"It's wonderful to finally see all of you," PD said smiling. "Come on into the conference room."

Whew, Billy Jo thought. *That was way easier than expected.*

EVERYONE GOT SEATED AND PD PASSED THE SANDWICHES to Billy Jo who swiped their cling-wrappings with a bleach wipe before handing them out. "The purpose of this meeting is to bring everyone up to date on both the pandemic and our cases. As you know, the Governor just rescinded the Stay at Home order, so we can get back to work on site. We need to wash our hands, or use hand sanitizer, and remove our shoes whenever we come into the office. Clients need to do the same thing. We will be seated six feet apart at the conference room table and wear masks. Agreed?"

Dory and Billy Jo nodded as did Wayne. Living with Lucy, an ER physician had made him very conscious of the recommended precautions.

"I bought one of those thermometers you use in the air by a person's forehead. I'll swipe all the clients when they arrive," Billy Jo said.

"Good idea. Now as far as cases go, I've kept in touch with Billy Jo by phone and we've had several Zoom meetings with folks in the last month. Unfortunately, most of our new clients decided to wait until they could meet with us in person, so I'm hoping for new cases soon."

"I have a question. What if anything is happening with that girl, Lexie Lovell? Was she the one who wanted us to find her unforeseen brother last spring? That case really captured my interest," Wayne said.

"She was here earlier," Billy Jo said. "I didn't let her in but said we would discuss her case and get back to her today."

"If she and her mother are still lying, it will be a waste of time," Dory said.

"Lexie got into her father's office a few days ago and brought me some promising material." Billy Jo set the brown accordion-pleated file on the table and passed the contents around.

PD reached for the Pre-Nuptial Agreement. Dory looked carefully at the photo of the woman who was probably the mother of Lexie's half-brother, turning it over and reading the date on the back. Wayne read the birth certificate, making some notes as he did so.

"What have you done so far?" PD asked.

"I put the photo of Pansy Jane Delaney through facial recognition. She didn't come up under that name, but her image did. She is also known as Poppy Anne Delaney who has quite a record of assault, solicitation, etc. In the photo taken at her arrest, her face was badly bruised."

"Interesting," PD said calmly. He had been in law enforcement for so long that nothing shocked him anymore, certainly not a prostitute who had been abused by a client or a pimp.

"No Marriage Certificate?" Dory asked. "Too bad. That would have been helpful. And where, may I ask is this woman with two names at present?"

"Serving time," Billy Jo said.

"For which offense?" Wayne asked.

"Solicitation. The guy she offered her services to was an off-duty deputy."

"Please tell me it was Deputy George from our Sheriff's Office here in Rosedale," Dory said, trying valiantly to stifle a chuckle.

"Would you like to check on that, Dory?" Wayne asked in a teasing tone.

"It will be a distinct pleasure to mercilessly badger George about being solicited by a prostitute," she said with an evil grin.

"We'll need to talk to Miss Delaney, but no visitors are allowed in prisons at present. When the prison ended in-person visitation in Tennessee, they implemented Zoom meetings. All the prisoners have to do is sign up for open slots and list the caller on their approved visitor list," PD said.

"Shall I call Lexie and ask her to come later in today?" Billy Jo asked.

"Yes. And ask if, during her foray around her father's papers, she found a marriage license," Dory said.

"What about Lexie's mother? Should I see if she can come to the meeting?"

"Certainly not. That woman did nothing but fib to us before. I have a feeling we will get a lot more out of Lexie if her mother isn't in the room."

"I've asked Dr. Lucy to come in to do an in-service about the recommended COVID-19 protocols in our state," PD said. "She'll be here around 5:00."

AN HOUR LATER, LEXIE LOVELL KNOCKED on the front door of the building. It was still raining and she was holding an umbrella. It was black on the exterior but the interior was blue with puffy white clouds. Billy Jo thought it was a clever design.

"Hi Lexie, come on in," she said, pulling up her mask and taking the girl's raincoat and umbrella. "I love your umbrella. Where did you get it?"

"From the MOMA catalog."

Billy Jo didn't recognize the acronym but would find it later. "Do you mind taking off your boots and using hand Sanitizer? We're asking everyone who comes in to do that. And I'm going to run this electronic thermometer over your forehead, okay?"

"Not a problem," Lexie said and removed her boots. Billy Jo checked to see that she didn't have a fever and held out the hand sanitizer which she used.

"Did you find a marriage license in your dad's office?" Billy Jo asked as the two young women walked down the hall.

"I didn't and I'm wondering if my father even married this woman. It could be a scam. If he wasn't married, does that give me any ammunition to fight splitting his money with this kid?"

"I'm not a lawyer, but I am taking night school classes toward my bachelor's degree in criminal justice. From what I know, if a man acknowledges a child, it doesn't matter if he was married to the mother. However, if DNA evidence proves the child wasn't his, it could make a difference," Billy Jo said.

"An excellent thought," Lexie said, raising her right eyebrow. Even wearing a mask, Billy Jo could see her little feline smile.

They entered the conference room and Lexie greeted the team. As the group said hello, Billy Jo wondered why Lexie would be so reluctant to share her father's money with her brother. Did Lexie want to hang on to every penny out of greed? Or perhaps to give the money to her mother, who told them she hadn't been left a thing from the marriage? Or was Lexie still furious with her father for leaving her and her mother? Why else want to deprive a baby brother of his share? As an only child, Billy Jo had always wanted a sibling. As the case progressed, she was determined to convince Lexie Lovell to agree to a relationship with her brother.

THREE

"**T**HANK YOU FOR SEEING ME," Lexie said, taking a seat at the far end of the conference room table.

Wayne nodded as did Dory and PD but none of them offered her coffee or tea. Billy Jo suppressed her normal tendency to see if the client wanted something to drink. Apparently, the senior team was still irked with the young woman.

"How can we help you, Miss Lovell?" PD asked in a cool tone.

"As you know, I hired your firm some time ago to find a boy my father told his legal executor was his son. I didn't believe it was true and neither did my mother. It's probably some clever ploy on the part of the kid's mother to get dad's money."

"Were you able to find a marriage certificate or license?" Wayne asked. "Or your parent's divorce decree?"

"Neither one. My mother says she and my dad were still married, despite being separated forever, so he couldn't have married this Delaney woman. Mom is going to talk to a lawyer and assert her rights to my dad's estate. I'm only here to get some advice and possibly to stop you from searching further for this boy."

"That's certainly your right, Miss Lovell, but you will owe us for the time and effort we put in to date," Dory said.

"As far as I can tell, you haven't done any work at all," Lexie said. "You didn't find him or you would have contacted me."

"Do you recall signing a contract with the agency when you came in last year?" Dory asked and Wayne looked at his partner appreciatively. He recognized that purring tone of voice, it was the one she always used when some dopey thug was just about to step into a giant mousetrap.

"I'm pretty sure I didn't," Lexie said. Her cheeks flushed.

"You did. Let me remind you. The contract, which you signed and dated, states that if you wish to terminate the services of Rosedale Investigations, you will owe the full amount we estimated as the cost of finding your brother. The contract stated that if we found the boy, Rosedale Investigations would receive 5% of your father's estate or the equivalent dollar amount."

The room was very quiet. Outside the rain was still coming down. PD drummed his fingers on the conference table until Dory cast him an irritated glance.

"I don't have that kind of money," Lexie said, sounding subdued. "Billy Jo said if the kid wasn't my father's biological son, I might get all Dad's money."

All three senior partners swiveled their heads to look at Billy Jo who squirmed, feeling like a butterfly pinned to a display board.

"Well that's what I said, but to prove the boy wasn't your brother, Lexie, we would first have to find him. That's the only way you could get a DNA test done and officially determine whether you two are related. Last spring you gave us nothing to work with. Until you gave me the file folder earlier today, we didn't even know the boy's or his mother's name. Now that we have his birth certificate, it shouldn't take long to track him down," Billy Jo said.

Lexie hesitated a moment before saying, "Well, I'm not happy about it, but it seems you will need to find him, I'll take another look at my father's papers at his house tonight. If I find a marriage license or a divorce decree, I'll let you know."

"I'm not sure you should hold out much hope that Theodore Chase Lovell isn't your brother, Miss Lovell. The birth certificate lists Edward James Lovell as the father," Wayne said.

Lexie sighed and stood up. "You have my phone number. Let me know when the boy is located. I'm going to talk to my dad's lawyer about getting a DNA test done."

"I'm not sure you can legally force that to happen, Miss Lovell," PD said. Lexie didn't respond but her face grew even pinker as she stood up, said good-bye, and hurriedly left the room.

"Coffee, anyone?" Dory asked and at nods from Wayne and PD went to the kitchen. She returned with coffees and a soda she slid across the table to Billy Jo.

"As I mentioned, Dr. Lucy is coming in later to give us the COVID-19 protocols for businesses in Tennessee. She's pretty pressed for time, so it's going to be a short presentation," PD said.

"Rosedale General's ER has been overwhelmed with cases. All of the first responders are working around the clock. That must be her now," Wayne said hearing the doorbell. He stood up and went to open the door for his long-time girlfriend.

Lucy Ingram was wearing green scrubs, having just left the ER. She was a lovely woman, tall with long brown hair, but had dark circles under her eyes. She got seated at the table and Dory handed her a cup of coffee.

"Thanks, Dory. Hello everyone. I appreciate you having me visit to talk about this issue. All Rosedale's first responders are trying to help educate the community. As I'm sure all of you know, the virus is a real threat. It's likely evolved from an animal virus and made the jump to humans. It's a flu virus in the SARS family, but far more transmissible and deadly. It appears to strike people of color hardest, as well as the elderly, but we all need to be vigilant. And keeping people from congregating is the only way we know to keep COVID from spreading to the point where the health system is overwhelmed. Our best hope to control COVID-19 is a vaccine. Getting 70% to 80% of the population vaccinated is the optimal way to keep the virus at bay. I'm passing around two pieces of paper. One lists the COVID-19 guidelines for businesses in our state and the second lists the symptoms you need to look for if you think you might have been exposed. If any of you believe you have been exposed, you need to wait five days and then get tested. Since we're no longer on lock-down, just wear your masks when you leave the office, to enter any businesses, or to question anyone." At that moment the group heard Lucy's pager ring. She turned away and talked briefly on the phone. "Sorry, people. I wanted to have time for questions, but it seems I'm needed. Thanks for having me in." Wayne rose and escorted Lucy out the door.

"Please read over the material carefully everyone," PD said. He waited as the team perused the hand-outs before saying, "Here are the assignments for the Lovell case. Billy Jo, we're going to need to see Mr. Lovell's emails. Since they were living together, I'm assuming Ms. Delaney used his email account. Dory, can you go through County and State records for divorces and marriages? And since the father is dead and the mom is in prison, try to figure out where this little brother would have been placed. I'm assuming Child Protective Services has stepped in. Wayne, please use your contacts to find out which prison Miss Delaney is in and if we can talk to her via the video conferencing system. I'm going to visit the florist Mr. Lovell ordered his flowers from and the travel agency listed on the Greek Islands brochure." PD picked up the florist card and the tri-fold from the table. "That's it, people."

As the senior team disbursed and Billy Jo sipped her soda, she wondered how the heck she was supposed to get into Mr. Lovell's computer and obtain his emails. There hadn't been a crime, so she couldn't work through the Sheriff's Office, and a warrant could only be obtained with the help of the cops. There was only one option. She would have to follow Lexie Lovell when she went back to her father's house and try to convince her to let her inside. She picked up the Pre-Nuptial Agreement from the conference room table and made a note of Lexie's father's address. Walking out to her desk, she pulled a brand-new flash drive from her bottom drawer, making sure to get one that had a large memory capacity. Running upstairs to her apartment, she collected her raincoat and boots. Wishing she had a cool umbrella like Lexie's, she came back downstairs, grabbed her mask, and went out to her car.

BY EVENING, THE RAIN HAD STOPPED. The sun was setting, drawing the moisture up from the earth. The outdoor air was warm and humid as Billy Jo drove to Lexie's mother's house. She knocked and when Lexie answered the door asked if she would allow her into her father's house. With her mother standing behind her, Lexie refused, even when Billy Jo said they needed to get inside the house to obtain the documents that would help locate her brother.

Her first plan having been quashed, Billy Jo drove down the street and waited until Lexie and her fiancé came out of the house. She tailed the couple to a restaurant with outdoor dining and ducked behind a row of shrubs from which point she could see the tables. When she heard the waitress ask for their drinks orders, Billy Jo assumed she had a good hour before they would be finished eating. Lexie had mentioned she was going to her father's house after dinner. Her new plan was to try to get into the house ahead of Lexie and, if possible, to copy Mr. Lovell's emails before she arrived. She was aware that entering the house without the permission of the owners was illegal but was determined not to fail PD—no matter what it took.

Edward Lovell's house was located in the White Oaks subdivision where all the homes were nearly a hundred years old, having been built by the original lumber and liquor barons. The mansion where Mr. Lovell lived was made from red sandstone and had multiple cupolas and chimneys on its roof. Billie Jo parked her car several blocks away and walked nonchalantly down the street.

Parents were calling young children into their houses and older kids were riding their bicycles home for dinner. Reaching Mr. Lovell's mailbox, Billy Jo stopped and looked around. Seeing no one, she opened it, and pulled out several pieces of mail, noting the addresses. There was one letter with a return address of the Tennessee Prison for Women. She held it up to the light, but the paper was too thick to see through. She put it back in the mailbox, noting that the date on the envelope was one week ago.

The house had originally been beautifully landscaped with dogwood trees, lilacs, giant snowball shrubs, and mock orange. Nobody had been tending the shrub and flower beds recently, however, and it was wildly overgrown. The scents of the plants were heavy, nearly visible in the soft air. The pine trees at the back of the property were enormous; they towered over the house. The grass was long and curled in waves. The house itself had the air of neglect that dwellings always got when uninhabited. She saw three soggy rolled-up newspapers strewn on the sidewalk leading up to the front door.

Walking around to the back of the house, she spotted a screened-in porch. The screen door was locked, but when she tugged on it felt flimsy. Billy Jo pulled her pocket knife from her jeans and sliced carefully along the base of the screen. Inserting her hand through the opening, she unlocked the door. It squeaked as it opened, and she walked inside. The sunroom was filled with old-fashioned porch furniture, a settee that swung back and forth, a wrought-iron table with a glass top, and several very dead violets. Dust lay over everything.

Once in the main part of the house, Billy Jo opened door after door without finding anything that looked like an office before climbing a flight of stairs and finding a room in one of the turrets with a large walnut desk and a computer. She entered several versions of Lexie's birthdate before finding one that worked as the password. She then inserted her flash drive and started copying the email files. It was warm in the room and the humming sound of the computer made her feel relaxed and sleepy.

It was completely dark when the sound of giggling woke Billie Jo. She had fallen asleep with her head on the desk. She recognized the sound of a couple, a deeper man's voice, and a higher-pitched girl's. It was Lexie and her fiancé. On the other side of the room from the desk was an old leather couch. She quickly darted over to it, pulling it slightly away from the wall. The thin eel-like space would be claustrophobic, and Billy Jo hated small spaces. Nonetheless, she crawled behind the couch and laid down. She could hide there until the couple left the house. Then she remembered the flash drive and the blinking lights on the computer. It was a dead giveaway. Concealed behind the couch, she heard the sounds of Lexie's high heels clicking as she walked up the stairs.

"Hold on a minute, Lex," the fiancé's voice said. "I just noticed there's a small bedroom off the landing here. It's got a bed all made up. Come take a look, Sweetheart."

"Stop trying to distract me," Lexie said with a husky laugh. Billy Jo heard the sounds of kissing and then footsteps walking into the room. She heard giggling, shoes landing on the floor, bedsprings squeaking and then a soft moan before one of them closed the door to the bedroom.

She slid out from behind the couch and walked to the desk. The window on the monitor said 98% copied. It would have to do. She ejected the flash drive quickly, slipped it into her pocket, clicked off the computer, and opened the door leading to the staircase. The bedroom door off the landing was closed and the sounds of rising passion would drown out any sounds her feet made. She had almost reached the landing when she heard the front door to the house open.

"Lexie, Honey, are you here? It's Mom."

Trapped between Lexie's mother walking into the front room and what would certainly be the sudden opening of the bedroom door, Billy Jo Bradley had no place to run.

FOUR

T HE RAIN HAD CONTINUED FALLING WELL into the evening. Dory Clarkson loved drifting off to the sound of the rain hitting her metal roof. She was dreaming about walking her dog in a field of sunny white ox-eyed daisies when the sounds of pounding fists and loud shrieking woke her. She sat up in bed, wide awake and seriously irritated. The Flower Pot district was known for its enforcement of complete silence after ten p.m. and any parties that went on too late earned the acrimony of neighbors and often calls to the Sheriff's Office. There was even a newsletter the snoopiest neighbor, Caroline, had started that gave 'Bad Neighbor: Too Noisy' ratings to residents who violated the rules. Whoever this was had to be silenced immediately—before anyone else was roused.

"Help me," the high-pitched voice yelled. "Help!"

Knowing she had no choice but to investigate, Dory got out of bed, slipped on her long blue velvet robe (she always slept fully naked), and walked to the front door. Her little white dog, True, followed behind her, toenails clicking on the floor tiles. The cries for help continued unabated as Dory clicked on the porch light and opened the front door. Her young colleague, Billy Jo, looking like a wet muskrat in the pouring rain was standing on the porch. Her car wasn't in the driveway.

"What on earth? It's two o'clock in the morning. Stop that yelling right now. Keep your voice down." The girl was sobbing so hard she didn't react. Dory wondered if she had even heard her. She put her arm around the kid and pulled her into the entryway. She was soaking wet, crying and breathing hard. Pulling off Billy Jo's jacket was a struggle. Once accomplished, Dory led her over to a bench in her entryway and putting both hands on her shoulders managed to get her seated. Dory knelt and untied the girl's high-top red sneakers, pulling them off. Her wet jacket and shoes leaked, making a puddle on the floor. The dog licked at the water, looking hopefully up at Dory who absent-mindedly reached into her robe pocket and handed the dog a treat. The girl was still crying, but her tears were combined with sniffles and occasional hiccups now.

"Stand up and follow me," Dory said firmly and Billy Jo did so. They walked into the kitchen where she opened a lower cupboard and extracted a bottle of brandy. She took a shot glass from the upper cupboard and filled it. "Drink this," she said, and although Billy Jo still hadn't spoken and her eyes were glazed, she took the glass and swallowed the liquor. Realizing it was going to be a long night, Dory poured herself a shot of the brandy and downed it. Brandy was medicinal after all.

"Sit down at the island," she said. "I'm going to make you some hot chocolate." She touched Billy Jo's fingers to assess her temperature. They were ice cold. Stirring some milk and adding chocolate syrup to a saucepan, Dory kept up a stream of meaningless words of comfort. "It's all right, Honey. You're going to be fine. Everything's all right. There's nothing to worry about. You're safe now." She poured the hot chocolate into a mug and added miniature marshmallows to the top. Still crooning reassurances, she handed the mug to Billy Jo and told her to drink it. She had stopped crying by then but was frowning and looking confused.

"You're at my place, Honey. How did you get here? I didn't see your car."

Billy Jo's face wore a sudden look of horror as her eyes widened and she said, "Trapped, trapped. Couldn't get out. Burning papers. Fire, fire."

"Where were you, Billy Jo?" Dory asked calmly.

"Lovell mansion," she said and for the first time met Dory's eyes with recognition.

"You went to the Lovell place? Were you trying to get the emails from Mr. Lovell's computer?"

"Files, so many files. The cupboard. The dark cupboard. He had a gun!" She shrieked the last words, her dark eyes huge in the dim lighting of the kitchen.

It was clear that Dory wasn't going to get much more out of her for a while. Noticing that the girl had finished most of her hot chocolate, Dory resumed her kindly patter. "I'm going to put you into bed now. Follow me." They walked down the hall to Dory's guest room and Billy Jo sat down on the bed. She looked up helplessly at Dory, who realized she needed to get the rest of her clothes off. She couldn't let the kid sleep in cold wet things. "It's okay now. You're completely safe. I'm just going to pull off that shirt." It was difficult to remove Billy Jo's shirt and wet jeans, but at last she was down to her undies. Dory pulled back the covers and pushing gently against her, laid her down. When Billy Jo curled on her side, Dory raised the puffy yellow quilt over her young body and started to leave the room.

"True," she hissed. "Get down and come here." The dog, who had a mind of her own, had climbed up into the bed. "Fine then," Dory whispered, realizing the dog's small compact body would help warm the girl.

She picked up Billy Jo's clothes from the floor and walked back to the entry where she added her jacket and sneakers to the pile in her arms. She switched off the front porch light and locked the door. Walking to the laundry room at the back of the house, Dory started the machine, adding hot water and soap. She was about to drop Billy Jo's jeans into the water when a sudden warning qualm stopped her. What if there was something important in her pockets?

She reached into a back pocket and pulled the flash drive out. "OMG, that was close," she said, before checking the rest of the pockets and removing the girl's pocket knife. It was open, the tip of the blade was bent, and a little wood shaving was stuck on the end. *What had the girl used it for?*

Back in her bedroom, Dory divested herself of her robe and climbed back into bed. She picked up her cell phone from the nightstand and sent a text to her partners, Wayne and PD.

"Billy Jo is spending the night here. Something practically scared her to death. Will come to the office in the morning when she's lucid."

She clicked 'Send' and laid back on her pillow wondering what on earth had happened to her little work friend at Mr. Lovell's mansion?

DORY WAS UP BEFORE BILLY JO WOKE, made a pot of coffee, and put her oven on pre-heat. She cracked open a tube of cinnamon rolls and put them in a pan to rise. She walked to the laundry room and put Billy Jo's clothes in the dryer, hoping they wouldn't shrink. Kids were funny about that stuff. Then she took a shower and got dressed. Returning to the kitchen, she sliced some strawberries and set two places at her kitchen table before walking to her guest room and opening the door. Billy Jo was still sound asleep, but True was wide awake. The dog thumped her tail in recognition.

"Get down," Dory said quietly and the dog jumped down from the bed. "You have to go outside and go potty." The dog followed her to the back door and Dory released her into the fenced backyard. The rain from the previous night had moved off, leaving a stunningly beautiful day with a singing blue sky. A soft breeze was hard at work drying the grass. Dory's neighbor was standing on her back porch. She waved and smiled. Dory waved back. Hopefully, the nighttime disturbance hadn't been a problem or, God forbid, woken her snoopy neighbor, Caroline, who did the wretched newsletter.

Walking back inside to the guest room, Dory was pleased to see Billy Jo's eyes were open. "Good Morning, Billy Jo," she said in a calm cheerful tone. She was trying to mimic her veterinarian—a woman capable of calming large racehorses and maddened dogs with just her voice. Billy Jo looked at her and blinked in recognition, but didn't speak.

"You got here around two o'clock last night, Hon. I gathered you were at the Lovell mansion." Alarmed wide eyes met her statement. "You can tell me about it later. Right now come get your clothes. I washed them last night. They are in the dryer in the laundry room. Take a shower if you want. I'm going to put some cinnamon rolls in the oven to bake."

Just as the timer rang, indicating the sweet rolls were done, Billy Jo walked into the kitchen. She had taken a shower and her long hair was still wet, but she was dressed. Her soggy sneakers and damp jacket were in her hand.

"Have a seat. I'm going to pour you some coffee. Here you go. I put three sugars in it. Sugar is good for people who've had a shock. I gather you ran all the way here last night from the Lovell mansion? I looked it up on my cell phone. It's six miles! No wonder you were crying and looking out of it. I'm sure you did a great job getting those computer files though," she said, handing Billy Jo the flash drive, relieved she'd remembered to empty the girl's pockets. "Can you tell me what happened?" she asked.

Billy Jo gave her an open-eyed blinking look and then wailed. "No."

"Okay, okay. Never mind. Let's get some food into you. After breakfast, we're headed to the office. You can tell all of us what happened then."

PULLING INTO THE DRIVEWAY AT ROSEDALE INVESTIGATIONS, Dory noticed that Billy Jo had perked up when she recognized her home and their place of business. It had been a bit tense getting the girl into the car. Just as Dory had her in the front seat and reached to buckle her seatbelt, the girl pushed her hands away, opened the car door, and got out again. Finally, it occurred to Dory that Billy Jo wanted the dog to go with them. True was only too happy to oblige. Little Runt loved riding in cars.

Wayne and PD had stepped out onto the front porch of Rosedale Investigations and Billy Jo, beginning to cry again, ran right to Wayne and threw herself into his arms. He met Dory's eyes over Billy Jo's back looking alarmed. Like most men, Wayne was disconcerted by female tears and they were supposed to be keeping six feet apart.

"Just keep telling her everything is going to be fine and that she's safe," Dory told him and in his pleasant voice, Wayne Nichols did exactly that.

Fifteen minutes later, with PD holding her hand and Wayne patting her on the shoulder, Billy Jo walked into Rosedale Investigations. Her eyes were bright and in response to Dory's question about whether she could tell them what happened, she nodded. In due time, they would get the whole story.

FIVE

By THE TIME DORY GOT HER DOG OUT OF THE CAR, tied her up to the wrought-iron porch railing, and walked into the conference room, the team was already seated.

"I am so grateful to you, Dory," PD said. "Something must have scared Billy Jo to death last night. Thank you for helping her. She said she will tell us what happened but would like to hear the rest of our reports first."

"Good idea," Dory said. "I'll start. I found the registered divorce decree between Edward Lovell and Lexie's mother. It was in the Vital Statistics office. The divorce took place over a decade ago. I knew Lexie's mother was lying. I did not, however, find a marriage license for Edward Lovell and Ms. Delaney, but they could have gone out of state to be married. I will keep looking. I ran into a major roadblock, though, when I contacted Child Protective Services. They have no record of a Theodore Chase Lovell being taken into care or placed with a foster family. I thought I was being given the run-around and drove over to the administration building and personally met with the Director. She convinced me. They have no record of the child."

"That's really weird. The father is dead, the mom is in prison, and Lexie said there was no other family. Where could the boy be?" PD looked around the table, looking concerned. "I hope to hell the kid isn't dead," he said quietly.

"I guess I could check death records," Dory said. "He's just a baby." She rubbed her hands over her eyes wearily, trying to wipe the painful thought away.

"My assignment was to find Poppy Delaney," Wayne said. "Thanks to Billy Jo's search of the criminal database, I knew she was in the Tennessee

Prison for Women. I contacted the Warden directly. He used to be a cop and knows me. He asked Ms. Delaney to put PD and me on her list of approved visitors. She did so, and we have a video conference set up with her tomorrow afternoon. I also called Sheriff Bradley and found out it was the cops from Nashville, not Rosedale, who picked her up for solicitation. What I don't understand is why Poppy Delaney would take to the streets selling her skills in the world's oldest profession when she had a child and presumably a home in Edward Lovell's manor?"

"This case just gets odder and odder," Dory said. "What did you find out, PD?"

"I went to the travel agency that booked their trip to the Greek islands. Mr. Lovell had paid for a cruise for two adults and one child, but the tickets were never used. I also called the Vital Records office and they gave me the date Lovell died. It was just shortly before they were going on that trip."

"Why would the woman not go on the trip and take her son with her?" Dory asked. "I sure as hell would have. Greek islands, sunshine, beaches. She was nuts to waste the tickets."

"She was in custody the day they would have left. What else did you find PD?" Wayne asked.

"Remember that Lexie gave us a tag from a florist? I went to that florist and found something equally obscure. The girl at the front desk remembered the order as soon as I showed her the card. Mr. Lovell came into the store to pick the flowers up personally. He read the card the florist had written and said there was a mistake. The girl had written the words, 'You are prettier than *a* poppy.' He had her re-write it, saying it was supposed to read, 'you are prettier than Poppy.' He told her to capitalize the letter P."

"If the flowers were for her, why would he say that? Who was prettier than Poppy?" Billy Jo asked, looking perplexed.

"Maybe we'll find out after our video conference with the woman. I have a question for you, Billy Jo. On the first case we worked together, when Dory and I joined the firm, you had an analogy for what we do. You said our job was like mending a hole in a spider web for our client. After we solved that one, you changed your mind and said we were more like a safety net, with each of us holding on to a corner. Everyone had to keep their corner up or the whole thing would fall. Have you thought of a name or a metaphor for this case?" Wayne asked.

"I call this case the Blind Split because Mr. Lovell split his money between his two children—blind to the consequences for his daughter, Lexie, who was kept in the dark about having a little brother. Her mother was blind to what her ex was up to, and we seem to be working in the dark as far as finding the kid goes."

"Let's take a break, people," PD said. He stood up and walked over to Billy Jo, putting a comforting hand on her shoulder.

AFTER A BRIEF BREAK, THE TEAM REASSEMBLED. Looking at their expect-ant faces and taking a deep breath, Billy Jo swallowed and began. "When I left the office yesterday, I was planning to copy the email files from Mr. Lovell's computer. That was the assignment you gave me, PD and I was determined to succeed. I tailed Lexie to her home and asked her if she would let me into her father's house. She said 'no', so I followed her to a restaurant where she was having dinner with her fiancé. While they were dining, I drove over to Edward Lovell's address and parked a couple of blocks away. I took a picture of the old mansion, take a look." She passed her phone around. "Making sure nobody saw me, I went around to the back of the house and got inside."

"Should I ask how?" PD said.

"You don't want to know. Anyway, I got in and found his office. It was in this high tower on the top floor. I got his password from Lexie when she was here and started copying files. An hour or so later, I heard Lexie and her fiancé coming in through the front door." Billy Jo paused and took a sip of coffee. "They were walking up the stairs, but luckily went into a bedroom just off the landing for a little one-on-one time. That allowed me to get the flash drive out of the USB port and turn off the computer. I was tiptoeing down the stairs when I heard Lexie's mother enter the front door directly below me." Billy Jo was breathing faster by then and her cheeks were flushed. "I was terrified, thinking I had nowhere to go but there was a built-in linen cupboard on the landing. I opened the door and crawled inside. I had to lie down in a fetal position below the bottom shelf. I barely fit," She was breathing unsteadily and trembling.

"That must have been pretty tough for you. You're claustrophobic right?" PD asked.

Billy Jo nodded. "I didn't pull the door fully closed, so it wasn't too bad at first. Lexie, her mom, and her fiancé had a conversation on the landing. They were just inches from me and Lexie's mother was talking about some files she wanted to get rid of. Then they went upstairs to the next level and into Lovell's office."

"So, you were able to escape then?" PD asked.

"God, I wanted to, PD, but I knew you would want me to learn everything I could. And I just couldn't let you down," Billy Jo's face crumpled and she started to cry.

Wayne cast an exasperated look at PD.

Billy Jo then grabbed a tissue from the conference table and resumed her narration. "When they came back down to the landing from the office, one of them closed and latched the door to the linen cupboard. It had one of those latches made from a bar of wood that slides across on the outside of the door."

"OMG. You poor kid," Dory said. "How did you ever get out?"

"It was just so small and dark and I was afraid I'd panic and scream. I could hardly breathe. I thought I was going to have a heart attack! But I had my cell phone and I planned to wait until they left and call you guys. It seemed like hours before I heard them leaving the house. I was frantic by then. I started to call you, but couldn't figure out how you would get into the house and rescue me without Lexie and her mother seeing you. So, I just kept putting the blade of my knife through a crack in the door, trying to lift that wooden bar. It took forever before I was able to raise it. When the door opened and the air poured in, it seemed like a miracle." She took a long trembling breath.

"Did you leave the house then?" PD asked.

"I couldn't go out the front door because I was afraid they would be in the driveway or loading file boxes or something, so I went downstairs through the kitchen and back out through the screened porch. It was very dark, but I saw two, or possibly three people standing in the backyard. They had made a bonfire and were burning papers. While their backs were turned, I snuck out. I must have made some noise though, because a man's voice said, 'Who's there?'" She stopped talking and just looked at them, breathing hard and finding it almost impossible to continue.

"Go on. What happened then?" Wayne asked.

"He came after me, Wayne. I ran as fast as I could, but it was very dark and the shrubs and trees in that yard are huge. I ran into one big shrub and he caught me by the shoulder. The moon was out and I could see a snake tattoo on his wrist. He dragged me back toward the fire. I was struggling to escape and managed to bite his hand. Even that didn't make him let go of me and then he . . . pulled his gun." She stopped talking, her eyes were huge.

"Did he fire the gun at you?" Wayne asked, his voice dark with rising anger.

"Before he could, I kicked him in the knee and he fell. I started to run again. That's when he fired. He was on the ground so the bullets went high." She stopped talking, tears were running down her face. The rest of the team was silent, caught up in the story.

Billy Jo cleared her throat and said, "He must be a terrible shot because even when he stood up and shot again, he missed. The bullets made an awful noise when they whizzed by my head. I'll never forget that sound." She shuddered.

"Do you think he got a good look at you, Billy Jo? Did he know who you were?" Wayne asked.

"I don't think so."

"Could you identify him in a suspect line-up?" PD asked.

"If it's Lexie's fiancé, I could. I got a good look at him at the restaurant and his picture was in the paper with their engagement announcement."

"You said there were two or three people by the fire. Do you remember for sure? Was it two or three?" Dory asked.

"I'm not sure. There might have been only one man and a woman. I was desperate to get to my car, Dory, but it was parked on a nearby street and I knew if I ran under street lights, he would get me. He just kept coming. I could hear him breathing hard. I was running through back lawns and climbing over hedgerows and fences. I got lost a hundred times and all that time I could hear him crashing into trees and bushes before he finally gave up. It still took several hours before I made it to your house." Billy Jo stopped then and put her face down in her hands. She was sobbing and her shoulders shook.

"We're so glad you made it, Sweetie," Dory said. Turning to PD she said, "I believe you owe Billy Jo an apology. She put herself in real danger because you assigned her to get Mr. Lovell's emails."

"Everything she went through was to show you how committed she is to the business," Wayne said, shaking his head and frowning at his colleague. "You didn't tell her not to enter the house without permission and she found a way inside. You should have thought about the possible consequences before giving her that task. She isn't a fully trained cop you know."

"You're both right. Billy Jo, I'm sorry. I should never have given you such a difficult assignment. Please forgive me," PD said.

"Of course I do," Billy Jo said, but her voice was very small.

"When Lexie first came to us last spring, I thought this was going to be a simple case. She brought us a picture of herself as a baby holding a teddy bear. Going through her father's wallet, she found a picture of a different baby with the same teddy bear. To her, it was the worst betrayal of all, that her father gave his new baby the same teddy bear. In the beginning, all we had to do was find the brother and collect the fee. I certainly didn't expect anything like this," PD said.

"Do you folks remember the quote that says, *In the country of the blind, the one-eyed man is king?*" Wayne asked and everyone shook their heads. "It seems to me in this Blind Split case none of us have a single working eye," he said and Billy Jo shivered.

SIX

A FTER SPENDING SOME TIME WITH DORY upstairs in her apartment,
Billy Jo returned to the main floor calmer and more in control. Dory
had made a serious effort to cheer her up by making some notes about
the colors of the girl's tops. There was a seamstress in her neighborhood
who was making color-matched masks. She'd have her make some for
Billy Jo. When the partners started discussing their next assignments,
however, and Billy Jo realized they were all about to leave the building,
she started to tear up. She was afraid to stay by herself, she admitted.
Dory offered to stay with her. There were the emails to go through and
more research to do on the whereabouts of Teddy Lovell.

Wayne and PD stopped in the kitchen for a second cup of coffee
before setting out. Billy Jo waylaid them and handing Wayne her keys,
asked if they would get her car from the White Oaks neighborhood and
drive it back to Rosedale Investigations. He agreed, saying they would
locate her car and PD would drive it back to the office.

"In your opinion, Wayne, do we have a crime here?" PD asked.

"Hell, yes, we have a crime," Wayne responded irritably. "We need
to go to the Sheriff's Office and report it as attempted murder, or at least
felonious assault. They will protect Billy Jo and track down the perp. It's
going to be a slam dunk because we know who it was."

PD was frowning. "Hang on a minute before you get on your big
white horse and lead the cavalry charge, Buddy. We don't know for sure
that Lexie's fiancé was the guy who shot at Billy Jo. For another thing, the
Sheriff will need Billy Jo to report the crime herself, and she's still very
shaken up. She won't be able to provide a coherent narrative."

"I thought she did a pretty good job," Wayne said, sounding defensive.

"She wasn't sure exactly how many people were at the bonfire and can't tell us whether they were male or female. It's all circumstantial at this point. I think the key to understanding what happened is in those files. I'd like to go back to the Lovell mansion and see if there is anything left that didn't completely burn. And we can look for bullets and shell casings," PD said.

"Okay, let's look into it but just for a few hours. I want to get this reported today," Wayne said, sounding determined. He set his coffee cup down in the sink with a thunk and they departed. Walking down the driveway to his truck, he added, "You know, PD, this was a missing person's case at the outset, but we didn't even have the kid's name or the mother's. It was such a dead-end that we never fully investigated Ed Lovell. As I recall, you went to his bank and tried to get fiscal information, but without permission of the account holder, we got nowhere. I'm also wondering what the executor for Lovell's Last Will and Testament knows about his business and who his clients were."

They made the remainder of the drive in silence until PD said, "If we find some shell casings at Lovell's house, we will have hard evidence to support reporting the incident to the Sheriff. And we'll know what kind of gun was used."

"But not who owns it," Wayne said darkly.

DRIVING INTO THE TREE-LINED WHITE OAKS NEIGHBORHOOD, the two Detectives easily located the Lovell mansion and pulled into the driveway. Wayne looked at the old red stone place with its towers and chimney pots, intrigued by the air of mystery and neglect surrounding it.

"Lexie said her father owned an accounting firm, right?"

"That's right."

"Have you ever known an accountant who made enough money to afford a house like this?"

"I understand if the head of a firm employs a lot of junior accountants, the CEO can make a ton of money, but from what Lexie told us about her dad, he ran a solo practice," PD said.

The men got out of the truck and walked through the expansive grounds to the backyard. They noticed the screened-in porch and PD gestured significantly to the slice in the screen on the door. "The work of Billy Jo Bradley, I assume," he said. Wayne nodded.

They continued ambling around the backyard, listening to bird songs and seeing squirrels scamper up the old oak trees as they approached. A wild rabbit ducked under some shrubbery. Another one, completely unafraid, chewed meditatively on a piece of grass. The sunlight shone through his near-transparent ears. When they came upon the bonfire, they found a mess of burnt and blackened scraps of paper. A small tendril of smoke emerged from the pile when Wayne kicked at the remnants.

PD took a picture of the bonfire and several of the house and grounds, circumspectly avoiding pictures of the door to the screened-in porch.

Wayne picked up a stick and poked it tentatively into the darkened mess, dragging out one unburnt piece of paper. It was a tab for a manila file folder and it read "State Line." He showed it to PD.

"That's the old name for the mob," PD said. "When I was growing up my uncle, who was in law enforcement, told me that's what the cops called it. State Line ran the usual enterprises—extortion, racketeering, prostitution and drugs along the Mississippi/Tennessee border. That's where the State Line name came from."

"I thought the mob was pretty much out of business," Wayne said.

"Pretty much, but I've heard there are still some minimal ties to it right here in Rose County."

"Do you think Edward Lovell could have been an accountant for the guys who are still in the mob?" Wayne asked.

"Yup, and if we're right, mob money probably bought this house."

"Given that prostitution is always one of their income lines, it explains how Edward Lovell likely met the Delaney woman," Wayne said.

"We can't forget our appointment to talk to her on video conferencing today," PD said.

"Right. Let's try to find some shell casings and bullets."

The two men prowled the grounds for over an hour, acquiring two shell casings and a single bullet. Wayne always carried plastic gloves and evidence bags. Putting on gloves, he put the bullet and casings into the plastic sleeves. "I'll bring these into the Sheriff's office. Do we still need to talk to Lovell's attorney?"

"Might not get much, but if he's also working for the mob, we will probably be able to tell by how he reacts to our questions," PD said. "I'll give him a call. We need to get Billy Jo's car while we're here. Let's do that now."

AFTER MAKING AN APPOINTMENT TO SPEAK with Lovell's attorney, the two men located Billy Jo's car. PD drove it back to the office with Wayne following him in his truck. After dropping off her car and texting her that they were leaving her keys under the matt, they got back in Wayne's truck and drove to a recently re-opened sandwich shop with a drive-up option. Eating their sandwiches in the vehicle, the two detectives headed to the outskirts of Rosedale and parked at a strip mall. One business in the row of stores had a sign reading "Bradley Carver, J.D. Attorney at Law." Mr. Carver, a forty-something man opened the door at their knock. He was casually dressed, wore glasses with dark rims, and had a small pencil mustache.

"Afternoon, Mr. Carver, I'm Detective Pascoe and this is my partner, Detective Nichols. We represent Alexa Lovell. She hired our firm, Rosedale Investigations, to find her brother." PD handed his card to Carver.

"Come in, gentlemen. It's getting warm outside, but my office is air-conditioned, and I took the liberty of chilling some cold brews."

P.D. and Wayne followed him into his office that had a no-nonsense wooden desk and three chairs. There were absolutely no papers on his desk, just a laptop. It looked to Wayne like a front for an office, rather than an actual workplace. He didn't even see a phone and most legitimate businesses still kept a landline.

"Please have a seat. What can I do for you today?" Bradley Carver pulled three beers from a small refrigerator tucked under a granite countertop. Wayne accepted one and thanked him. P.D. declined.

"Are you are the executor for Edward Lovell's will?" PD asked.

"That's correct. Now that Probate finished their job and the business has been sold, I can disburse his assets to his children, Lexie and Teddy—as soon as you find the boy and his mother, that is."

"I see you know his name," PD said. "Mr. Lovell discussed his paternity for the boy with you then?"

Mr. Carver nodded.

"Did Mr. Lovell give you any information about the boy's whereabouts?" Wayne asked. "We've not turned up much in our initial inquiries and wondered what happens if we fail to find him?"

"In that situation, the money will remain in the account for the foreseeable future. I got a call from Lexie's mother a few days ago. She plans to challenge the will, but it's unlikely she will get very far. Mr. Lovell told me she received the majority share of his business at the time of the divorce. No Judge is likely to re-visit a completed divorce settlement from a decade ago."

"How did you come to be Mr. Lovell's executor?" Wayne asked. He was curious about the connection between the two men.

"I'm his attorney and have been for decades," Carver said. "It was a logical choice to make me his executor."

"I have something I'd like to show you," Wayne said, sliding the partially burnt file tab in the plastic evidence envelope across the desk. "I assume you know the words *State Line* refer to the mob."

"I didn't know that," Carver said with a studiously blank face.

"It's an old term," Wayne was watching the man closely. Carver's eyes shifted to the right. It was his "tell" his nonverbal reaction to telling a lie. Supposedly, when asked a question, if a person honestly tried to remember something, they invariably looked to the left. If they looked right, they were lying. Wayne knew he had him, but he couldn't interrogate him. His loss of the privileges he had as an officer of the law continued to pinch. Becoming a private investigator had been a tough adjustment.

"I have no idea what you are talking about. Honestly, Mr. Lovell ran an above-board business and I'm just his lawyer," Carver said. "Please let me know as soon as you find Ms. Delaney."

They talked a bit longer but got nothing more.

Walking back out to his truck, Wayne said, "I've noticed that most people who begin sentences with the word 'Honestly' are lying."

"I agree," PD said. "It's almost time to put the squeeze on Ms. Delaney."

"I thought it was interesting that Carver asked to be informed when we located Ms. Delaney," Wayne said.

"I noticed that too. Found it a bit odd."

THEY ARRIVED BACK AT THE OFFICE in time to see Billy Jo click the link for the Zoom meeting on the computer in the conference room.

"Sure hope the boy's mother knows where he is," Dory said. "I keep coming up empty."

"I take it you didn't find any evidence he is dead?" PD asked.

Dory shook her head. "Not so far. Do you two want to handle this conversation by yourselves? Should Billy Jo and I make ourselves scarce?"

"The prisoner only listed PD and me on her approved visitors' list," Wayne said.

As the two women left, the Zoom image flickered and came on, showing a prison guard leading Poppy Delaney by her upper arm and seating her at a table.

"You can talk to these guys," the guard told her and took his position standing in the far corner of the room.

Poppy Delaney looked thoroughly defeated. Her bruises were fading, but her eyes were dull and unfocused. Her dyed blonde hair with dark red roots was pulled back in a scraggly ponytail. She seemed completely uninterested in what was happening around her.

"Are you Miss Delaney?" PD asked.

She nodded.

"You are speaking with Detectives PD Pascoe and Wayne Nichols from Rosedale Investigations. We have been employed by Lexie Lovell to locate your son, Theodore." Both men watched the woman carefully. She frowned, but even her frown was slow to arrive. It looked as if she was having a hard time processing their questions, or maybe was on drugs. Even in prison, they were fairly easy to acquire.

"I don't have a kid," she finally said.

"Do you have any information about the whereabouts of Theodore Chase Lovell?"

"He's my sister's kid," she said.

"You two certainly look alike," Wayne said.

"Twins," the woman said. "I'm Poppy, she's Pansy."

Wayne and PD met each other's eyes. Their being twins explained a lot. "We need to find your sister and the boy. Can you tell us where they are?"

"I have no idea. Are we done?" she asked.

"When was the last time you spoke with your sister?" Wayne asked.

"We had lunch the day I got arrested. Asked her for some money, but she said she didn't have any. I don't know where she is. Can I go back to my cell now?"

"In a minute. How did you come to get picked up?" Wayne asked.

"It was evening when I saw this dim-witted looking guy walking along the alley in Rosedale. I asked him he wanted to party. As you know, it's the normal pick-up line we use. The idiot said he would love to go to a party, but wanted to know who else was coming and what he should bring." She shook her head in disgust. "I drove back to Nashville and got picked up by the cops later that evening."

"What did your sister do for a living, Poppy?"

"Real estate. Worked for Centennial Realty in Rosedale. She met Lovell when she got him that big red-brick manor house."

"Does your sister have a car?" PD asked.

"She did, but it broke down. Don't think she had the money to fix it. Are we finished? I have a headache."

"If you think of anything, however trivial, about where your sister and her boy might be, please contact us," Wayne said before agreeing that, at least for now, they were done.

Miss Delaney stood up and the guard came forward to lead her from the room.

Wayne clicked off the Zoom meeting and walked into the kitchen for some coffee.

"Twins. That's why facial recognition thought they were the same person. I didn't think she was lying, did you, Wayne?" PD asked.

"No, I don't think she has a clue where her sister or her nephew are," Wayne said as he returned with his coffee mug to the conference room.

"At least the mother and child are alive or were on the day Poppy got picked up for soliciting," PD responded.

"Unless they've been murdered and the bodies haven't been found yet," Wayne added and the two men looked at each other . . . saying nothing further in the hungry silence of the empty room.

SEVEN

THE FOLLOWING MORNING WAYNE CAME BY Dory's house and picked up Billy Jo who had spent the night there. They were headed for the Sheriff's office. The previous evening, as everyone was preparing to knock off for the day, PD asked Billy Jo if she would be okay staying in the building alone. She said "yes" but there was a little quaver in her voice. The three senior partners immediately decided that until they knew who had shot at her during her sortie to the Lovell mansion, she needed protection. Dory volunteered, saying that Billy Jo was welcome to stay with her until the situation was resolved. Despite Billy Jo's rather feeble attempts to convince them she would be fine alone, Wayne thought she looked mightily relieved.

Wayne had worked as a Detective for the Sheriff's office for nearly twenty years before his recent retirement to join Rosedale Investigations. It hadn't been an easy transition and as they drove into the parking lot that morning, he realized seeing the old building again and greeting his former colleagues was continuing to be difficult—especially since he knew he would be seeing Undersheriff and Detective Rob Fuller sitting at was used to be *his* desk.

Wayne's mask was lying on the seat of his car. Lucy had insisted he wear one but he usually took it off while driving.

As they parked the car, Billy Jo said, "How are you and Lucy dealing with the pandemic? I know she's a first-responder and you two live together."

"We are lucky because coming into the house from the garage, the laundry room is on one side of the hall and there's a bathroom on the other. When Lucy comes home from the hospital, she strips off all her clothes, puts them directly into the washer, and then takes a long shower. We both spray our shoes with bleach and wash our hands when we come into the house. Plus, Lucy's screened every time she enters the hospital and gets tested frequently. Let's head inside."

"Please note the sign on the door to the Sheriff's office that says you won't be allowed in without a mask," Billy Jo reminded him, and Wayne, feeling dumb for forgetting, put his on.

ONCE INSIDE, THEY GREETED THE RECEPTIONIST, Mrs. Coffin, who was wearing three masks. One was the fabric type. She wore a re-breather mask on top of that and there was a flip-down plastic shield over the others.

"Good Morning, Mrs. Coffin," Wayne greeted her. "I'm here to talk with Ben. Is he in?"

The woman responded, but the triple mask made it all but impossible to understand what she said. She tipped her head toward the hall. Wayne and Billy Jo walked down the corridor with its old tile and fluorescent lighting. The building was a time capsule from the 50s. Wayne's usual feelings of ambivalence about leaving his former life as a detective punched him in his gut.

Knocking on the Sheriff's door, they heard him say, "Come in."

Sheriff Ben Bradley was sitting at his desk, eyeing his computer monitor and wearing his uniform. Wayne knew he was considered by women to be very good-looking. Lucy said he was, but Ben just looked like a regular guy to him. He wasn't much of a judge of male attractiveness. He did notice that Ben had dark circles under his eyes. He and his wife, Mae, had twin baby girls. No doubt the little ones, as well as the demands of his job, were causing the sheriff's fatigue.

"Good Morning," Sheriff Bradley said. "What can I do for you two this morning?"

"As I mentioned when I called yesterday, Billy Jo got herself shot at during her investigation for our most recent case. We're calling the shooter Snake Wrist, because he has a snake tattoo, one of those where the snake bites his tail. As background, Rosedale Investigations was hired by a Miss Lexie Lovell to find her brother, Teddy, the son of Mr. Edward Lovell, a recently deceased accountant and a Ms. Pansy Delaney. Billy Jo was at Lovell's house looking for information that would tell us where the boy was when she was attacked. PD and I went over to the house where the incident occurred and found two shell casings and one bullet. Here they are," he said handing the plastic envelopes to the Sheriff.

"Right. I'll get these down to the lab. Did you want to report a crime, Billy Jo?" Sheriff Bradley asked.

She glanced at Wayne who nodded. "I guess," she said.

"I'm going to have my Under Sheriff and Detective, Rob Fuller, join us to take your statement." Ben got up and left his office, returning shortly thereafter. Detective Rob was tall with silver-rimmed glasses and an intensely focused gaze. He was still fairly new to the rank of Detective and Wayne considered him inexperienced, but knew he was smart and focused.

"Rob, this is Billy Jo Bradley. She's here to report a crime and we're taking an official statement from her," Sheriff Bradley said.

Wayne stood, and despite the social distancing recommendations, shook Rob's hand. They needed no introduction as they had worked together for several years. Wayne tightened his grip hard, meeting Rob's eyes. Rob looked startled and Wayne felt ashamed of himself for trying to assert his physical superiority in the situation. It wasn't Rob's fault that when the Sheriff's office took some recent budget cuts, Wayne was encouraged to take early retirement, and Rob was kept on the payroll.

An hour later, Billy Jo's statement had been taken and she had signed and dated it. As Wayne knew it would be, the session had been intense. Both Sheriff Bradley and Detective Fuller bore down hard on the number of people she had seen by the bonfire. She wavered, sometimes saying there were two people, sometimes three. When she described the man who came after her, she was only able to say he was a white guy and had a strong grip. He was able to chase her for over an hour before she could no longer hear his harsh breathing. Because the attack happened in the dark, she was excused from the usual drill of looking at headshots.

When they were about to leave, Billy Jo said she needed the Ladies' room. Sheriff Bradley and Rob waited with Wayne in the area by the reception desk. A standing Plexiglas shield had been rigged up in front of Mrs. Coffin's desk and strips of yellow tape on the floor indicated the recommended six-foot distances.

"What's your take on this one, Wayne?" Ben asked.

"PD and I think Mr. Edward Lovell might have been an accountant for the mob. I believe his ex-wife knew he worked for them and was burning his files so that no proof remained of his involvement. As you know, if his money came from illegal activity, it would be confiscated and couldn't be passed down to her daughter, Lexie. Billy Jo thinks that Lexie and her fiancé left the house before the bonfire was started, and the people she saw standing around the fire were Lovell's attorney, a man named Brad Carver, his ex-wife and if there was a third man, it was probably the guy who shot at Billy Jo."

"I agree. I'll look into this and contact Captain Paula in Nashville. They have a Gang Squad and one of those guys could know something— if indeed we are dealing with the mob. Possibly we'll get lucky and there will be fingerprints on the shell casings or the bullet. I'll let you know as soon as I get the report. Thanks for reporting Ms. Delaney and her son being missing. I'll inform Nashville."

Billy Jo came out of the Ladies' room and walked up to the men.

"I just remembered two more things, Sheriff. I bit the man who grabbed me, so he might have a mark on his hand and he wore a ring. It wasn't a wedding ring because it was on his right hand."

"Good work," Rob told her. "Was it just a plain band or did it have a stone?"

"There must have been a stone on it because at one point while we were scuffling, the stone cut into my hand." She held out her hand which had a small scratch.

THEY DIDN'T TALK MUCH ON THE DRIVE BACK to Rosedale Investigations. Reporting the crime to the Sheriff had left Billy Jo shaken and subdued. Wayne was deep in thought about Edward Lovell. The man was probably planning to get remarried on the trip to Greece. He had a baby son by then. Perhaps he was sick of working for the mob and wanted out. Or he might have been turning State's evidence. If so, his death was extremely convenient and Wayne wondered if it was due to natural causes. He needed to find out if Lovell's body had been cremated. If he had, an exhumation would be useless, as virtually all evidence of a murder would have been lost.

Then his mind turned to the woman in the case, Pansy Delaney. She was the realtor who handled the sale of the red stone mansion to Lovell. Was she also employed by the mob? It would make sense if both she and her sister were connected to them. The mob often ran prostitution rackets and perhaps both women were recruited for that purpose. Pansy Jane had been smarter, or luckier, and had managed to get a real estate license and avoid the sex trade that had been so hard on her twin. And where was Pansy now, he wondered? And where was her son, Teddy? Hopefully, Dory had come up with something in her review of the missing person's register. A woman alone who went missing was sadly all too commonplace, but a missing woman with a toddler would have raised a lot more eyebrows.

REACHING ROSEDALE INVESTIGATIONS, they saw DORY standing on the porch and waving them down. Exiting the car, Billy Jo and Wayne walked up the sidewalk toward her.

"What gives, Dory?" Wayne asked.

"We have a new client in the conference room, but I wanted to hear what happened at the Sheriff's Office before you came inside. Didn't want them to hear what was said. I scanned them both with the thermometer and made them use hand sanitizer. What happened, Billy Jo?"

"I gave my statement to the Sheriff and Detective Fuller," she said quietly.

"Good work," Dory said. "What does Ben think?"

"We discussed the incident and Ben's going to talk to the Gang Squad in Nashville. Some of Nashville's Finest might be undercover with the mob. If we're right and it is the mob, their enterprises normally cross state lines. In which case, the FBI will have to be informed."

"The feds?" Billy Jo grimaced, looking fearful.

"Let's not get ahead of ourselves here. We are only guessing it's the mob. We could very well be wrong," Wayne said as the three of them walked into the building.

WHEN DORY OPENED THE CONFERENCE ROOM DOOR, Wayne saw a couple seated at the far end of the table. The woman was in her late thirties, the man a bit older. The man stood up when they entered.

"I'm Garth Roberts," he said. Roberts had a round face and was just turning gray at his temples. He was a big man, fleshy but not fat. "This is my wife, Jill." The woman smiled and nodded.

"I'm Detective Nichols and this is Billy Jo Bradley," Wayne said.

"Mr. and Mrs. Roberts are here about her grandparents," Dory said. "Both are deceased, but they died in different states. Their names are Vivien and Charles Carson. Vivien Carson is buried here in Rosedale. Charles Carson is, in theory, buried in Waseca, Minnesota."

"In theory?" Wayne asked, turning to the couple.

"Yes, we recently traveled to Minnesota to visit his grave, but we couldn't find it in the cemetery where he was supposed to be," Jill Roberts said. "I brought copies of both their death certificates. I'd like my grand-father's body found, brought to Rosedale, and re-buried next to his wife. My mother Angela, has asked me to take care of this."

"Is there any particular urgency about this matter?" Wayne asked. He was hoping it could be put off.

"There is. My mother is in critical care in the hospital at present. Before she leaves us, she wants to visit her parents' graves and have both of them interred side by side in the same cemetery. We have a family reunion planned for her 80th birthday. It's in a month and it's going to take place at the park next to the Rosedale cemetery. Everyone is planning on visiting the graves then, provided you can find my grandfather."

"I already told Mr. and Mrs. Roberts that we would start the process of locating her grandfather right away," Dory said, looking intently at Wayne.

Wayne, who never disagreed with his partner in front of anyone, nodded reluctantly. They would discuss the matter later, but he wished Dory had deferred their case. The attack on Billy Jo, the possibility of mob involvement in the life of Edward Lovell, and a missing woman and little boy dominated his thinking. In his mind, there was nothing urgent about reuniting a *deceased* couple—not when compared with finding a missing child. Then he remembered the fragile emotional state of his young colleague. Perhaps if they made Billy Jo the lead on this case, it would keep her busy and staying put in the office where they could keep an eye on her.

EIGHT

WAYNE WENT TO THE SANDWICH SHOP down the street to get three lunches and when he returned they ate at the conference room table. Afterward, Dory cleared away the sandwich wrappings and paper cups. Billy Jo got out her bleach wipes and wiped down the table. She handed around the hand sanitizer.

"I've been thinking about our next steps. Since I'm the senior partner whenever PD is out of the office, I'm going to assign tasks," Wayne said.

"For the Lovell case or the Missing Grandfather case?" Dory asked.

"Both. I'd like to make you, Billy Jo, the lead investigator on the Missing Grandfather case."

"Really? Lead?" she brightened.

Wayne nodded. "Here's where I'd start. First, I'd carefully review Mr. Carson's death certificate. It should list where and when he died. Other important information includes the person who pronounced him dead. That's usually a doctor or a nurse, but depending on the circumstances could be a coroner or medical examiner. There's often a funeral home, a crematory, or someone listed who took charge of the remains. That's the starting point for locating the body."

Billy Jo had been quickly making notes as Wayne spoke and raised her hand.

"Questions?" Wayne asked.

"Yes. What if he was in the military? Is that important information too?"

"It is, especially if he had a military funeral. If no one was there from the family to take charge of the remains, the military could have claimed the body."

"I'll get on it right away. How often do you want reports, Wayne?"

"Once a day is enough, Billy Jo. And if I'm out of the office, you can give your report to Dory. Now, as far as the Lovell case goes, it appears that the Blind Split is a particularly apt analogy. We seem to be bumbling around in the dark with no leads at all on the whereabouts of Pansy Jane or her little boy. Dory, you were going to check the Missing Person's Register. What did you find?"

"Nada. Not a thing. And before you ask, I also checked all the suspicious deaths in the entire county for the past year. No Jane Does whose vital stats matched Pansy Jane. And I checked children with suspicious deaths, too. Nothing showed up."

"Unfortunately, we didn't get much out of her sister. She was withdrawn and apathetic when PD and I talked to her, but might be more amenable to talking to a woman. I'd like you to see if she will agree to add you to her list of approved visitors, Dory, so you can have a video meeting. Maybe the twins had a special place they liked to go as children. I also wondered where Pansy and Ed Lovell were going in Greece."

"Not a problem, but Pansy didn't go to Greece, remember? The tickets weren't used," Dory said.

"I've been thinking about that. Possibly she was in such a hurry to get out of town that she didn't use the tickets, but she might have flown. See if she and the boy took a flight to Athens."

Dory nodded and asked, "What are you going to be up to, Partner?"

"I have a request for Dr. Lucy. She has the day off and I'd like to get her to pose as my wife and go with me to Centennial Realty. I thought we might ask whether the red stone mansion is for sale, and to work with a particular agent named Pansy Delaney."

"Asking Lucy to pose as your *wife*, leads me to another question," Dory said.

"Yes?" Wayne raised his eyebrows innocently.

"Have you proposed to the woman yet or is there still something that prevents your stupid knees from bending," Dory said and both she and Billy Jo grinned.

Wayne shook his head, starting to gather his belongings, his cell phone, and sunglasses.

"You have had that ring for a year!" Dory said in an exasperated tone. "It's going to wear a hole in your pocket or Lucy is going to find it."

"I hide the box in my bottom drawer at night," Wayne said smugly and started leaving the room.

"Right, like Lucy isn't going to find it there, Moron!" Dory called after him, raising her eyes heavenward.

Billy Jo hummed the Beyoncé song "If you like it, put a ring on it."

"What happened to opera?" Dory asked, remembering Billy Jo's love for the musical entertainment which led to her purchasing a very expensive gown the previous year.

"I love it, as you know, but *singing* opera, as opposed to *listening* to opera, is way above my skill level," she said.

"Moving on, let's review what you learned from Lovell's computer," Dory said.

"I feel so dumb. What I should have done was remove the hard drive and leave the house right afterward. If I had, I wouldn't have had to go through being locked in a cupboard and being attacked by a gunman," Billy Jo blanched and clenched her teeth.

"True, but when Lexie or her mother noticed the hard drive was gone, they would have called the Sheriff immediately and even in little Rosedale there are CCTV cameras at the entrance to pricey neighborhoods. They would have ID'd your car right away. And then there would be extremely awkward questions about how you got into the house, which was illegal you know, and you'd have to turn over the hard drive."

"Thanks, Dory. That makes me feel better. Anyway, I think one of the most important things I found were the names of Pansy Jane's OB/GYN doctor and the name of little Theodore's pediatrician. They might have more information for us."

"Yes they might. When you were at the Sheriff's office, Wayne said he reported both Pansy and Teddy as missing persons. Without such a report, the doctors can't release information."

"While I was in the Lovell mansion, I managed to copy about 98% of Mr. Lovell's emails. PD presumed Pansy used his email account and if so, we could find out who she was emailing before she disappeared. I skimmed through them very quickly. I need to print them off and read them carefully."

"What else did you notice?"

"Well, we thought the red stone mansion belonged to Edward Lovell, but it didn't. He had a month-to-month rental agreement with Centennial Realty's Rental Management Division."

"Text Wayne right away. He needs to know that the house was a rental before he and Lucy get to Centennial Realty."

"Will do. There was a contact person listed for the rental. Guess who?"

"Don't have a clue," Dory said.

"It was Lovell's lawyer, Mr. Bradley Carver."

"That makes sense. If we're right and this is the mob we're dealing with, they like to keep their friends close . . . and their enemies closer."

"What should we do first?" Billy Jo asked.

"If you want to print those emails off, I'll start reading them," Dory said. "Why don't you call the doctors? Start out by telling them that Pansy and Teddy have been reported to the Sheriff's Office as missing persons. That way they won't have HIPPA issues in telling you what they have on file. See what address and phone Pansy Jane listed with them and the dates of her last appointments. Oh, and one other thing. Ask the little boy's pediatrician if he had any serious conditions, birth defects or diseases and if he had been immunized for measles, chickenpox, etc."

DRIVING OUT OF ROSEDALE TOWARD THE HOME he shared with Dr. Lucy Ingram, Wayne knew Dory was right. He'd stalled for a whole year on proposing. Both of them had just been so busy, it had been hard to carve out any time to go to some special place where he could pop the question. *That's a pretty flimsy excuse, Dumbass,*" he told himself. Lucy's birthday was coming up at the end of the summer and he made a mental pledge to propose on her birthday. Meanwhile, since he was about to ask her for a big favor on one of her few days off, he stopped at the grocery store and bought a large bundle of flowers. *Couldn't hurt,* he thought.

He arrived home, parked his car, and entered the home from the garage. He washed his hands before looking through several kitchen cupboards to find a vase large enough to hold the bouquet which included lilies, roses, some blue spiky flowers, and ferns in the tissue-papered bundle. He put the flowers into a big crystal vase and added cold water.

"Lucy?" he called. Hearing no response, he walked through the house carrying the flowers and out to their screened-in back porch. They had recently bought a comfy couch for the area and Dr. Lucy was sound asleep, snoring faintly, on the bottle green velvet sofa. She was wearing a nightgown which meant she had been awake but then had fallen back to sleep. He knew it was risky to wake her for any reason, she worked long hours and was often exhausted, but the life of a small child could be at stake. "Wake up, Honey," he said and touched her shoulder.

"What?" Lucy sat up suddenly and then to his surprise, he had been expecting profanity, she smiled. "What are you doing home?" she asked.

"I just wanted to see you. I brought some flowers." He placed the vase on the coffee table in front of the sofa.

Lucy's eyes narrowed. "You brought flowers? That means either you have done something stupid or you want something, which is it?" she asked.

"I'd like us to go house hunting and know the real estate agency I want to use."

Lucy looked startled. When Wayne moved into Lucy's house, they had briefly discussed finding a new place together. However, that topic had quickly been abandoned and hadn't resurfaced in several years. She settled back on the sofa and asked the pertinent question.

"Would this house be for us? Or for a case? Never mind, I can see from the expression on your face that it's for a case. This had better be good, Detective Nichols." She frowned.

"Would saving the life of a little boy be good enough?" Wayne asked

"I'll get dressed," she said and immediately rose from the couch.

"Don't you want the details?" he called.

"You can tell me in the car," she replied, her voice floating back from their bedroom.

That kind of instant response is only one of the reasons I want to marry the woman, Wayne thought and smiled.

WALKING OUT TO THE GARAGE, Lucy scooped the keys from Wayne's hand saying, "I'll drive while you tell me what this is all about." He thought she looked particularly attractive in her white sundress splashed with black flowers and a black jacket. She'd brought him a sport coat and tie. He struggled to put them on in her small car.

"You were going to tell me about the case," Lucy said.

"We've been looking for a missing person, a woman named Pansy Jane Delaney and her son. She was going to be married to Edward Lovell, they already had a little boy together. It was a second marriage for him and a first for her. Before they could marry, Lovell died and his will specified that his estate was to be divided between his daughter, Lexie, from his first marriage and his son, Teddy. Lexie was the person who came to Rosedale Investigations last spring asking for help finding her brother. Until the will was read, she had no idea she even had a brother. According to Lovell's executor, the money can't be disbursed until Teddy is found."

"Go on," Lucy was driving fast, navigating around a pokey little blue car and just barely making it through a yellow light. Wayne was surreptitiously pushing an imaginary brake pedal to the floor and wishing she would slow down.

"Bottom line, we can't find the woman or the child. The mother, Pansy, has a twin sister who's in jail for solicitation. We've talked to her, but she has no idea where her sister and nephew are. There are no other family members that she knows of. Pansy was, and hopefully still is, employed by Centennial Realty, so when we get there we're going to ask to work with her. Lovell rented the big red stone mansion and she was the agent who arranged the deal. That's how they met."

"Is the red mansion the house in the White Oaks subdivision you described to me?" Lucy asked.

"Yes, but here's the kicker. We think Pansy Delaney may have worked for the mob."

"The mob?" Lucy raised her eyebrows as she laid on the horn, swerving around a pick-up truck.

"Lucy, for God's sakes slow down! You are not here to set a land speed record. And yes, we think the mob could be involved."

"Sorry, Wayne," she said, slowing down to a crawl as they entered the city limits of Rosedale. "I gather we're hoping Pansy Jane is still working at Centennial and has her little boy with her. Right?"

Wayne nodded and concentrated on directing her to the office of Centennial Realty. They pulled into the parking area shortly and Lucy turned off the car.

"For this covert operation, we are newly married and want to get a home together. We have heard good things about Miss Delaney and want to work with her. Got it?"

"About to get married are we?" Lucy said looking directly at Wayne who quickly turned his head, hiding a wry grin and avoiding eye contact.

NINE

"MAY I HELP YOU?" THE BLONDE receptionist at Centennial Realty asked as Wayne and Lucy entered the office. The place was a replica of multiple other realtor agencies. There were chairs around the perimeter of the waiting room and photographs of houses adorned the walls. The pictures had little written tags on them, showing the price and the date sold.

"Yes, thank you. I'm Wayne Nichols and this is my lovely wife, Lucy. We've recently gotten married and are looking for a home. She's not happy with my bachelor pad. It's full of old black La-Z-Boy chairs," he said, smiling fondly at Lucy.

"No, she's not happy with his taste in chairs," Lucy said crisply. "And he's not comfortable with all the floral wallpaper and the multiplicity of throw pillows at my house. We need a new place and we're hoping to work with Pansy Delaney. Is she working here?"

The receptionist frowned. "No, not any longer. She left about a month ago. And she wasn't a real estate agent paid by Centennial. She was an independent contractor."

Wayne frowned. He didn't want to say he was a private investigator, but he needed more information. To his surprise, Lucy jumped in.

"We are friends with some people who know Pansy Jane. We've just moved to Rosedale and promised we'd look her up. Could you give us her address and phone number?" she asked.

Beautiful, Wayne thought. *Hope it works.*

"I'm not sure I should," the receptionist said, hesitating.

"We wouldn't ask you under normal circumstances, but my dumb husband here has just gotten around to informing me that he's the

Godfather to her little boy. I haven't met Teddy, and we have a gift for him," Lucy smiled.

Woman's a natural. She should work undercover, Wayne thought.

"I guess it would be okay then. She adores that little boy," the receptionist said and clicked on her computer. "Here it is. She was living in the White Oaks neighborhood for a while, but last I knew was going to have to move. Ed's attorney wouldn't give her any money until the business was sold. The house was a rental and she didn't have enough money to pay the rent. I couldn't believe the attorney wouldn't help her. Seemed fishy to me. I don't have her new address but here's her phone number." She read it out and Lucy copied it down.

"Thank you so much, Christy," Lucy said, having read the name plaque on her desk. "We will be sure to come back and work with your agency as soon as we locate Pansy Jane."

Taking Wayne's arm, Lucy led her fictional husband from the office.

"You are just amazing, Lucy," Wayne said. "Can you call that phone number? I'll drive."

Lucy dialed but there was no answer. She left a message saying she had recently moved to Rosedale and had been given Pansy Delaney's name as the person to contact about renting a house in Rosedale. She said they were interested in renting the red stone mansion in White Oaks.

"I knew it was unlikely she would answer, but it was worth a try. I'll find out who the phone number belongs to and whether it's a burner. If by chance Pansy does call back, set up a meeting, will you?" Wayne asked.

"Have you forgotten that I have a *job*? If she returns the call, I'll give her your phone number, but that's all. You'll have to take over at that point. I'm on-call starting at 4:00 today."

Wayne nodded and thanked her. As they drove through the outskirts of Rosedale on their way home, he said, "At least Pansy Delaney was alive a week ago."

"You thought she might be dead?" Lucy asked.

"I've got a bad feeling about this one like maybe the woman is dead and that little boy is all alone in the world. Father dead, Mother missing and his only blood relative, besides his half-sister, is the mom's twin. And she's in jail."

DORY HAD BEEN READING THROUGH THE LOVELL EMAILS steadily for an hour without learning anything significant. They were singularly uninformative. She was about to get up and ask Billy Jo to go with her to the Flower Pot district and walk her dog when she finally came upon something interesting.

"*I'm getting scared. Can you meet me tomorrow? Coffee Shop on Main Street and Green. 10:00.*" The email had been sent to LWells1897. Dory flipped quickly through the few remaining pages. There were no other emails addressed to LWells1897 and no return emails from that address.

"Come in here a minute, Billy Jo. I found something."

Billy Jo came into Dory's office with news of her own. "Just got off the phone with Teddy's pediatrician. I talked to the person who answered the phone, said I was from Rosedale Investigations and told her that the boy was missing. That got her attention and she checked with Dr. Jenkins. He wanted to talk to me. He asked me a bunch more questions but finally said he hoped we would find the child soon. Teddy needed medical attention routinely and at their last appointment, he had referred them to a pediatric cardiologist. The little boy has a heart murmur."

"This is scary. A kid in my extended family died of complications from a heart murmur," Dory said quietly.

"What did you want to show me?" Billy Jo asked and Dory pointed to the email.

"We need to show this to Wayne and PD. Have you heard from PD by the way? I thought he was supposed to be in today." Billy Jo frowned and chewed on her fingernail.

"He was and no, I haven't heard anything. I'll call his cell." When there was no answer, Dory left a message. Then she called Wayne.

"What's up?" he asked.

"We have some things we need to discuss. Have you heard from PD?"

"Yes, he called me. He had a doctor's appointment for a check-up today and the doctor said because of his age he should work from home instead of coming into the office. He's agreed and will be staying at the cabin for the next two weeks. I'll come by the office in about an hour," he said.

WHEN WAYNE ARRIVED, DORY ASKED HIM what he'd learned from his visit to the realtor's office.

"Lucy and I went to Centennial Realty and found out Pansy Jane hasn't worked there for a month. We got a phone number, but there was no answer."

"When I went to the Lovell mansion, I rifled the mailbox," Billy Jo said. Seeing identical frowns on the faces of Wayne and Dory, she said, "Don't worry. I didn't *take* anything, just looked at what was there. I found a letter with a return address of the Tennessee Prison for Women. It was dated a week ago."

"So, Poppy wrote her sister a letter and sent it to that address a week ago, when she told us she didn't know where her sister was living since she got picked up. Did you get an interview set up with her, Dory?" Wayne asked.

"I had Sheriff Bradley call the Warden. You and PD got Pansy to add you to her list of approved callers without an official request, but the Warden doesn't know me. Ben called the Warden and had her add me. Our appointment's tomorrow. I was going through the emails and found one Pansy wrote to someone with the email address of LWells1897. In the email, she said she was scared."

"This is all helpful stuff. It tells us that Pansy Delaney was alive a week ago and that she has a friend named Wells with a first initial L. When you talk to her twin sister tomorrow try to find out who that is," Wayne said. "What have you got Billy Jo?"

"I called the boy's pediatrician. He's very concerned because the boy has a heart murmur. I also got the name of the pediatric cardiologist he was referred to and called their office. They were very reluctant to tell me anything at first, but I finally learned that Teddy's mother had never taken him to his scheduled appointment."

"That's troubling. I'm thinking we need a bit of police help on this one. I'm going to call the Sheriff and ask him for any information they might have on Edward Lovell. I also called Mark Schneider and asked him to come in."

"Who is that?" Billy Jo asked.

"A young computer geek they have on staff in Nashville. We've borrowed him several times for cases I worked at the Sheriff's office. I'm going to ask him to look over the email data you found and also see what he can learn from Pansy Jane's phone number. I think that's Mark now," Wayne said, hearing a series of quick rhythmic knocks on the door.

MARK SCHNEIDER WAS A SKINNY COLLEGE-AGE KID with a thatch of black spiky hair. From times when he helped with earlier cases, Wayne remembered he had a multi-colored dragon tattooed on his back. When

Mark bent down to remove his shoes, Wayne could see the dragon's mouth with its fiery tongue sticking up out of the neck of his t-shirt.

Dory came up and said, "Hi, Mark." She handed him some hand sanitizer and ran the thermometer in the air across his forehead. "It's 97.6 degrees. No fever," she told him.

"Thanks for coming over, Mark. We could really use your help," Wayne said.

"No problem. Glad to make a bit of extra cash. The Nashville post hasn't needed me much since the epidemic started. What do you want me to do?"

"Come into the conference room. We are trying to find a little boy named Teddy Lovell. His father is dead and his mother is missing."

"We've already checked Missing Persons and Jane Does. No unknown toddlers dead, or women who match the boy's mother in relevant details," Dory said.

When all of them were seated at the big table, Wayne pulled out the thick file of printed emails Billy Jo had obtained. "These are from Lovell's computer. He's the missing boy's father. The mother's name is Pansy Jane Delaney."

Mark Schneider frowned. "All I can give you is the IP address of the computer from these, and make a list of the names of people they were emailing, but I'm guessing you already know that much. It would be better to check their phones. Do you have the guy's cell phone? Or the woman's?"

Wayne shook his head. "No, I only have Pansy's cell phone number. What I'm hoping is that you can get the cell service provider to give you the last few numbers she called. It looks like she didn't pay her bill, and the company recently shut off her service."

"I take it you're asking me to do this because you're unwilling to ask Sheriff Bradley or Captain Paula from Nashville for those contacts?"

"You got it," Wayne said. "I'm retired now and hate to ask them for favors."

"Well, we should have a subpoena, but since the cell service people know me, I can probably get the numbers she called. Wish you had the phones themselves, but will that help?"

"It certainly will, Mark. Plus, you've just given me a good idea. I assumed when Edward Lovell died that his personal effects were given to his fiancé, but I didn't check. I do have an 'in' with Rosedale General. I'll go over there tomorrow and see what I can find. I'll leave you to it," Wayne said.

TEN

SITTING AT THE CONFERENCE ROOM TABLE the following afternoon, Dory glanced at her watch. It was almost one o'clock, the time for her Zoom appointment with Poppy. She clicked on the link Billy Jo had set up and in just moments the door at the back of the room at the prison opened and a guard, holding the upper arm of the woman tightly, entered the room. She was dressed in the usual orange jumpsuit issued to prisoners. Orange was definitely not her color. Dory prided herself on knowing what colors went best with which complexions.

"Sit," the guard said and seated her forcibly.

"Let go of me," she said angrily, pulling her arm out of his grip.

Dory waited a moment while the woman regained her composure before greeting her saying, "Hi Poppy, I'm Dory Clarkson. Thank you for agreeing to this meeting. I'm one of the investigators looking for your sister and her little boy. You talked to two of my colleagues recently, Detectives Nichols and Pascoe. Do you remember meeting with them?" She stopped speaking then, waiting for the woman's reaction. Wayne had said she seemed withdrawn and depressed.

"I remember," Poppy said. "I told them I didn't know anything."

"So they said, but they were men and I think, given your profession, you probably don't have much respect for the male gender. And sometimes after a person is interviewed, they remember something else they could have said. We're very concerned about your sister and her little boy."

"I haven't talked to her," she said with a sullen expression.

"That's probably true, as far as it goes, Poppy, but you wrote a letter to your sister just a week ago and sent it to the house where she was living with Edward Lovell." Poppy Delaney looked as if she was going to deny the charge but Dory continued saying, "We've seen the letter and its postmark date."

Poppy slumped a little, caught in a fib.

"Even if you haven't had contact with your sister, I've heard that twins, especially identical twins, often have a kind of psychic connection. I have friends who are twins (a complete fabrication) and they always know when the other one is in trouble. I'm wondering if the reason we can't find your sister, Pansy Jane, is because she's left the country or is hurt. Is she . . ." Dory took a shaky breath.

"I know she's alive," Poppy sounded certain and Dory felt immensely reassured.

"I knew you could help us. My twin friends also told me that if one of them is in pain, the other one often feels it too. Is Pansy injured?"

Poppy shook her head. "Just scared," she said.

Dory deliberately made her voice kind and supportive saying, "I sure hate to see you in this place. It's hard for a gal to make a living as a working girl, isn't it?"

"It is," Poppy said. "I get beat up and then I'm the one in trouble with the law. Why the hell aren't the cops looking for the creep who did this?" she gestured, pointing to the fading bruises on her face.

"I agree with you. You give me his name and I'll see what I can do. I worked for the Sheriff's office in Rosedale for a long time and have lots of cop friends."

Poppy shook her head. "Can't do that. If I go to the cops, he'll beat me again. Worse next time."

"Well, if you change your mind about that, call me and I will do my best to lock the asshole up," Dory said, showing the woman her card by lifting it up to the Zoom camera. Poppy wrote the number down. "Back to your twin sister again, if you were in trouble where you would go?"

Poppy sighed and was quiet for some time. Dory waited her out. Finally, the woman took a deep breath and said, "Our folks owned an 80-acre farm north of Appleton. It's on Healy Road, about ten miles out of town. When they died, neither of us wanted to take it on. I don't think anybody ever bought it. She and the boy could be out there. The house is pretty much falling apart, but we lived there our whole childhoods."

"Good. That's helpful. I just have one other question for you. I'm also looking for a friend of your sister's whose last name is Wells. Her first name starts with the letter L. Do you know who that is?"

"Lucinda Wells. She lived near us when we were growing up. We all went to the same rural school. Her folks own a farm down the road. She's a student-teacher now," Poppy paused and a bit of a crafty smile came across her face. "Since I've helped you, Miss Dory, can you pull some strings and maybe get me out of here early?"

"The problem is, Poppy, I saw on your record that you took a knife to the john who beat you up. And you robbed him. That's not going to work in your favor."

"I was only defending myself and the bastard owed me that money. Isn't there anything you can do?"

Dory was quiet for a few minutes before saying, "I personally consider prostitution a victimless crime and wish it would be decriminalized, but to get the case re-opened, you would need to talk to the Rosedale Sheriff. I'll see if he's willing to help, but you have to tell him the name of your pimp. Don't worry, you can trust him to keep it to himself. He's a good guy."

"Thanks, Miss Dory," Poppy said. "Anything you can do is mighty appreciated."

"I want to thank you for your help. You may have saved your twin sister's life, and her little boy's, too. When we find her, I'll be sure to let you know," Dory smiled at the woman and said goodbye. The guard moved forward and took Poppy by the arm, as the smile faded from her face. Dory clicked "end meeting," and walked out to Billy Jo's station.

"I may just have found Pansy Jane and her son," she said. "Could you find out the address of the old Delaney farm on Healy Road? It's about ten miles north of Appleton. I also need an address for a nearby farm belonging to the Wells family. I want to go out there yet today."

"That's great news! I'll get right on it. I've made some progress on the Missing Grandfather case, too," Billy Jo said.

Dory thought she sounded almost back to her old self. "What have you found?"

"I called Mrs. Roberts and found out that Charles Carson had a summer cottage in Minnesota. He always took a fishing trip up there in June. Normally, his wife or a friend went with him, but sometimes he went alone, especially after his wife passed away. The cottage was on a small lake and he was careful about wearing a life vest, so his daughter didn't worry."

"Go on," Dory said.

"The hospital tried to identify a next of kin. They had an address from his wallet, but when they called the phone number, nobody answered. They left multiple messages. After forty-eight hours without hearing from the family, they contacted the local funeral parlor. Mr. Carson had a card in his wallet requesting cremation in the case of his death. Now here's where it gets interesting," Billy Jo paused to take a sip of her soda.

"Need to stop you there for a moment, Billy Jo. I want Wayne to go to the Delaney farm with me in case there's any trouble. Can you call him and tell him to come to the office?" Dory asked.

"Sure thing," Billy Jo said.

WAYNE NICHOLS WAS EN ROUTE TO ROSEDALE GENERAL hoping to search the Lost Property office. He felt incredibly stupid assuming Edward Lovell's personal effects had gone to Pansy Jane when he died. His assumption meant he had missed a chance to get ahold of Lovell's phone. He remembered what his mentor in the Detroit Police Department had told him as a rookie. "Never assume. *Assuming makes an Ass out of u and me.*"

He parked his truck near the visitor entrance. Just inside the large glass door was a young man seated at a table. Walking up to the door, Wayne pulled his mask from his pocket and put it on. Once inside, he opened his wallet to his Private Detective ID card and showed it to the security guard.

"Hi. I'm Detective Nichols. I'm here to obtain some property left by a patient who died in the hospital. This is a criminal matter so I assume you can permit me to enter the hospital. Can you tell me where I should start?"

"Let me make a quick call," the young man said. Wayne waited while he talked briefly to a supervisor. When he ended the call he said, "Take the elevator to the fourth-floor nurses' station."

"Who would I talk to?" Wayne asked.

"Ward staff or department heads are responsible for patient property. The items are put into an envelope with the patient's name on it and then locked in the safe."

"The patient died of a heart attack, I believe."

"Then you will need Cardiology, or possibly the ICU. I'd start with the Nurse Administrator for Cardiac Care. Her name is Susan

Wolfe-Campion."

Wayne thanked him, walked over to the bank of elevators, and punched the button for the fourth floor.

"I need to speak to Ms. Wolfe-Campion. Is she here?" Wayne asked the woman sitting at the nurse's station in Cardiology. The nurse looked up, appearing harassed and displeased at the interruption. The pandemic had taken its toll on everyone, but none were hit harder than the front-line health workers.

"Room 420," she said, turning back to her computer, obviously glad to get rid of him that easily.

THE DOOR TO ROOM 420 OPENED TO AN OFFICE. The desk had a name-plate that read Wolfe-Campion. A slim woman with shining dark hair cut short was standing with her back to him. She was opening a file drawer.

"Director Campion?"

She turned around saying, "How can I help?"

She was very attractive, dressed in a forest green business suit, a white blouse and heels and she wore a mask. Wayne introduced himself and pro-ducing his credentials, said he was in search of property left at the hospital after a Mr. Edward Lovell had died. Remembering Lucy's instant response when he said a little boy's life could be at stake prompted him to say, "His fiancé and little boy are both missing. I've been hired to find them."

"Oh dear," a worried expression chased across her fine features. "When did the patient die?"

Checking his notebook, Wayne gave her the date.

"After that long, property is transferred to the Patient Lost Belongings office," she said.

"I'd like to check that office then," he said.

"Unfortunately, you can't get to that area of the hospital unless you are an employee."

"Do you know Dr. Ingram from the ER?" he asked, playing his trump card.

"How is she involved?"

"Assisting us with the case," he said. He started to say she was his girlfriend but found himself increasingly unwilling to use the term, it seemed so juvenile.

"Dr. Ingram has an excellent reputation with the nursing staff. I'll give you a pass." She picked up a pad of passes and wrote his name down.

"This should get you past the dragon ladies on the first floor," she grinned. "The office is in room 104 B."

"Before I go, do you remember Mr. Lovell by chance, or the name of anyone with him when he died?"

"Sorry, too long ago, but I'll check my computer." Director Campion took a seat and looked up the patient's name. "Here he is. I remember him now. A Miss Pansy Jane Delaney was with him that day and told me she was his fiancé. Anyway, she had left for the cafeteria to get something to eat. While she was away, one of the food service people brought the patient his lunch and saw that he looked bad. She called a nurse who came to the room and listened to his heart. He was barely breathing and she immediately called for help. The resuscitation team came and worked on him for almost an hour before he expired."

"So, Lovell was alone while all this was going on?" Wayne asked.

"No. There was a man in the room when the team arrived. He was asked to step out while they worked on him. After I received the information that Mr. Lovell died, I went back to his room. I was hoping to find Ms. Delaney, express my condolences and tell her what had happened. She wasn't there, but the man still was, although he was about to leave. He was gathering up Mr. Lovell's possessions. He already had the patient's phone in his hands and would have taken it without authorization, if I hadn't returned. I hope I didn't make a mistake. I told him it was okay to take the phone."

"Did he give you his name?" Wayne asked, but he already knew who it would be.

"Yes, it's right here in the computer record. His name was Bradley Carver. He said he was Mr. Lovell's attorney. There was another odd thing that happened that day . . ." Her phone rang and she apologized but said she had to check on something urgent and had no more time to talk.

Leaving her office, Wayne realized it would be a waste of time to visit the Lost Property office now. He'd discuss his suspicions about Lovell's death with Sheriff Bradley and ask him to look into Lovell's death and to talk with Director Wolfe-Campion. She clearly had more to tell them.

As he was leaving the hospital, Wayne's phone rang. It was Billy Jo who said she was giving her phone to Dory.

"I just finished my video conference with Poppy," Dory said. "Unlike you menfolk, *I* got some excellent information. I know where Pansy Jane and Theodore are. It's an old farm belonging to the twins' parents. I need you to come to the office ASAP."

ELEVEN

WHEN WAYNE ARRIVED BACK AT ROSEDALE INVESTIGATIONS, Dory was standing by Billy Jo's desk.

"You said this farm belonged to Pansy and Poppy's parents?" Wayne asked.

"Yes. The girls were raised on the farm and Poppy thought her twin sister might have gone there. In going through Lovell's emails, Billy Jo found a message sent by Pansy Jane saying she was scared. The person she sent it to was Lucinda Wells. Her parents have a nearby farm. All three girls were friends growing up."

"We better get out there," Wayne said.

"What should I do while you two are gone?" Billy Jo asked. "I should stay here because I'm waiting for a call back on the Crematorium for the Missing Grandfather case."

"Not by yourself, you're not. We don't want you alone after dark and it's already late afternoon. You are coming with us," Dory said. Billy Jo started to protest but the words died in her throat at Wayne's expression.

The three of them trooped out the door. Dory drove, Wayne sat in the front seat and Billy Jo navigated using her cell phone and calling out instructions from the back seat.

It took over an hour on dusty country roads to find the old Delaney farm. The numbers on the battered mailbox, hanging halfway off its post, were nearly illegible, but according to Billy Jo, it was the right place. The long driveway leading back to the decrepit farmhouse was narrow and potholed. Over time, Nature's vegetation had encroached on the laneway. Blackberry canes in full white bloom cascaded in arcs, clicking against Dory's car. She swore under her breath that the business was damn well paying to fix her new vehicle if it was scratched.

When they pulled up in front of the house, there was no evidence of human habitation. Originally a white farmhouse, the weather had peeled off most of the paint, turning the wood siding a silvery patina. The house's roof shingles were covered in moss. An uneven slanted overhang shaded the front porch. The front door was locked, but walking around the house, they came upon a small broken window to a back bedroom.

"I'm going to pull the rest of the shards of glass out of this frame and you can boost Billy Jo inside," Dory said, reaching in her purse for some gloves.

"We need a warrant," Wayne reminded her.

"We're not cops now, remember?"

He remembered. It was one of the few times being a PI had worked in their favor, but he felt uneasy, violating such a basic precept. He was in search of two missing persons though. If they found the woman or the child, the risk would be worth it.

Dory pulled the splinters of glass out of the frame one by one until Billy Jo could climb inside without cutting herself. Once through the small window, they heard her calling.

"Hello? Is anyone here?" Returning to the bedroom with the broken window, she said "Nobody answered. Go around to the front and I'll let you in."

When Billy Jo unlocked the front door, Wayne and Dory walked inside. They split up and searched all the rooms, meeting back in the kitchen.

"Somebody had been here recently," Wayne said. He'd found food in the refrigerator with current date stamps. There were unwashed dishes in the sink.

"There were some women's clothes in the big bedroom closet, and clothes for the boy in a dresser in the back bedroom. I saw his teddy bear too," Billy Jo added.

Keep looking. Check to see if there's a cellar for the house or an attic. I'm going to search the barn and the garage," Wayne said. He took his time searching thoroughly, even opening up the large metal trash container beside the garage, feeling a tremor of fear, but found nothing inside. Returning to the house a wave of discouragement settled hard on him.

"Did you find anything?" Billy Jo asked when he reappeared.

"Nothing. There was only one set of tire tracks in the dust. I took a picture of them. No cars in the garage. Looks like Pansy and the boy were dropped off here."

"All of this seems to suggest they took off in a hurry," Dory said. "I'm going to leave her a note." Rummaging in her large purse, she came up with a piece of paper and a stubby pencil.

"We've been searching for you, Pansy. Mr. Lovell left your son a substantial inheritance. Call as soon as you read this." Dory signed her note and put her card on the table.

"I want to add something," Billy Jo said and quickly scrawled the words, "Don't worry. We can protect you."

They left the house unlocked, headed out to the car, and drove down the driveway to the road with Dory complaining about the blackberry canes damaging her car all the way.

TEN LONG MINUTES LATER, LITTLE TEDDY LOVELL crawled out from behind a box hidden deep underneath a double bed. He was covered in dust and silent tears made tracks on his chubby cheeks. His mommy had told him not to make a sound or to go with any stranger. He hadn't. She promised she would come right back. He climbed up on the bed, sucked his little thumb and waited.

"SHALL WE VISIT THE WELLS FARM NEXT?" Billy Jo asked.

"Good idea," Dory said and they continued driving down the country road and until they located the farm. It was a dairy; they could hear the sound of cows lowing.

"I'll check the barn," Wayne said. Dory and Billy Jo walked up the driveway toward the house.

Mr. Wells was seated by the flank of the cow he was milking. He was using an old-fashioned milking machine, one that had to be attached to the cow by hand. No tubes collected the milk and no computers calculated the output here. Wayne called out "Hello" softly, not wanting to startle the man or frighten the animal. He remembered from his young years in Michigan's Upper Peninsula that cows could kick hard.

Wells stood up abruptly, looking startled. The milking stool tipped over, upsetting the cow who mooed and looked at them balefully. He was an old guy, unshaven and dirty, dressed in wrangler overalls with no shirt and mucky boots.

"Who the hell are you?" he asked, sounding suspicious.

"My name's Wayne Nichols, I'm a Detective looking for Pansy Jane Delaney. She's a friend of your daughter's I believe. Have you seen her recently?"

"Not in a couple of years."

"What about your daughter, Lucinda. How long since you've seen her?"

"Not around much since her mother died," the old man said. He reached down and sat the milking stool upright. Turning back to Wayne he said, "Can't you see I'm busy here? I have a dozen cows still to milk. I got nothing more to say. Get on your way."

"Just a couple more questions, Mr. Wells. Do you have your daughter's phone number? We're pretty worried about Pansy. She has a little boy and they are both missing."

"Don't have her number."

For a moment Wayne longed for the old days when he could have grabbed the truculent filthy man by his overall straps, pushed him up against the wall of the barn, and pounded on him until he told him what he wanted to know. He wasn't without options, though. Intimidation still worked. Grabbing the old guy by his skinny arm, Wayne pulled Wells abruptly away from the cow.

"You are going to give me your daughter's address, and where she works right now or you and I are going to have real trouble."

"You cops are all alike," Mr. Wells said spitting out the words and shaking his arm free of Wayne's grasp, but by the time he left the barn, Wayne had the information he needed. Lucinda Wells was a student-teacher at the Pioneer elementary school in Mount Blanc. She lived in a townhouse at 1236 Mill Trace and Wells had her phone number. Wayne wrote the information down in his notebook and left, calling back over his shoulder that if any of the information was false or contributed to the death of a woman or her little boy, he would see him go down.

"You and what army?" Wells yelled and Wayne clenched his fists. He felt his anger rise and almost turned back, but Dory and Billy Jo walked up and he regained his composure.

"I got what we needed," he told them and they walked back to the car.

Driving back past the old Delaney farm, Wayne had a sudden prickling feeling in the pit of his stomach. He sensed they'd missed something and asked Dory to go back down the Delaney driveway.

"Absolutely not," she said. She wasn't about to ruin the finish on her brand-new car by driving down that driveway again. Not for love nor money.

"You're sure you searched everywhere?" he asked as they sped past.

"Sure did," she said. "Pansy Delaney isn't there."

As it turned out later, she had been right, but she couldn't forgive herself for a very long time and would spend the rest of the case dealing with her guilt and doing all she could for Pansy Delaney's little boy.

"HEAD FOR MONT BLANC," WAYNE SAID. The sun was going down and a muggy haze had settled in the air by the time they reached Pioneer Elementary. The school was closed but by knocking repeatedly, they roused a janitor. He didn't know Lucinda Wells but said there were a lot of student teachers in the school.

"Call her phone number, Billy Jo," Dory said.

"Already did. I'm not getting an answer, but it says I've reached Lucinda's phone. I left a message."

"Find the location of her address on your phone, can you?" Wayne asked.

As Billy Jo navigated, complaining from time to time about being hungry, they drove to the address Mr. Wells had given them and found the townhouse without difficulty. Knocking repeatedly failed to rouse anyone.

"Now can we get some food?" Billy Jo asked.

"Yes, and after that, we need to take you to Dory's," Wayne said.

"I have dinner planned with my boyfriend," Dory said plaintively. "Could Billy Jo stay with your and Lucy tonight?"

"This is ridiculous, I can stay in my own apartment since Dory doesn't want me, and I *don't* need a babysitter," Billy Jo said. Wayne and Dory exchanged glances.

They drove to Rosedale Investigations. Dory departed immediately but since it was already dark by then, Wayne didn't leave until he had called the Sheriff's Office and with Ben's permission got Deputy George to guard the place. The sheriff called George to give him the news and said Wayne would call with specific instructions.

When George answered the phone, Wayne said, "You need to guard Billy Jo Bradley at our business tonight. And wear your uniform, Buddy. It makes you look slightly more official. You can take your gun, but no ammo. Did you hear me, no bullets. Can you come over to Rosedale Investigations now? I'll wait until you get here and will check back around midnight. I can relieve you then."

Wayne waited until Deputy George arrived before setting out again for the Delaney farm. It was Lucy's night to work the graveyard shift. She wouldn't be home until around 4:00 a.m. The nerve-jangling feeling on the back of his neck that all officers of the law get from time to time had grown stronger. They had missed something. And whatever it was, it was important.

TWELVE

IT WAS COMPLETELY DARK BY THE TIME Wayne drove back down the driveway of the old Delaney farm—for the second time that day. Given their concerns that Pansy Jane might be involved with the mob, he'd come armed. He could feel the reassuring bulk of the gun against his chest in its shoulder holster. Upon leaving the Sheriff's Office, Wayne had been required to turn in his detective's badge and gun. It had been tough. He felt his identity as a detective, as an officer of the law had been erased, leaving him feeling defenseless. *Who was he, if he wasn't a detective anymore?*

Since then, he had legally purchased a Glock semi-automatic handgun. Unless he needed the weapon, the gun and bullets were locked in the safe at Lucy's house. Today, he needed it. He parked his truck and pulled a flashlight from his glove box.

Exiting the car, he looked carefully at the pattern of tracks in the dust by the garage. Nobody had been there since he, Dory, and Billy Jo made their visit earlier in the day. *It was probably a waste of time to come back out here,* he thought, but since they had left the front door unlocked, he walked up on the porch and stepped inside. For just a moment, he thought he heard a tiny sound. The hair on the back of his neck rose. He waited.

Again he heard something. It was so insignificant, he doubted it was anything but an animal that had taken up habitation when the people left. He walked into the kitchen, hearing the refrigerator come on. Perhaps that was what he had heard. Taking his time, he opened every cupboard in the minimal kitchen, including the broom closet. He moved on to the living room, carefully checking around and behind furniture, opening the coat closet, stirring the hanging clothes. Then he heard it again. Just the faintest sound, like a muffled cry.

He walked down the hall to check the bedrooms, switching on the overhead lights in each room and then turning them off again after looking under beds and in closets. He checked the under-sink cupboard in the bathroom and pulled aside the shower curtain. It was stiff with mold. Some echo of the sound he'd heard kept returning to his mind, bothering him. He went back to the largest bedroom. As he switched on his flashlight, the pillows on the bed seemed to move, just the slightest bit. He blinked and they were still. Had he seen them move or was it just that his instincts were on such high alert. He stood at the foot of the bed barely breathing and played the narrow flashlight beam across the bedding. The pillows moved again. Reaching down, he yanked the blankets off the bed. In the dim light, he saw something moving. Was it an animal? No, it was the boy.

The child wailed and tried desperately to scramble away. Crawling and crying, he struggled to get back underneath the covers.

"I'm not going to hurt you, Teddy," Wayne said calmly. "I'm here to help you. Where is your Mommy?"

"Mommy," the little boy wailed. He shrieked and then started to sob hysterically as if his whole world had come to an end.

Wayne reached down and scooped little Teddy Lovell up in his large arms. The child fought like an enraged tiger. He grabbed Wayne's thumb and bit it. He kicked and screamed. Having subdued many criminals in his life, Wayne had to give it to him. He was a fighter all right. Carrying the struggling child to the kitchen, he managed to hold him tightly with his left arm while writing on Dory's note. "We have Teddy. Call ASAP."

He carried Teddy out to his truck and strapped him in the back seat. It was a serious effort getting the seatbelts tight enough to hold him without squashing him. Once the child was contained, he sat brooding furiously, still shrieking from time to time. Wayne looked at him carefully under the dome light in his truck. He looked like a miniature Jabba the Hut, dangerous and pale. He knew he should call Child Protective Services and wait until they arrived, but it had been hours since they left the house earlier. Teddy could have been alone in the house for days. He didn't know a lot about small children, except that they needed to eat often. There was no time for the ponderous bureaucracy to kick into action. He knew where to take him.

Once back on the road, Wayne glanced at his watch. It was almost midnight, but despite the hour, he dialed Sheriff Ben Bradley's home phone.

"Bradley," he answered sounding sleepy.

"It's me," Wayne said.

"For Pete's sake, Wayne, do you know what time it is?"

"Sorry, but I've found the boy we've been looking for. I need your okay to take him straight to the ER rather than call Child Protective Services."

"You have it. Where's the mother?"

"Didn't find her. But I doubt she would leave the kid alone in a deserted house unless something very bad happened. Can you call George and ask him to drive Billy Jo to Dory's house for the night? I'd call him myself, but, as you know, I'm not his superior now. Dory had a romantic evening planned and didn't want Billy Jo to stay with her originally, but her boyfriend's probably left by now. I promised George I'd relieve him by twelve, and I don't want to delay getting the boy to the hospital."

"On it," Ben said tersely and hung up.

WAYNE PULLED INTO THE ER LOT OF THE HOSPITAL, turned off his car, and sat there wondering if he would be allowed inside. He heard the buzz for an incoming text and saw it was from Deputy George. It read, "Dropped Billy Jo off with Dory. Boyfriend already left. Quiet all night at Rosedale Investigations."

He looked in his rearview mirror and saw Teddy continuing to struggle mightily against the seat belts, biting at them. *What a little warrior*, Wayne thought in admiration. Pansy Jane must have warned her son not to go with strangers and little as he was, he was doing his utmost. Once he reached the hospital, he lifted the struggling wildcat out of the truck and walked toward the entrance. The desk was manned, but when the guard saw Wayne's credentials, he said they could come in.

Wayne asked the woman at the intake desk if Dr. Ingram could be informed that Detective Nichols was there and took a seat in the waiting room holding Teddy tightly in his arms. Fifteen minutes later, Dr. Lucy Ingram, wearing slim black trousers, a pink blouse, and a long white lab coat walked quickly into the waiting area.

"Hello there," she started to say, but the word dwindled on her lips when she saw the struggling child in Wayne's lap.

"You *did* say you hoped to be a mother one day," Wayne said with a grin.

"I *didn't* say you could steal one!" Lucy replied, with wide eyes.

IT TOOK OVER TWO HOURS FOR TEDDY LOVELL to be admitted for observation to the Pediatrics Ward. Ultimately, and not without active opposition, he was bathed and fed, dressed in a tiny gown, and put into a hospital crib. The sedative the pediatric resident gave him and the presence of several nurses seemed to bring him to the realization that resistance was futile. When they were finished with his examination, an exhausted Teddy Lovell laid back in his hospital crib, put his clean thumb in his mouth, and closed his eyes.

"Okay, let's go to the family waiting area now. We need to meet with the social worker," Lucy whispered. A young woman, whose name was Hayley Drummond, joined them. She had long shiny hair—dark as licorice—that fell on either side of a central part, a tiny gold nostril ring, and beautifully expressive eyes. Her face was almost perfectly round. To Wayne, she looked about as old as a middle-schooler and he was tempted to ask if her mommy had given her milk and cookies after school. He stifled himself. Hayley donned her tortoise-shell glasses, which made her look a bit older, opened up her laptop computer, and started asking the questions needed to complete the necessary paperwork.

"You understand that you aren't going to be able to *keep* Teddy," Hayley said, raising her eyes and looking at Wayne sternly.

"Of course. I was only kidding." She'd overheard him say that Teddy would need a family. While there was still some hope that his mother was alive, by now Wayne had grave doubts. When he and Lucy visited Centennial Realty, Pansy's colleague told them how much she adored her son. It was unlikely she would have left him voluntarily. Unless mothers were insane, high on drugs, or hopelessly alcoholic, they didn't leave little children alone in deserted farmhouses to starve to death.

After getting what minimal information Wayne had about Teddy, including the mother's name, the aunt's name, and his half-sister's name, Hayley closed her laptop.

"That will do for now," she told them. "Teddy needs some medical attention but in a few days he's likely to be physically fine, grieving the loss of his mother, but okay."

"I agree. He's only scared, hungry, traumatized, and dehydrated," Lucy said. "Without Wayne's dedication to finding him, though, little Teddy would probably have perished in another few days." She smiled as she reached to take Wayne's hand.

"I'll get started looking for a foster home for him tomorrow. By the time Pediatrics is ready to discharge him, I'll have something lined up. You mentioned his half-sister, Lexie Lovell, and that she's getting married soon. Do you think I should contact her and ask if she and her husband-to-be would like to have her brother live with them?" Hayley asked.

"Please hold off until we can get in touch with her," Wayne said.

"Perhaps once she's married, she'll want to have Teddy with her," Lucy said hopefully.

"Doubtful," Wayne said and took a shaky breath. He knew what Teddy needed was his mother and that meant he had to find Pansy Delaney, dead or alive. If dead, despite not being a police officer any longer, he felt duty-bound to find and bring to justice the person who forced her to abandon her little boy alone, frightened and hungry.

Lucy walked Wayne out to the parking lot. "I'm so proud of you. Just remember your promise," she told him.

"What are you referring to?" he asked.

"No putting your life at risk by investigating violent crime again. Not if you *ever* plan to put a ring on this finger," Lucy said smiling, before turning back to re-enter the hospital. She was still on duty.

Returning to Rosedale Investigations, Wayne called Dory. It was nearly dawn and the pale gray skies were lightening.

"Why are you calling me at this hour?" Dory's sleepy voice asked.

"Sorry to disturb you, Dory, but I wanted you to know what's happened. I found Teddy Lovell. Just checked him into the hospital."

"What? You found him? Where was he?"

"In the deserted Delaney farmhouse."

There was silence for a bit before Dory's voice caught and she said, "No way. How is that possible? We searched everywhere."

"When I got there, he was hiding under the covers on the double bed. When we were there earlier, my guess is he was under the bed behind a box I saw."

"Oh, no. I feel just awful," Dory said. Remembering Wayne wanting her to go back to the house and her voice saying firmly that she, '*wouldn't drive her car down the driveway again for love nor money*.' She grimaced. In a tear-filled voice, she said, "I can never forgive myself. Never . . ."

In the final moment, before she hung up, Wayne caught the sounds of strangled sobbing.

THIRTEEN

"I'M CALLING PD," BILLY JO SAID as she and Dory walked into Rosedale Investigations the next morning. Dory was surprisingly dressed in gray and wearing absolutely no jewelry. She'd done nothing with her hair either. It was uncombed and messy. The gray dress wasn't a good look against her golden-brown skin. Searching her mind for the proper adjective, Billy Jo could only come up with *drooped*. Today, Dory's normally bright sassy personality positively drooped.

"Good Morning, PD," she said as she heard his voice answer the phone. "I have some good news for you. Wayne found little Teddy Lovell last night out at the Delaney farm."

"Alive?" PD asked.

"Yes, of course, alive. We took him to the hospital and he's going to spend a few days in Pediatrics. According to Dr. Lucy, he's dehydrated and traumatized, but should be okay, physically at least. Once we find his mother, they will be reunited."

"If . . . If . . . we find his mother," PD said.

"If anyone can find her, it's Wayne," Dory said.

"How's working from home going, PD?" Billy Jo asked.

"I was home for two months before Rose County re-opened you know, and being alone all this time is getting hard." He paused before saying, "Think I'll stick it out here, though, don't want to get exposed to COVID. Sorry, have to go. Just getting a call."

Turning to Dory, Billy Jo said, "What are you going to be doing today?"

"I want to have another conversation with Poppy. She needs to know that her nephew is okay. What about you?"

"I'm still waiting for a call back from the Crematorium in Minnesota. If I don't hear from them shortly, I'll call them back," Billy Jo said. "Are you okay, Dory? You look sort of . . . peaked."

"Still feeling dreadful that I was thinking about my stupid car when that little boy was alone and terrified." Tears came into her eyes and she wiped them away. Billy Jo was stunned, she had never seen her even misty-eyed before.

"He's just fine now, Dory. Please don't cry," Billy Jo said and patted her on the shoulder. She handed her a tissue. "You don't seem yourself this morning, Dory. You aren't wearing any jewelry and I didn't know you even owned a gray dress and shoes."

"Bought for my father's funeral," Dory said, still looking despondent.

"I'll get you coffee and a blueberry donut," Billy Jo said.

WHILE DORY WAS ARRANGING FOR THE VIDEO CONFERENCE, Billy Jo called the Crematorium in Minnesota. "Good morning. I'm the person who called previously from Rosedale Investigations. We are in search of the remains of Mr. Charles Carson. I spoke with Mr. Grayling. He was supposed to call me back."

"Yes, Miss. I'm his son, Robbie. My father is the person you talked to yesterday. When Mr. Carson's body was sent here after his death, we tried to contact the family with no success. The only number we had was for a landline that had been turned off. He had a signed card requesting cremation, so we proceeded."

"Where are the cremains now?"

"His driver's license listed his home address and there's only one funeral home in Rosedale. We sent the ashes to that facility."

"There's a problem," Billy Jo said. "Mr. Carson's ashes aren't in Rosedale. Neither the hospital nor the funeral home has them. What kind of delivery service did you use?"

"We employ a dedicated courier service. It's shared with several other facilities like ours and is used only for transporting a body or cremains. We have the shipping receipt. I'll find it and fax a copy to you. The date, the driver's name, and the destination are all on the receipt."

Billy Jo gave Mr. Grayling's son the fax number, thanked him, and said goodbye. While she waited for the fax to come through, she took the coffee carafe and a mug into the conference room. Dory was just sitting there, doing absolutely nothing until she could speak to Poppy via video conference. *Very atypical*, Billy Jo thought and patted her shoulder, feeling concerned.

She was leaving the room when she heard the sound of the incoming fax. Walking back to her workstation and pulling it from the machine, she looked it over carefully. Mr. Charles Carson's cremains had indeed been sent to Rosedale. Billy Jo frowned. Then her expression cleared. Mr. Carson's ashes had been sent to Rosedale, all right, but not Rosedale, *Tennessee*. They were sent to a funeral home of the very same name in Rosedale, *Texas*.

SIPPING HER COFFEE, DORY WAITED for the Zoom meeting to start. She was still feeling awful about herself. Her attachment to her possessions and especially to her new car (it was the nicest one she had ever owned, a little red convertible) had endangered a little boy's life. The only way she could feel better about her stupid materialism was to help Teddy now.

Watching the guard escort the prisoner into the room by holding onto her upper arm, Dory crossed her fingers superstitiously, hoping Poppy had thought of something which would help them find her twin sister.

"Hello, Poppy. It's Dory here. I have some good news for you."

"Have you talked to the Sheriff yet? Or the Judge?" Poppy asked.

Dory had forgotten to mention the matter to the Sheriff and feared it was likely to cause a rift in her efforts to build trust with Poppy. "I am seeing him this afternoon," she lied. "Are you prepared to tell him the whole story? You're going to need to report the incident as self-defense, tell him the name of your pimp and you'll need a lawyer. Legal Aid will provide your counsel."

Poppy sighed.

Hurriedly, Dory continued saying, "The good news I had to tell you is about your nephew. He was found at the old Delaney farm by my partner. It was your tip that led to finding him, so thank you so much for that."

"What about my sister?" Poppy asked

"That was the odd thing. She wasn't there and surprisingly had left her son alone in the farmhouse. We took the boy to the hospital where Teddy's being treated for dehydration and trauma."

"She left him alone?" Poppy asked and frowned. "She wouldn't do that."

"We know she is devoted to him and were surprised not to find them together. I'm wondering if you have any more ideas about where she might be."

"I'm not a mind-reader, you know," Poppy said with asperity. "Have you talked to the Wells family down the road?"

"We went there and spoke to Mr. Wells. He gave us the address and phone number of Lucinda, but we haven't spoken to her yet. We hope to hear back from her today. Can you think of any reason Pansy Jane would have left the farm?"

"Leaving Teddy alone in a deserted house? What the hell kind of people do you think we are?" The woman was clearly outraged and Dory felt her stomach fall, her connection with the woman was disintegrating. She had to do something to get her back.

"I didn't mean to imply your sister would have left voluntarily. Of course not. What I wondered was if you had an idea about anyone who could have forced her to leave the farm?"

Her hasty thrust in the dark backfired because Poppy stood up, pushed her chair aside angrily, walked to the back of the room, and called "Guard, Guard," until a man appeared and led her from the room.

As Poppy left the room and the video call clicked off, Dory's remorse deepened. She grabbed her coat and purse. Saying a hurried goodbye to Billy Jo, she left the building. She would go by the Sheriff's Office. Maybe she could talk him into agreeing to review Poppy's case.

DETECTIVE WAYNE NICHOLS KNEW FINDING PANSY DELANEY was not going to be easy. His head was buzzing with thoughts swirling around in circles, swarming like wasps, coalescing, and then breaking apart. He considered going to talk with Sheriff Ben Bradley. He and Ben were good friends. They respected each other's strengths in investigative work. They could discuss the case, share ideas and the natural authority of the Sheriff would defuse any objections people might have about talking to them. It wasn't fair to ask him though. It would be pushing their friendship too far. He wasn't an officer of the law anymore. Requesting Ben's help would be crossing a line.

Earlier in the investigation, when he asked whether Edward Lovell had a record or was the subject of ongoing investigations, the sheriff had back-pedaled. "I'd like to help you, Buddy," he had said, "But you know how it is. You're a civilian now and no crime has been reported to my office regarding Mr. Lovell."

Wayne knew he was right, but it still hurt. Only a year ago, he'd been Chief Detective. Now he was *only* a civilian.

Driving toward the Delaney farm once again, he wondered what could have made Pansy leave her little boy. He reviewed his usual mental list. They had found nothing to indicate mental illness, there were no empty bottles of liquor in the house, no medicines for depression or anxiety, and no opioid prescription bottles or drug paraphernalia. That left forcible abduction as the only possibility. Someone had taken the woman, but he'd seen no tracks in the driveway other than the one set, which was probably from Lucinda Wells' car dropping them off. He forced his mind down new paths. Could Pansy have gone outside and been attacked by an animal? A bear perhaps? Or a coyote pack? He shook his head. It was just too unlikely. He needed to look at the evidence around the house more closely.

The sky was clouding up and the rain was on its way from the west. Driving the deserted lane, he rolled down his window. The world had gone silent in the lull before the storm. If the woman was alive, he knew she didn't have long. Either Pansy was already dead or being held somewhere against her will. The click and scrape of blackberry canes against the sides of his truck felt like minutes ticking away, a countdown leading toward a bad ending. Finding her was now critical.

Once in sight of the old place, Wayne pulled his truck over to the side and parked in the weeds. He got out and started walking very slowly, eyes on the ground. He was Native American but had never been in the tribe. There had been no elders to teach him the skills of tracking. All he had was excellent eyesight, a retentive memory, and the determination of a bloodhound. He worked his way slowly up to the house, seeing nothing more than two sets of tire tracks, Dory's from the previous day, and the earlier set which were probably Lucinda's. He pulled out his cellphone and took pictures of the imprints. Then he walked behind the house toward the barn. There was a dumpster beside the shed. He'd seen it earlier and opened it, his heart filled with dread, but it was empty.

Today he viewed the container with new eyes, walking all around it, looking at every blade of grass on which it stood. Then he stopped, seeing a tiny smear of brownish-red on the ground. He touched it with his finger. It was sticky and thick, the consistency of congealed blood. He checked the nearest corner of the receptacle. Yes, there was dried blood on the metal edging, too. He studied the ground more carefully. The grass was flattened as if a body had fallen and lain there a while. Then he saw other drops of blood leading away from the dumpster toward the cornfield. A sudden clap of thunder rent the sky.

Simultaneously, he felt the flush of adrenaline hit his bloodstream. That surge was unmistakable. He felt the impenetrable darkness of this damned case begin to open, a pinpoint of light appeared, and he knew what had happened to Pansy Delaney. Until that moment, he'd never considered the possibility that the woman could have tripped and fallen against the metal corner of the dumpster. She'd probably hit her head and had a concussion. He wondered if people with concussions had memory loss. If not, perhaps she had experienced transient amnesia. He'd have to ask Lucy how common it was. It would explain why she'd left her little boy.

His impulse was to start immediately following the trail, but aware that finding the woman could take him hours if not days, he took time to go back into the house. He grabbed a handful of stones from the ground in front of the porch. He had found a rolled map of the property in a closet during his earlier search for Teddy. He unrolled the map on the kitchen table and used the stones to hold the corners down. The trash container was on the east side of the house and he put several small pebbles on the map in the direction he intended to start. He found bread and peanut butter in the cupboard, quickly made himself four sandwiches, and filled his thermos with cold water. It was hot outside, so he removed his jacket and left it on the back of a kitchen chair. Glancing at his cell phone, he saw that the power was low, but put it in his pants pocket anyway.

Knowing the rain could start any minute and with it, all the evidence leading to Pansy would be washed away, he ran awkwardly out the back door and into the cornfield. Lucy said he needed a knee replacement and his knee was killing him, but with his eyes fixed steadfastly to the ground, he jogged unsteadily down the near-invisible blood trail.

FOURTEEN

Dr. Lucy called the business on the second day since anyone had heard from Wayne. She'd finally gotten a call from him.

"He's on the trail of Pansy Delaney, certain she's still on the farm belonging to the family. He wanted to know how long a person could live without water. I told him three or four days before they started to hallucinate and then inevitably become comatose and die."

"Weren't you angry with him? You made him promise not to investigate violent crime again," Dory said.

"He assured me that the disappearance of Pansy had likely been due to an accident. He was just trying to find her before it was too late. I wasn't upset, except when he didn't come home that first night. He asked me to let you both know he wouldn't be back until he found her. He didn't want to be reported as a missing person or to have Sheriff Bradley informed. I have to say, I'm tempted to disregard his wishes."

After agreeing with Dr. Lucy that someone needed to check on Wayne, Dory said, "I'm calling Ben. Probably should have called before this, but I knew Wayne would be pissed. Stupid to be thrashing around in the heat and that woods for days. He's not a young man."

"Younger than you, though," Billy Jo said quietly.

Dory gave her a blistering glare as she dialed the Sheriff's Office and flipped the phone on speaker.

"Sheriff's Office, Mrs. Coffin speaking. How can I help?"

"Good Morning, Mrs. Coffin. It's Dory calling. Could you put me through to Ben?"

"He's in a meeting with several important people. I don't wish to disturb him," she said primly.

"And I don't give a *rat's ass* whether you do or not. This is important. Put me through now!" Dory said. Her face was mutinous.

"Dory? What's going on?" Ben Bradley's voice on the phone sounded irritated. "If this is still about Poppy Delaney, I told you I will review her case once she gets her Legal Aid attorney."

"It's not about her. Your former Chief Detective is missing. He's north of town on an old farm that once belonged to Pansy and Poppy Delaney's parents. As you know, he found the little boy out there and took him to the hospital. Now he's hunting for the mother."

"How long has he been gone?"

"Two days. Dr. Lucy called to say he didn't want to be treated like a missing person. He specifically said *not* to contact you."

"That sounds serious. Whenever Wayne says *not* to contact help, it's because he knows he's in over his head."

"What do you want to do?" Dory asked.

"I'll take Rob and George out there and we'll fan out and search the property. I'll borrow a search dog from Nashville. Do you want to join us, Dory?"

"I sure do. Thank you, Sheriff."

"Come over to the office and I'll get the troops together."

Hanging up the phone, Dory told Billy Jo to lock the business and stay inside. She would be back after they found Wayne.

BILLY JO WORKED ON THE COMPUTER FOR AN HOUR after Dory left. She located the Franklin Funeral Home in Rosedale, Texas, but got no answer when she called. She considered calling the Missing Grandfather people—she had been made the lead on the case after all—but decided to wait. It would be better to *locate* Mr. Carson's cremains before contacting the family. She tapped her fingers on her desk. Half an hour later, she left a message on the machine telling callers that they were out of the office, locked the doors to Rosedale Investigations, and headed out in her car. Dory wouldn't have approved, but she wasn't there to stop her. She was going out to check on PD.

Billy Jo was a half-hour from the cabin when it dawned on her that PD might need groceries. She pulled off the road into a small roadside park and started checking for the location of the nearest grocery store. Only minutes later, she glanced up from her phone. Another car had pulled in. It was a black sedan with tinted windows. The driver's face was turned away. He was checking for other cars as he backed out, but his arm was visible on the steering wheel. His wrist had a tattoo of a snake biting its tail. It was the same tattoo the shooter had. Billy Jo swallowed, feeling fear gnaw at her insides. *He hasn't seen me*, she thought and ducked down, quickly dialing the sheriff's office.

"Mrs. Coffin, it's Billy Jo. Remember when I reported a man who tried to shoot me? He's parked beside me right now!"

"There's absolutely nobody here right now except for me and the lab techs. Do you want me to call the Mont Blanc post?"

"Yes. I'm at the little roadside park by the Cedar River just off RR 29."

"Lock the doors to your car. Stay down. Wait there. I'll get someone to come out."

SHERIFF BEN BRADLEY, DETECTIVE ROB FULLER, Deputy George Phelps, and Investigator Dory Clarkson were standing in the kitchen of the abandoned Delaney farmhouse. It was a muggy morning with sullen blue-bottomed clouds that moved slowly across the sky. Thunder rumbled far off in the distance and the air was heavy.

The search and rescue dog, a large Bloodhound whose name was Chestnut, whined impatiently. The dog was almost completely russet-colored which accounted for his name. He was excited, thrashing his large tail, eager to begin working. Sheriff Bradley called Chestnut over and had him smell Wayne's jacket, glad his former Chief Detective had left it behind. A plat map for the property was unrolled on the heavily scarred kitchen table.

"I assume Wayne found this map and brought these stones into the kitchen to mark the area where he was headed," Sheriff Ben said. "Each of us can begin in a corner of the eastern quadrant and work toward the center. I think searching these twenty acres will take us about two hours. I brought some brightly colored stakes. Use them to whip the brush as you make your way through. It isn't going to be easy walking. Nobody has lived here for a long time and thick vegetation has grown back. You'll be fighting through tall brambles and the ground will be uneven," he said.

"Who gets the dog?" Rob asked. "I did a short training course on dog handling before I took my Detective's exam."

Dory gave him a narrow-eyed look as Ben said, "Dory gets the dog."

"Serves you right for bragging," Dory said.

Ignoring the interaction between Rob and Dory, Ben said, "One last thing, keep calling Wayne's name as you walk. If he's fallen, hurt or broken a bone, he will hear your voice and call back. Let's pray we find him and soon," the sheriff said as he solemnly handed out the long orange-colored stakes. The presence of the dog, the ceremonial passing around of colored stakes, and the missing man made them all feel as if they were on the eve of a battle.

Then Ben noticed George putting on his mask. "For God's sake, George, you don't need a mask when you are outside in the country and over six feet apart. Take it off."

Dory chuckled and the interchange lightened the atmosphere as they set off into dense undergrowth.

Dory was standing atop a small rise in the northeastern quadrant of the Delaney farm. She was breathing hard, covered with mosquito bites, and bruised from tripping over tree roots. *I'm too old for this*, she thought.

"Wayne," she yelled as loud as she could, given her shortness of breath. Chestnut had pulled his lead from her hands some time ago and run away. Dory could hear him barking excitedly in the distance. She hoped he had found her partner and wasn't just chasing some ditzy raccoon up a tree. It was times like these when the people you loved were lost, ill, or injured that you realized how much they meant. This stupid case had already damaged Billy Jo emotionally, PD was in quarantine at his cabin, and Wayne had seemingly vanished. Their team was coming apart. When Dory got control of her breathing, she and set off down the knoll, trekking carefully toward the sound of the dog. Chestnut's barking got louder and louder as she approached.

"Wayne," she hollered again, and then she saw him. He staggered out of a thicket with a 3-day stubble, bruised and limping. He scowled, but Dory felt her face break into a delighted grin.

"I suppose you brought the whole of law enforcement in Rosedale here," he said irritably, reaching down to grab the dog's harness. "I told Lucy I didn't need a damn search party."

"Well, you were wrong. It's so good to see you, Partner. Don't you dare run out on me like that ever again! It's been too hard doing this job without you." She had hoped for a grateful hug or at least a smile, but Wayne just looked down at the ground.

"I didn't find her," he said wretchedly.

"Why didn't you come back to the house? Or call?" Dory asked.

"I was afraid I'd never find the trail again, it's so faint now. And I've been worried the rain would wash away the blood, but the showers have been intermittent and so far none have hit here directly. Sorry about not calling, my phone was out of charge. You can leave if you want to, Dory, but I'm not leaving until I find her." He looked incredibly determined and a muscle pulsed in his jaw.

"I'm sure you have done your best, Partner, but now we have the dog."

"The dog?" Wayne said, looking down at him.

"He's a trained search and rescue dog," Dory said.

"OMG, that's great," Wayne said, sounding elated. "What's his name?"

"Chestnut."

"Here you go, Chestnut, take a sniff of this." Wayne tapped an infinitesimally dark spot on a leaf of a nearby shrub. The dog did so and before they could stop him, set off again baying.

Half an hour later they reached the far edge of the Delaney property. It ended at a road. Wayne was disheartened to see it was paved. The dog ran back and forth across the place where Pansy Jane's scent disappeared, whining in frustration. Wayne led Chestnut to the other side of the road and had him search the area. He could tell by the dog's behavior that he found nothing.

"It's okay, Chestnut. You did your best," he said, patting the dog and grabbing his harness. He felt so discouraged he could have howled himself.

"What do you think happened?" Dory asked.

"I think somebody saw her emerge from the woods, noticed she was injured and picked her up."

"Where would they have taken her?"

"Unless it was a bad guy, they would have taken her to get medical attention."

"The closest emergency room is in Rosedale," Dory said. "We better get going."

Wayne nodded and the three of them—Wayne, Dory, and a dejected Chestnut—made their way back to the Delaney farmhouse.

As they walked, Wayne mentally counted the days Pansy had left, before she slipped into a coma and died. The pediatricians estimated that Teddy had been without food or water for twenty-four hours before he was found. Since then, days two and three had gone by while he searched the farm. *It was now day four on the hunt for Pansy Delaney.* Lucy said

people could only live three or four days without water and there were
no streams or ponds on the Delaney property. Time was now his enemy.
He felt the days, hours, and minutes counting down to the inevitable
moment when he would discover her dead body.

FIFTEEN

WAYNE AND DORY STOPPED FOR LUNCH on their way back to Rosedale Investigations. They found a place with outdoor dining and ordered a sandwich to go for Billy Jo. They were sitting at the picnic table, discussing their next steps, when Dory's phone rang.

"Mrs. Coffin, slow down. What happened?" she listened while mouthing to Wayne that Billy Jo had seen the man with the snake tattoo again. "So, when the Mont Blanc deputy got there she was still hiding in her car? He was gone, but she didn't get it? That's unfortunate. She's back at the office? Okay, we're on our way there now."

"What was all that about?" Wayne asked.

"Billy Jo was at a roadside park when Snake Wrist pulled in next to her. She hunkered down and called Mrs. Coffin at the Sheriff's Office. She knew it would be useless to call us since we were all out looking for my Partner—*a total Moron*—who doesn't know enough to call for back-up," Dory narrowed her eyes at him. "Mrs. Coffin called a Mont Blanc deputy. He went to the park where Billy Jo was, but the black sedan was gone by the time he got there. The deputy followed her back to the office. He is going to stay there until one of us shows up."

"Let's go," Wayne said, refusing to rise to the bait of Dory calling him her 'Moron Partner.' He knew she was right. He should have called for someone to search with him, but his phone was dead, the blood trail was so faint, and the rain so close, he couldn't take the risk. He sighed deeply, feeling profound remorse weigh on him. Despite three days of searching, little Teddy's mom was still missing. He looked at Dory and asked, "What didn't Billy Jo get?"

"The license plate number on the car," Dory said.

Wayne grimaced. They paid for their lunches, picked up Billy Jo's take-out, and departed.

BILLY JO'S CAR WAS IN THE DRIVEWAY at Rosedale Investigations, and the Mont Blanc deputy was listening to the police band radio in his car when they arrived. Dory went inside. Wayne stayed to talk with the deputy, thanked him for his help, and told him he could leave.

Dory went upstairs and knocked on Billy Jo's door. Trying the knob, she found it locked. To her knowledge, the apartment had never been locked during business hours before. "Billy Jo, it's Dory. Let me in."

The door handle turned and Billy Jo, dressed in pj's, her eyes red from crying, opened the door. She reached for Dory and despite the social distancing rules, hugged her tightly. "I was so scared," she said.

"You're all right now. Wayne's here. He's telling the Mont Blanc deputy he can leave. Tell me what happened." After hearing Billy Jo's description of the incident, Dory started to say, "Well, I have to say it's very unfortunate that . . ."

"I didn't get the license plate number. I know. *I know.* Keep kicking myself. Can't believe I was so stupid. Let's go downstairs," Billy Jo said, wiping her eyes.

Wayne was in the kitchen putting Billy Jo's sandwich on a plate. "Are you okay?" he asked her.

Billy Jo nodded and thanked them for the food.

"I wonder if Snake Wrist was looking for you. What do you think?" Wayne asked.

"It could have been a coincidence I guess," Billy Jo said uncertainly.

Wayne and Dory exchanged glances. Neither of them believed in coincidences when it came to a criminal investigation. "He didn't pull a gun, you said. And he never got out of his car to come over to yours?"

"I don't think so. Mrs. Coffin told me to lock the car and stay down, so I did. When I poked my head up later, the deputy was pulling in and the black car was gone."

"My guess is either he didn't see you or was just trying to scare you," Wayne said.

"I'm sorry about the license plate," Billy Jo said.

"Hard to remember to get a plate number in the heat of the moment," Dory said patting her back. "Don't beat yourself up about it. You go ahead and eat."

TEN MINUTES LATER, THE PHONE RANG and Billy Jo grabbed it saying, "Rosedale Investigations." She gestured wildly to Wayne and Dory to come closer. "Hello, PD. So glad you called. We've been hoping to talk to you. Hang on. I'll put the call on speaker." She pushed the 'hold' button as Wayne and Dory joined her. She then clicked the speaker button on the phone saying, "We're all here now."

"Glad you're back among the living, Wayne. I want an update."

"Of course. I've spent the last few days trying to find Pansy Delaney. I noticed dried blood on the corner of the metal dumpster at the farm and a blood trail leading away into the overgrown fields. I followed it, but the traces were so faint it was a slow process. When Dory, George, Rob, and Sheriff Bradley showed up and we had the search and rescue dog, the dog led us right to a paved road at the edge of the property."

"Damn. I figured something like that could have happened. I'm sure both you and Dory want to keep looking for Ms. Delaney, but as the head of the agency, I'm calling off the search. Are you all listening? No more searching. You are done."

Wayne and Dory looked at each other with raised eyebrows and equally outraged expressions.

"Why are you stopping us?" Dory asked.

"In case it hasn't occurred to you, we have accomplished what we were hired to do. You found Teddy Lovell, Wayne. He's in the hospital and will shortly be in a foster home. We can collect our fee from Carver and move on." He paused and then said, "In fact, Billy Jo is the only person who is working on a *paying* case at the moment."

She couldn't help a bit of a complacent grin.

"I take your point, PD, but here's the thing. Nobody else is searching for Pansy and she's still missing. It's the fourth day since she left Teddy. That little boy is alone in the world," Wayne said, recalling the day when a uniformed police officer came to say they were looking for his mother.

"I get it, Buddy, but why not submit a missing person's report to Nashville and Sheriff Bradley in Rosedale. That will get it on their radar and you can bow out."

"I already reported them missing the day Billy Jo made her report about the shooter to the Sheriff. He was going to inform Nashville. But with so many officers both here and in Nashville assigned to enforcing public health rules, keeping social order and protecting themselves, they haven't been able to assign any officers to the case."

Saying this, Wayne cast a desperate glance at Dory and she nodded. "Since the whole country is still in the grip of a pandemic, and we don't have any more pressing cases at the moment, I'm not willing to give up either," she said.

PD made a grunt of irritated acknowledgment before saying, "So what do you propose, Wayne?"

"I'm hoping that a Good Samaritan picked her up from the road. From my pictures of the blood evidence on the dumpster, Lucy concurred with me that Pansy likely fell and hit her head. She could be semi-conscious, and possibly amnesiac. Unless it was the mob who grabbed her, anyone who found her would take her for medical care," Wayne said.

"Dory, what's your opinion about this?" PD asked. "You know the state of our finances since the shutdown."

"I'll inform Lovell's attorney that Teddy has been found. That should get us our fee, but I have my own reasons for wanting to help." Her conscience was still bothering her that she had been more concerned about her stupid car than finding Teddy.

"Let me think about this while I bring you up to date. By calling around, I found out that Edward Lovell was doing financial management for a well-to-do woman. Haven't got her name yet. The Good Samaritan idea is a long shot, but I'll give you a week *unless* another paying customer arrives. Now I'd like an update from you, Billy Jo. You saw the Snake Wrist guy again, I hear?"

As Billy Jo and PD continued their conversation, Dory turned to Wayne. "What's your next step, Partner?" she asked quietly.

"Lucy said if Pansy was unable to talk coherently, she would have been taken to an ER. I'm going to ask for her help calling the ER's in Rosedale and Nashville. I'm not letting this go," he said stubbornly.

Walking out to his truck, he felt haunted by his private demons, the voices in his head that kept whispering he was a failure. He would never find Pansy Delaney, or when he did, she would be dead. If that happened, Teddy Lovell would never get his mother back. If it was humanly possible, Wayne wouldn't allow that to happen.

DR. LUCY INGRAM WAS AT HOME when she received Wayne's call. She let it ring for a bit, but then unable to stand the ringing phone any longer, she answered saying, "So you're back."

"I am. I'm on my way home. Need to take a shower and talk to you."

"Why do I get a distinct impression that you need my help once again?" she asked.

"Because you are brilliant as well as beautiful?" he said hoping a compliment would ease the tension. He knew from her tone of voice that she was furious. He'd kept his promise about not investigating a violent crime, but by searching for Pansy for days alone, he had put his life at risk.

"Ha! If I weren't so glad to hear your voice, I'd happily strangle you," she said.

"Almost home," he said and rang off.

Just as he pulled into the driveway, PD called. "Can you talk?" he asked.

"For a few minutes. I got the sense you weren't telling Dory and Billy Jo everything."

"The Assistant DA had an appointment with Edward Lovell about a crime he wanted to report, but before that meeting took place, he died. I found the timing convenient. Do you think he could have been murdered?" PD asked.

"It occurred to me. I don't know if I told you, but Pansy Delaney wasn't with Lovell when he passed away. She'd gone down to the cafeteria to get something to eat. The only person in the room before Lovell expired was his attorney, Bradley Carver."

"Now that's interesting. I don't suppose you know whether or not Lovell was buried."

"Cremated."

"Damn. Whatever evidence there was on his body is gone then," PD said.

"I'd like to talk longer, but I'm in my driveway and my lovely but irked girlfriend is standing on the porch with her arms crossed across her chest, tapping her fingers on her upper arms. I best go."

"Indeed," PD said. "Call me later."

"Will do," Wayne said and ended the call. He got out of his car. He considered slightly exaggerating his limp, but after taking a few steps, found he didn't need to. He could hardly walk. "I didn't find her," he said as Lucy reached him, and a wave of despair swamped him.

"Sometimes all it takes to be a hero is showing up. You did that in spades," Lucy said, as she slipped an arm around his torso and helped him into the house.

SIXTEEN

W**AYNE AND LUCY TALKED BRIEFLY** about his unsuccessful hunt for Pansy Jane and what he hoped she could help with before he was unable to keep his eyes open any longer. He hadn't slept in three days and seeing his eyes closing, Lucy sent him to bed. By the time he woke up an hour later, slightly recovered from days plunging around in the deep brush, she had checked with the ER at Rosedale General as well as the ER's at all the Nashville hospitals.

"How's it going?" he asked.

"Nothing so far. I've already eliminated Rosedale General. The Nashville hospitals are calling me back. It's going to take them a while since we don't know the exact day she would have come in. Plus, she wouldn't have had any ID and was probably confused. What would help the staff, since you think she might not have been able to identify herself, would be a photo."

"That's a great idea. We have one of her identical twin. It's a mug shot and would have to be cleaned up a bit. I can ask my computer guru, Mark Schneider, to handle that. What else?"

"I have to go to work in an hour," Lucy said. "I'm assuming Pansy would have been taken to an ER, but if the person who picked her up wasn't sure what to do, they might have taken her into an urgent care clinic. Why don't you call Dory and Billy Jo? I've made a partial list of the urgent care clinics in and around Nashville. They can start calling this list of phone numbers."

"I'll get Dory on the calls and Billy Jo onto the photo of Pansy Jane. With Mark's help, they should be able to get something to us later today or at least by tomorrow."

"And what will you be up to?" she asked, giving him a sidelong glance with narrowed eyes.

"I never got to talk with Pansy's friend, Lucinda. Her father told me she's a student-teacher at Pioneer. I'll go over there and see what she knows."

"I don't suppose even *you* could manage to risk your life going to an elementary school. But, if you come up empty and decide you need to go to the farmhouse again, promise me—hand on heart—that you'll take Dory or someone from the Sheriff's office with you." She looked so sweetly at him, he couldn't help nodding his head in agreement.

By the time Wayne reached Pioneer Elementary School and found the Principal's Office, the students were getting on buses, and teachers were organizing their materials for the following day. He donned his mask, walked in, and was directed to the Principal's office. He introduced himself to Mr. Molson, showed him his Private Investigator license, and asked if he knew the room number for a student-teacher named Lucinda Wells.

"I'm going to need a lot more information before I release a room number," Principal Molson said crisply. He looked suspicious and Wayne was conscious of his appearance. He had forgotten to shave and must have looked pretty disreputable.

"Of course, I'm happy to give you the background. Rosedale Investigations has been engaged to find a woman by the name of Pansy Jane Delaney. She's missing. Miss Delaney grew up north of Mount Blanc and she and Lucinda Wells were friends as kids. Miss Wells might know something that would help us find Ms. Delaney."

"I see," Principal Molson took a pencil from behind his ear and tapped it on his desk. "May I ask why the Sheriff's Office is not doing this? I thought they did missing persons."

"It's a bit complicated," Wayne said.

"Go on."

Wayne told him only as much as he felt was needed to get the man on his side. He could see the buses leaving the school. Lucinda Wells would be taking off soon. "Could you give me her room number?" Wayne asked, trying not to let the man hear the urgency in his voice.

"I'll walk with you to the room. I'm not comfortable having you prowl around the school after hours by yourself. Lucinda could have left already though," Principal Molson said.

This is what comes of going through channels, Wayne thought. *I should have just asked a kid.* And indeed when they reached the room, it was empty and locked. He suppressed his anger as best he could, thanked the man, and left the building. His fatigue from his days in the woods made it hard to walk, impossible to think logically. He saved what was left of his mental faculties to call the office and ask Dory to start checking with urgent care centers and Billy Jo to get Mark Schneider working on the photo. He got in his truck and drove home.

MARK SCHNEIDER ARRIVED AT ROSEDALE INVESTIGATIONS about an hour later. Billy Jo let him in, checked his temperature, which was normal, told him to remove his shoes, and gave him some hand sanitizer.

"Thanks for coming over, Mark." She smiled at him.

"No problem. What can I do for you today?"

"When you were here before, we were focused on finding Teddy Lovell." Mark nodded. "I'm happy to tell you that we found him alive and he's in the hospital. Since then, Wayne's been trying to find his mother, Pansy Jane. She and her son were staying at her parents' old farmhouse, but she must have tripped and fell against the corner of a metal dumpster. Wayne thinks she cracked her head and wandered off, possibly with transient amnesia."

"How can I help?" Mark asked.

"We know that Pansy reached the road at the edge of the property and then vanished. Wayne is hoping a Good Samaritan found her and took her in for medical assistance. We need a photo to send out to all the urgent care clinics and hospitals to see if they have seen her. We don't have a photo of Pansy Jane, but she has an identical twin who's in jail. We have her intake photo."

"Let me see the mug shot," he said.

"I printed it off for you," Billy Jo said, handing it to him. She was thinking Mark had an interesting face. His cheeks slanted back from a sharply pointed nose. The planes of his face and his black spiky hair made her think of an eagle or a hawk, focused on its prey. She had a feeling he was highly intelligent. It would certainly be a change from Johnny at the Romanov Club who, due to a decade of drug use, had the IQ of a dishtowel. He could still dance, though.

Looking at the mug shot, Mark grimaced. "I don't think this is going to work," he said.

"Can't you just use Photoshop? Clean it up a bit?"

"It's too grainy and unclear. I'm thinking we should take new photos of the twin sister, full face, right profile, left profile, etc. There are so many people in and out of urgent care these days that unless we have a good image, they won't recognize the woman you're looking for. Is there a way we could do that?"

"Let's talk to Dory."

They walked into Dory's office where she was just concluding a call with Lovell's lawyer. "We will be sending you a bill later today or tomorrow, Mr. Carver, along with a report. I would appreciate your paying us as soon as possible."

"Has Pansy Delaney been located yet?" Carver asked.

"Not yet. Thank you and good-bye," she hung up the call. "What can I do for the two of you?" she asked Billy Jo and Mark.

"Mark wants to take new photos of Poppy Delaney. Would she be open to him taking pictures of her to help find her sister? Your last interview with her didn't go very well, you said. It might help her feel better about us."

"I've had an idea of how to get her back on our side. Poor thing looked a mess last time. If we got her some new make-up and hair stuff, I believe she would be very appreciative."

"Mark and I can go to the drug store and buy cosmetics. Maybe she would dye her hair red, too. That would make her look a lot more like Pansy Jane."

"You and Mark both?" Dory asked, innocently. She had already noticed the quick exchange of glances between the two of them. They clearly had chemistry. "You're willing to go with Billy Jo to pick out make-up, Mark?"

"Sure," he said, shrugging his shoulders.

"Not a very masculine errand, I'd have thought," Dory said, raising her eyebrows.

"He's coming," Billy Jo said firmly and taking Mark by the hand led him out of the building.

Dory couldn't help chuckling as they left. She dialed Sheriff Bradley and asked him to call the Warden of the Tennessee Prison for Women and get permission for Mark Schneider to take some photos of Poppy Delaney. She said Mark could shoot the pictures outside in the exercise yard, so it wouldn't be necessary for him to go inside the prison. Plus, the Warden, who had served with the Nashville police before taking the job at the Women's Prison, knew Mark's work from previous cases. The sheriff called back half an hour later. The Warden had approved the request.

"I got the Warden's okay for you to take your photos," Dory told Mark when he and Billy Jo returned with a plastic sack bulging with make-up and hair dye.

"Where can I shoot them?" he asked.

"There's one spindly Osage orange tree in the exercise yard. It's against a brick wall so I thought it would make as good a background as possible in the circumstances. Plus you wouldn't have to go inside the prison. Your appointment is in an hour."

"What about me?" Billy Jo asked.

"You aren't going," Dory said.

"I want to go, Dory. Please?" she said

"Life is hard, Girl. The Warden only approved Mark. You can drive out there with him and wait in the parking lot, I suppose."

Two pink spots appeared on Billy Jo's cheeks, but she didn't protest further. She picked up the bag of make-up, Mark gathered up his camera gear, and the twosome left the building. Watching them pull out of the driveway, Dory had a brief flare of worry. If Snake Wrist was following Billy Jo, he could trail them out to the prison and wait until Mark left the car. He could then force Billy Jo out of the car at gunpoint and put her into the trunk of his car.

"Stop being a ridiculous old worrywart. It's broad daylight and they will be in a busy parking lot," she told herself but sent Billy Jo a text anyway telling her to lock the car when Mark left.

AFTER LEAVING BILLY JO IN THE CAR AT THE PARKING LOT of the Women's Prison, Mark checked in with the security guard manning the Visitor door. He set the sack containing the cosmetics down on the table to be scanned as a second officer got his identification. He knew the drill, he'd been in the facility before.

"I'm here to drop off this make-up and a scarf for prisoner Poppy Delaney." The scarf had been Billy Jo's idea. If they wouldn't let Poppy wear street clothes, she could cover the upper part of the orange jumpsuit with the scarf. "Once she is ready, I'm approved to take some photos of her in the exercise yard," he said.

"I got the call you were coming," the Guard said. He removed everything from the bag and ran it through the x-ray scanner. Once done, he said, "Wait here while Sergeant Bruce takes the make-up to the prisoner."

"Will you ask her how long it will be before she's ready for the photoshoot?" Mark asked.

Sergeant Bruce nodded. A few minutes later he reappeared. "Going to be a couple of hours before she's ready."

"I'll come back then," Mark said.

When she saw Mark returning, Billy Jo unlocked the car to let him in. "That was quick. Did you already take the photos?"

"No, just got her the make-up. We have a couple of hours to kill. Let's get something to eat."

They settled on a Thai place that had several outdoor tables behind the restaurant. They ordered Phad Thai which was delicious and then walked to the ice-cream place next door. It had a walk-up window. Billy Jo ordered a chocolate ice cream cone with sprinkles. Mark ordered a flavor called rocky road. They sat talking in the car until it was time to drive back to the prison. Billy Jo locked the car as Mark walked toward the prison.

"SERGEANT BRUCE WILL ESCORT YOU TO the exercise yard after he gets the prisoner," the security guard told Mark when he returned. "Wait here."

Even outside the building, Mark could hear the sound of banging pans, angry cat-calls, and sobs. Something of the anguish of the women prisoners hit him at that point. It had always seemed inhumane to him, locking women up like animals in a zoo. *There has to be a better way,* he thought. Shortly thereafter, he saw the guard and the prisoner approaching.

"Hi, Poppy. I'm Mark. I hope someone obtained your permission to take pictures of you in the Yard. Is that okay?"

"Yes. Thank you for the make-up and all," she said and smiled at him.

"That was Dory Clarkson's idea." Dory had told him to try to use the occasion to heal their ruptured relationship. "She had another message for you, too. Once Legal Aid gives you an attorney, Sheriff Bradley's agreed to review your case and she'll try to get you before the Parole Board."

Poppy smiled and they walked along an external corridor with the guard who let them into a large fenced area. It looked to Mark like an enormous dog pen. In the far corner, he spotted the puny Osage orange tree Dory had mentioned. It had miraculously clung to life on a small strip of grass, casting minimal shade.

"We're going to take the pictures over by the tree. I was hoping you wouldn't have to wear that orange suit, but I see you did."

"No choice," she said, bitterly.

"Okay. Please stand over there and drape this scarf across your upper body and shoulders. We want to cover up the jumpsuit as much as possible. You look just great, by the way," Mark said. "Thanks a lot for doing this and for changing your hair color. It's going to help us find your sister."

Poppy's whole demeanor brightened at those words and she walked over to stand by the tree. At Mark's direction, she turned right, swiveled, turned left, and then gave him a brilliant smile as he took his full-face shots. He hadn't been able to use any studio lighting, but the sun was still out. Flipping through his digital pictures, Mark thought they would work.

Sergeant Bruce was about to lead them out of the human pen when something struck him. If Pansy Jane Delaney couldn't identify herself, the frantically busy health workers might fail to recognize her in the photos of her beautiful smiling twin.

"Hang on a minute," he told the Sergeant. "I think I'd better get some without her smiling."

Afterward, Mark walked across the parking lot to his car seeing Billy Jo wave. He felt tickled by her excitement. *I really like this girl,* he thought and grinned.

SEVENTEEN

I T WAS NEARLY SEVEN P.M. and Wayne was sitting in his parked truck on the street outside Lucinda Wells' townhouse. When he left Pioneer Elementary earlier, he was so tired he could hardly think. He'd gone home and crashed into bed.

When his alarm rang an hour later, he had been dreaming. In the dream, he was following a woman wearing a billowing white nightgown. Her long red hair floated behind her as she entered a dark forest. Barely awake, Wayne felt disoriented. He'd had so little sleep in the last few days and short naps seemed to make the fatigue worse. He got out of bed, went into the bathroom, and took a cold shower. It was brutal, but when he emerged, he was wide awake. Since it was a weeknight, he doubted Lucinda would be out partying. She would want to get a good review from her supervisor for student teaching and couldn't show up to work hung-over. She'd be home soon. To pass the time, and keep himself focused, he called Dory.

"Hey there, big guy," she said. "What's up?"

"I'm on stake-out in front of Lucinda Wells' townhouse. I've been here two hours with no sight of her. Can you talk to me for a while? I don't want to doze off and miss her."

"I can only talk for a few minutes. What did you want to know?"

"What happened after Billy Jo and Mark got the make-up for Poppy Delaney?"

"They took the whole kit and caboodle to the prison. Mark was able to give the Security Guard the make-up and he took it to Poppy. They are going to get some dinner and then will go back to take the photos. Billy Jo seems to think Mark is cute," Dory said.

"Mark Schneider?" Wayne sounded shocked. "Mark with the dragon tattoo? He just seems nerdy to me. Is he good-looking do you think?"

"Very cute, I'd say and a vast improvement on the boy Billy Jo claims is her current boyfriend who's high on drugs all the time. They haven't seen each other since the pandemic started and were never more than dance partners. In any case, our Billy Jo seems quite smitten with Dragon Boy. I wouldn't be surprised to hear that a dragon tattoo has appeared on her cute little bottom if the relationship takes off."

"Dory! Spare me. I do not need that mental picture," Wayne said.

"You're not her father, you know," Dory said, laughing at him.

Quickly changing the subject, Wayne asked, "Where is Mark going to take these photos?"

"The Warden approved the photoshoot to be done outside in the exercise yard."

"This whole thing just boggles my mind, especially the idea of Billy Jo and Dragon Boy as a couple. And I wonder what PD would say to your using business money to buy cosmetics and hair dye for a prostitute."

"I'm the CFO for the business, you will recall," she said austerely. "PD doesn't have to approve every purchase I make. Speaking of office funds, I talked with Bradley Carver today. Because you found Teddy, he's prepared to disburse Lexie Lovell's inheritance. Teddy's money is being held until such a time as he's in foster care or a more permanent situation. Carver's going to pay our fee, or so he says. He also asked me if we knew where Pansy Delaney was. I thought he seemed particularly interested," Dory said.

"Hmmm. He asked us about her earlier. I found it odd. Who is going to be with Billy Jo tonight?" Wayne asked.

"Sorry, Wayne, have to go." Dory rang off before Wayne could find out where Billy Jo was spending the night. He was still concerned about Snake Wrist's unexpected appearance in the roadside park. He started to push the button to call her back when he saw a young woman walking up the sidewalk to the townhouse at 1236 Mill Trace. She let herself in with a key. Lucinda Wells was home.

Dory had been calling Urgent Care clinics from Lucy's list asking the intake receptionists about a recent visit by a confused woman with no ID. She'd been told a very brusque, "Nobody like that showed up here," at three different clinics before she got the message. Dr. Lucy had done some of the original calls and as a physician, got good cooperation, unlike what Dory was encountering.

She considered leaving the office and going by the grocery store. Her boyfriend, Al, was in town and she was making dinner. They had spent the previous night together and he cooked, so tonight was her turn. Al had a Caribbean condo he stayed at several times a year, often for months. Dory rarely had time to go with him. When Al was in town, they spent all their time together. He had a favorite wine and she could go by the wine store and the dry cleaners. She wanted to wear her purple tea-length gown and hadn't picked it up. It went perfectly with her silver low-heeled shoes.

"What is wrong with me?" she said aloud, feeling her conscience prick like a stiletto. *Thinking about dresses and wine when Pansy Jane is still missing. I am a horrible person. Nothing is as important as locating little Teddy's mother.* She decided to call the urgent care nearest her home. She'd been seen as a patient there and perhaps that would get more cooperation.

"Rosedale Redi-Care East," the receptionist said.

"Hello. My name is Dory Clarkson and I've been a patient at your clinic. If you can pull up my chart, you will see that I'm an Investigator, formerly with the Sheriff's Office. I work for Rosedale Investigations now, and we are trying to find a missing woman. She needed help for a head injury and would have been brought in in the last few days, possibly confused."

"Stop right there, Ms. Clarkson. I can't give out any patient information. You know it's against the rules."

"I'm well aware of the patient confidentiality issues. I'm not asking you for a name. We are simply trying to locate her. She has a child who is in the hospital. I have a picture of the missing woman. Can you just tell me if it would be best to email clinics with the picture or FAX it?"

"Let me think," the receptionist said and put her on hold. She came back later saying she'd have to call her back. It turned out that the receptionist had to ask the nurses in the clinic, the nurses had to check with the doctors. Dory was pulling her hair out when she finally got a return call. It would be best to send the information by email. It was well past quitting time by then, and she had not added a single email address to Lucy's chart.

Sighing, she called Al and said she'd be working late. The romantic dinner she'd planned would have to wait. He wasn't particularly pleased and Dory remembered he'd been talking a lot recently about a woman he'd met who lived in his complex in the Caribbean.

WAYNE KNOCKED ON THE TOWNHOUSE DOOR and heard a voice call out, "Hang on a minute. I'm coming," before the door opened and Lucinda Wells appeared. She was slender with shiny brown hair, hazel eyes, and a nice smile.

"I'm Detective Nichols from Rosedale Investigations and I'm looking for Pansy Jane Delaney. She's missing and I'm hoping you can help me. Could I come in?"

It was immediately clear Lucinda knew something. It wasn't that she said anything, in fact, her silence itself was notable. She greeted his words with hooded eyes. And although she didn't invite him in, she stepped aside and opened the door wider. Normally people asked if you wanted something to drink, or asked you to take a seat. This woman did neither. They continued standing in the tight entryway.

"I have some questions I need to ask you," Wayne said and Lucinda took a deep breath.

"I wondered how long it would take," she murmured. "Guess you should come into the kitchen."

The townhouse kitchen was minimal but had a small round table and chairs. The window was open and an evening breeze lifted the sheer curtains.

"May I sit?" Wayne asked and Lucinda nodded. She picked up a glass of iced tea from the counter and asked if he wanted something to drink. He declined, not wanting to lose her attention. Their connection seemed precarious. "Why did you say you wondered how long it would take for someone to come asking questions about Pansy Delaney?" he asked.

"Because I'm worried about her and Teddy. I haven't talked to her in a while now." Her voice was clear and well-modulated but contained a hint of apprehension as if she expected to hear bad news.

"I don't know if you were aware but Poppy Delaney, Pansy's sister, is in jail. I talked to her and she said Pansy might have gone to their parents' old farm. I know you used to live out in that area. The bad news is that I searched the house, but she wasn't there."

Lucinda's face looked stricken and she bit her lower lip.

"The good news is that I found Teddy at the farm, and despite the little guy's strenuous efforts to escape and bite a chunk out of me, I managed to get him to the hospital." Lucinda's face cleared at that and her tight high shoulders came down a little.

"Did you find anything out about Pansy?" she asked and her voice was filled with trepidation.

"No, we didn't. A search dog was brought in and traced her scent to the highway just east of the property. The trail stopped at that road. My guess, my hope really, is that a Good Samaritan came along and took her to a medical facility."

"She would never have left the house without her son," Lucinda said and Wayne heard the certainty in her voice.

"I believe you. What I think happened was that she went out to put some trash in the big garbage container, probably early in the morning when the dew was still on the grass. She might have slipped on the wet grass, and fell against the corner of the dumpster, possibly hitting her head and causing a loss of consciousness. She wandered around in the fields for a long while until she reached the road on the east side of the property."

Lucinda put her hand over her mouth, looking like she was about to cry.

"I need you to tell me exactly when you saw Pansy last and whether you took them out to the farm," Wayne used a soft voice, but no one could have missed the steel that underlay his question.

Lucinda was quiet for a bit before saying, "She contacted me a couple of weeks ago by email and we met for coffee. I haven't talked to her since, but that day she said she was scared."

"Why didn't you turn her in as missing? A woman with a little child, alone and frightened? Why the hell didn't you contact the cops?" Wayne tried to control his accusatory tone but Lucinda looked like he had struck her.

"Because I was terrified that's why, and before you condemn me for it, I haven't been able to sleep since," she was breathing hard and blinked away some tears.

"Why were you so frightened?" Wayne asked more gently.

"Pansy said she thought the father of her child, Edward Lovell, had been murdered. He intended to meet with the District Attorney about a serious crime. He was going to identify the guilty party. I think he died before he could do so. I was terrified someone would come after me if I called the cops."

"I'm not judging you, Lucinda, but time is running out. Did you take them to the farm?"

Lucinda shook her head, but seeing his dubious expression, she said, "I'm not lying to you, Sir." Her voice was tremulous though, and Wayne could feel the shame rising off her slim young body.

Actually you are, he thought. "When the two of you had coffee, did Pansy have her purse and her cell phone?"

"She couldn't pay her phone bill, so her cell phone was dead. I asked her why she didn't have any money from Ed and she said his executor said he wouldn't give her anything until the business was sold. Seemed doubtful to me. I thought he could have helped her more."

"Okay," he took a deep breath. "If you think of anything else, like a description or the name of anyone who might know something about them, please call me. One last thing, is that your car parked across the street?"

"Yes, it's the green one. Third from the end."

"Thank you, Miss Wells." Wayne handed her his Rosedale Investigations card and although he could think of a hundred more questions, he left her standing in the kitchen. She was white-faced and trying very hard not to cry.

He walked over to the semi-covered parking area for residents' vehicles and looked at the tires on Lucinda's car, pulling out his cell phone and taking several shots. Her tire treads exactly matched the treads in the dirt in front of the Delaney farmhouse. Lucinda had taken Pansy and her son to what she considered a safe place. He walked back to his truck.

It was dark by then and his truck was warm. Before sleep could claim him, Wayne started driving home. He had been building a theory of the crime, but at that moment it seemed a shaky edifice—a house of cards that could be blown down instantly—by the slightest breath.

WAYNE ENTERED THE HOUSE he shared with Lucy completely exhausted. He hadn't had a full night's sleep in days and nothing to eat in hours. He checked the refrigerator and saw a white take-out box. He opened it hopefully but saw only half a pulled pork sandwich. He tossed it into the wastebasket. Feeling too tired to cook anything, he walked down the hall, managed to get out of his clothes, and fall into bed.

His mind was so agitated, he couldn't enter into deep sleep. He kept opening his eyes and checking the clock, seeing only an hour had gone by. Then the nightmares began. A naked girl with long red hair ran past him, panting. It was raining and her pale white body was filthy, covered with smeared blood and raindrops. In the dream, Wayne tried to reach her but was held by invisible vines that kept him trapped in a thorny bush. A wolf came out of the trees and ran toward the woman. A flash of lightning rent the sky and lit the animal's white fur. The woman screamed. He sat up, breathing hard.

That's it, he thought. *I'm getting up.*

He suddenly remembered the worrisome thing that wouldn't come to him earlier. It was Billy Jo. Nobody was with Billy Jo. He glanced at the clock. It was 2:15 a.m. He got dressed and walked out to his truck. Lucy wouldn't be home until 4:00. He had time to check on her.

ENTERING THE DRIVEWAY AT ROSEDALE INVESTIGATIONS, he saw Billy Jo's car. He glanced at the upper windows of the renovated house. There was a light on in her apartment upstairs. It was a good sign that she was home. He considered leaving her in peace but called her cell phone instead. There was no answer. Pulling his office keys from his pocket, he got out of the truck, walked up the sidewalk, and let himself into the building.

He distinctly heard two voices talking quietly upstairs and then a bubbly little giggle. She was all right, but who could she be with? He walked up the stairs to Billy Jo's apartment and tried the handle of her door. The girl's voice shrieked with laughter and the door practically fell open.

"Detective Nichols, Sir," Mark managed as Wayne stared him down noticing his shirt was unbuttoned and the fly on his jeans was partly undone. His spiky black hair was standing straight up. Billy Jo appeared behind Mark. She was hurriedly tying the sash on a pink terrycloth robe and trying to stifle her laughter. "Miss Dory was with her boyfriend, so there wasn't anyone to stay with Billy Jo and she was afraid to stay alone," Mark said.

Wayne glowered. "And you felt it imperative to stay here in her apartment, in a state of almost complete undress, rather than being on guard on the main floor?"

Mark flushed and managed, "You see, Sir . . ." He trailed off.

"Never mind. I get the picture," Wayne said dryly. "Billy Jo when you have some actual clothes on, I'd like a word with you."

He knew he was being ridiculous. The girl wasn't underage. He wasn't her father and Mark hadn't committed a crime. It was quite clear whatever the two of them had been up to, it was consensual. He needed to go.

He thumped back downstairs, leaving Billy Jo and Mark standing red-faced on the upstairs landing.

He yelled over his shoulder, "I will talk to you tomorrow, Billy Jo. And Mark . . ." He turned back to look at the boy, forked his fingers at his own eyes, and then pointed them at him, making the old sign for "I'm watching you."

As he left the building, he could hear Billy Jo squashing more giggles and Mark trying to shush her.

EIGHTEEN

IT WAS NOW THE FIFTH DAY IN THE SEARCH for Poppy Delaney and Wayne was in a black despair. Desperate to do something to help, he was driving to the Nashville police post to meet with Captain Paula. With her help, he got the CCTV from every street near *any* medical facility for the days since Teddy was abandoned. He locked himself in the conference room reviewing the footage, emerging only for coffee. Even the food Dory bravely left for him went uneaten. He hadn't spoken to either her or Billy Jo the entire time. Sometimes he left to catch a few hours sleep at home but usually stretched himself out on the couch in the entry. Billy Jo brought him a blanket and pillow. She and Dory had given up taking the bedding back upstairs every morning. It was a losing battle. They were all working round the clock.

Lucy called the office on day five of the siege. "Dory, it's Lucy. I know it's like grabbing the tail of a grizzly bear, but I must speak with Wayne."

"I'll take the phone in to him. Hope he doesn't bite my head off," Dory said. Opening the door to the conference room, she met a stone-cold expression on her partner's face. "It's Lucy. She wouldn't take no for an answer," she said, quickly sliding the phone across the table. She had put the call on speaker. Leaving the room, she kept the door ajar. Billy Jo joined her and they stood listening to the conversation.

"Hi Lucy," Wayne said. His voice was raw. Despite not smoking for thirty years, there was a pile of cigarette butts in the ashtray.

"I had an idea," Lucy said.

"What is it?" Wayne asked.

"Because Pansy Jane had a head injury, we focused on the Rosedale and Nashville Emergency Rooms and Urgent Care clinics. I got to thinking about that. Maybe the person who picked her up went further afield. Some of the rural hospitals in the state have Emergency Rooms."

"That's a really good thought, Lucy," his voice softened.

"Have Billy Jo make up a new list, and as payment for my idea, I insist that you come home tonight."

"Since I'm going blind looking at this CCTV crap, I think I will."

"See you soon. I'm cooking roast beef and mashed potatoes."

"With gravy?" he asked hopefully.

"Yes, Wayne, but I'm *not* eating this meal alone."

Wayne emerged blearily from the conference room, stuck the phone in Dory's outstretched hand, told Billy Jo to start checking ER's further afield, grabbed his jacket, and left the building. Driving to the house he realized how tired he was. It was not the sort of tiredness he felt when he was short of sleep. This was a bone-deep tiredness he felt when his reason for pursuing a case had vanished. Pansy Delaney was already dead. He was chasing a ghost woman.

DORY TURNED TO BILLY JO WHEN Wayne left and said, "I'm going to see Hayley, the social worker for Teddy. Can you call PD and give him an update?"

"I will, but when you get a moment, I have something personal to ask you," Billy Jo said.

The serious note in her voice made Dory turn around. "Sounds like we should talk about this now."

"Okay. Remember the night that Al was in town and I stayed here instead of with you?"

Dory nodded. "We talked about Mark staying with you."

"That's right and he did, but nobody told Wayne. He appeared here at 2:00 in the morning."

"So?" Dory asked.

"So, Mark was upstairs with me and we, well we weren't completely dressed when Wayne arrived." She colored in embarrassment.

Dory tried in vain to keep a grin from tugging at her mouth. "Go on."

"Mark said that he was guarding me, but Wayne wasn't buying it for one minute. It didn't help that Mark's shirt was unbuttoned and his zipper was part-way down."

Dory hooted with laughter and after a minute or two, Billy Jo couldn't help but join her. "Man, I needed that," Dory said when they stopped laughing.

"I've been thinking maybe Wayne wasn't speaking to me because of that night. I've been afraid to have Mark come back," Billy Jo said.

"Your being with Mark isn't the reason. He hasn't spoken to me in days either. Wayne can't stop blaming himself for not finding Pansy. I don't know how much you know of Wayne's background, but his mother ran out on the family. Finding Teddy's mom, if he succeeds, will lay some ghosts to rest for him. And speaking of one's conscience reminding us of our failures, I need to go."

"Hang on a minute. I have something else I wanted to ask. Don't be mad, but I can't figure out why you aren't focused on finding Pansy Jane like Wayne is."

A grave expression crossed Dory's face. "You're right. I have struggled with it. I've gone to church and prayed about it. I even met with my minister trying to figure out why I didn't feel compelled to help find her. Once we realized she made it to the road by her parent's property, I've had a premonition that Pansy Jane is either dead or will never be in a condition to be Teddy's mom again. I wish Wayne luck, but my failures had to do with Teddy, not his mother. Until I know he is settled, I won't be able to . . . forgive myself," she blinked back tears. "I'll see you at my house later tonight." Dory adjusted her mask and left the building.

HAYLEY DRUMMOND, THE YOUNG SOCIAL WORKER assigned to Teddy's case had been working to arrange a foster placement. Dory would have liked nothing better than seeing Teddy in person, but visitation was still prohibited at the hospital. Hayley was permitted inside because she was an employee and was able to take pictures to show Dory. They met in her office at the Community Mental Health facility.

"Hi, Hayley," Dory greeted her. The young social worker was wearing a yellow shirtwaist dress and flats. It complimented her dark hair. However, Dory knew her case numbers had increased many times over since the pandemic began, and she looked tired and a bit frazzled.

"Hi Dory," Hayley said.

"Have you made any videos or taken any recent photos of Teddy?"

"I have and will send them to your phone, but there's something else we need to discuss today."

"Am I taking up too much of your time, Hayley? I know your workload is ridiculous and it's already closing time. I don't mean to be a pest. I'm happy to talk with you on the phone or look at pictures. I brought some new clothes for Teddy," Dory gestured to a plastic sack she'd brought along.

"We might need to change how often we meet in the future, but right now I wanted to tell you about Teddy's latest issue."

"Is he okay? What about the heart murmur? Is the pediatric cardiologist going to suggest surgery?" Dory felt frantic every time she thought of the little guy going under the knife alone with no family.

"No, it's not that. The heart murmur is being treated medically. He won't have to undergo surgery for years, possibly never. The problem is his speech," Hayley looked worried. "The fact is Teddy isn't talking."

"Well, maybe he's just too young. Boys never talk as early as girls. And he was left in that farmhouse alone, maybe for several days," Dory grimaced, feeling guilt hit her all over again.

"We don't think it's developmental. He's plenty old enough to be talking. We've considered Autism, but don't think it's that. He doesn't have low intelligence, either. We believe he's very bright. The lack of speech is definitely due to the trauma of losing his mother. Detective Nichols said he only spoke one word during the tussle he had with the child. Teddy said, 'Mommy.' He hasn't even asked for her since. We've heard no speech at all since he arrived. He doesn't even cry when they take blood from him. It's very troubling. I've been talking with the child psychiatrist at the hospital and I've asked her to join us today. Her name's Dr. Juanita Marsh. She'll be here shortly."

"Before she arrives, have you decided on a foster placement yet?" Dory asked.

"That's another issue. I believe a home with young children would help Teddy, but Dr. Marsh doesn't agree. She wants him in a home with no other children so the parents can focus on him. I thought we'd discuss that today, plus have her tell you what else they've done to get Teddy to talk." They heard a brisk knock and Hayley got up to open the door.

When the introductions were complete, Dr. Marsh told them she'd arranged a specialist to meet with Teddy to help him start talking again. "The speech therapist has met with Teddy twice so far. They meet in the pediatric playroom which has a lot of toys and a little child's teepee. As soon as they get to the room, Teddy races over to the corner and hides in the teepee. He has so far refused to come out or engage with her in any way. She's not giving up, but isn't optimistic," Dr. Marsh said, sounding worried.

"Hayley mentioned that you and she are not in agreement about what type of foster home would be best for Teddy. Are there even a lot of choices at present? Given the pandemic, I'd think foster homes might be at a premium," Dory said.

"You're right. While young children don't often get Corvid 19, and if they do, usually don't get seriously ill, many of our best foster parents have said they can't take any more children," Dr. Marsh said.

"Are you both aware that Teddy's mother has an identical twin sister? Her name is Poppy Delaney. She's not available now, but she would like to be Teddy's guardian if the boy's mother can't be found. I'm trying to get her released."

"Released?" Hayley asked, frowning.

"Yes, she's serving a short sentence for prostitution, a trade she would happily swear off if she had any resources. I would have to discuss this with Child Protective Services, but she might be able to be appointed his guardian. The inheritance is probably big enough to support both of them."

"I have some reservations about that," Hayley said. "Prostitution is like any other addictive lifestyle. It's hard to get out of."

"I agree, but we are very short of options. Once Poppy is released, provided she's willing to go through the process of being credentialed as a foster parent, and . . ."

"She must agree to go to therapy," Dr. Marsh said firmly. "Hayley and I would both need to meet with her and assess her suitability, but the family connection could help expedite the process."

"Teddy's pediatrician would like to see him released from the hospital soon," Hayley said. "We will probably have to make interim arrangements."

"You two are the experts in placing children, but I did have one wild idea. Do you think Teddy might be helped by being with a young dog?"

"A very interesting thought," Dr. Marsh said. "Do you agree, Hayley?"

"I do. Sometimes children will talk to pets who won't speak to humans."

"Pets being much nicer generally," Dory said. "I have a small friendly dog. She's very sweet and loves kids. We could get them together and see how it goes. What do you think?"

"Nobody is going to approve such a visit, but I agree and think it might help him. It's a risk and I will be in huge trouble if anyone finds out, but maybe I can come up with a way to make it work," Dr. Marsh said.

NINETEEN

I T WAS EARLY MORNING ON THE SIXTH DAY of their looking for Pansy Delaney. Wayne had texted Billy Jo to say he was going back out to the Delaney farm. Calls requesting the services of Rosedale Investigations kept rolling in. Trying to preserve as much time as possible for Wayne to locate Teddy's mother, Billy Jo was scheduling initial client meetings for several weeks out. She'd received a call back from the Franklin Funeral Home in Rosedale, Texas. They had located Mr. Charlie Carson's ashes. She was tickled it had been so easy and called Mrs. Jill Roberts who answered immediately.

"Mrs. Roberts, this is Billy Jo from Rosedale Investigations. We have located your grandfather's cremains."

"That's excellent news, Billy Jo. Thank you."

"They are being sent to our office, and when they arrive I will personally take them to the Franklin Funeral Home. I'm sending you a report today along with our bill. Something amusing happened during the search. Your grandad's ashes were sent initially to a funeral home in Rosedale, *Texas* not Rosedale, *Tennessee*. That's why it took me a while to locate them."

Billy Jo had expected a chuckle, but Jill Roberts' tone was distinctly cool. "Are we certain they are the ashes of my grandfather then? I'm not burying a stranger next to my grandmother. I insist on having a DNA test to confirm that they are his."

Billy Jo hesitated. Could one even get DNA from cremains? "I think the only way to do a DNA test would be from tooth dentin. Did your grandfather have his own teeth?"

She heard a sigh. "No, he had false teeth from an early age. I'm not paying your bill until I am certain those ashes are my grandfather's."

"I'll look into our options and I'll call you back when I know something." Billy Jo set the phone down, wracking her brains about her next steps in the Missing Grandfather case.

IT WAS AFTERNOON BY THE TIME DORY GOT TO THE OFFICE. She'd had a hair appointment and decided on a braided African up-do. Patting her hair, she gave Billy Jo a quick once-over, noting a "Black Lives Matter" T-shirt and black jeans. As a woman of color, Dory could hardly object, although she would have adorned the outfit with some silver jewelry and a splashy belt.

"What's been going on?" Dory asked.

"We have new cases coming in, all of which I'm scheduling for next week or the following. I tracked down the missing grandfather's ashes in Rosedale, Texas and they're en route to our office here. I called Mrs. Roberts to give her the news, but she wants a DNA test to prove they are her grandfather's. She wasn't burying a stranger, she said. I knew you could test the dentin in teeth for DNA but he had false teeth. Not sure what to do next. Any ideas?" Billy Jo asked.

"Large bone fragments would do it. You're going to have to wait until the cremains arrive and have the Rosedale Funeral people see if there are any pieces of bone big enough to have viable marrow—that's what they need for the DNA test. Best check to see what the cost will be and tell Mrs. Roberts. What other cases have come in?"

"There's a cheating spouse. Interesting situation, it's usually the wife who suspects the husband of cheating, but this is a husband. He suspects his wife of having a *lesbian* affair. He seems far more outraged than he would be if it was a man," Billy Jo told her grinning.

Dory raised her eyebrows and chuckled. "I volunteer to do the surveillance and photos on that one. What else?"

"A woman called because her grandfather died and she has been going through his papers. He was in France during WWII and she thinks he might have had a daughter with a French woman. It's a bit tricky because his wife is still alive and would be devastated. They want us to track down the rumor and find out if it's true."

"That will be an interesting one. How old is the grandmother?"

"She's in her 90's."

"Frankly, women of that vintage aren't surprised by much. They lived through WWII with all the rationing. People complain about wearing masks, but in those years disposable diapers hadn't been invented and neither had formula or baby food. Young women, many of whom had babies, dealt with milk, butter, and gasoline shortages for four years. Gramma might just surprise them. She could even want to meet the woman. Lots of men stationed overseas had wartime relationships. Anything else?"

"Yes, a third case involves a painting. Not a lost painting, which would be more usual, but a painting a local woman inherited from a cousin. She wants to know what it's worth and whether it's dodgy."

"What does that mean, dodgy?" Dory asked.

"Stolen, or altered in some way. Anyway, I've scheduled the Lesbian Affair case and the Illegitimate French child case for next week. I put off the Dodgy Painting until next month."

"God, I love this job," Dory said with a grin. "Never a dull moment." She sashayed into the kitchen to see what there was to eat.

The phone rang again. It was PD. "Hi. How's it going?" Billy Jo asked.

"I've been making progress. The mob connection is looking more and more tenuous. I've thought from the beginning that money lies at the bottom of this case. That's what I'm concentrating on now. Bring me up to date, will you? What's Wayne doing about Pansy Delaney?"

"He met with Pansy's friend, Lucinda Wells, yesterday. She lied and told him she didn't take Pansy out to the old farm, but he took pictures of her tire treads and compared them to the pictures of the tire marks in the driveway. It was a match. He also had a brainstorm about where Pansy's purse and cell phone might be. He's on his way out to the farm again. Deputy George is going with him this time."

"Good. Anything else?"

"Teddy Chase Lovell isn't talking—literally. Dory wants to take her pup to the hospital to see if the dog might help. She's running into roadblocks. It's unclear whether dogs can get the wretched virus, although cats and even lions and tigers can get it. She might need to test the dog."

"What about the Delaney woman's twin? Any progress on getting her out of jail?"

"That's Dory's second big project," Billy Jo lowered her voice, and practically whispered as she said, "She's focused on getting Poppy out of jail because she's had a premonition that Pansy is dead and Wayne is chasing a ghost. In the absence of his mother, Dory thinks Poppy would be the best person to raise Teddy. Neither of us wants to tell Wayne. I've never seen him like this. He's always driven on his cases, but this one has him working around the clock. Lucy finally made him come home to eat and sleep yesterday. I could come out and bring you some groceries, PD. I was on my way out yesterday when I saw the man with the snake tattoo. It was pretty scary, but I'm okay now."

"I'll read you my grocery list," PD said.

WAYNE AND DEPUTY GEORGE WERE DRIVING into the old Delaney farmhouse driveway. Although it was a beautiful day with a cloudless blue sky, there were thunderclouds in Wayne's mind. It was day six and Wayne hadn't found a trace of Pansy. He had a sinking feeling he had already run out of time and now he was running out of ideas. Failure closed around his spirit like a bitter cloud.

"You think the Delaney woman's purse is in the house?" George asked.

"When we first searched the place I noticed a box under the double bed. I should have pulled it out and looked, but I was so focused on finding the mother and the boy that I let it go," Wayne said.

"Now this woman you're looking for, she isn't that *call* girl who asked if I wanted to party, is she?" George said, raising his eyebrows and looking horrified.

"No, that's her twin sister, Poppy. She's is the Women's Prison in Nashville. Dory is working to get her released. Don't worry, George, I won't let her invite you to any more parties," Wayne gave a teasing chuckle, grateful for anything to smile about. "Since you didn't catch on that she was a prostitute, I take it you didn't arrest her?"

"No, I didn't. She must have left Rosedale and gone back to Nashville where she was picked up. I know I'm not the sharpest knife in the drawer," George said gloomily.

"We just keep you around for the laugh factor, Buddy. However, next time a scantily-dressed woman on a street corner asks if you want to party, just say you're not interested. I have to know though, did you tell your wife about the proposition?"

George's face was a picture of horror. "God no! She would kill me, just kill me."

Wayne was not surprised. George's wife was known as a bit of a termagant and he was completely under her thumb. They pulled up to the Delaney farmhouse and got out of the car. Once inside, they walked down the hall to the master bedroom and looked under the bed.

George cast Wayne a pleading look. "Do I have to crawl under there?"

"As you know, I outrank you, so under you go."

"Not any longer," George said, standing up a bit straighter. "Not since you retired."

"Well, look who just got a backbone. See, George, you are smart. And besides, my friend, you are correct." Wayne pulled the bed away from the wall. Pulling on his gloves as he bent down, and ignoring the stabbing pain in his knee, he extracted the box. It was about the size of a boot box with a lift-off cover.

"Aren't you going to open it?"

"No. As you so rightly pointed out, I don't work for law enforcement any longer, so to preserve the chain of evidence, you get to open it." Wayne handed George a pair of plastic gloves. In the dim light on the bedroom, George put on the gloves and lifted the lid. Inside was a purse, a cell phone, and a leather-bound book. Wayne felt a surge of satisfaction. "Let's take this back to the Sheriff's office. Ben's going to want to see what's in this book."

"Ben said to tell you he got a call from Centennial Realty about the red stone mansion. The realtors went out to put up some 'For Rent' signs and did a walk-through on the property. It had been tossed, especially the office in the high tower."

Wayne nodded, it was all coming together now. Either the mob or the feds had been looking for evidence of a crime and he had the strangest sensation that what they had been searching for was inside the box they had found. It was a step in the right direction, but there had been no trace of her since she left the Delaney farm. Had he missed a shallow grave on the farm? His breathing quickened. Lucy's idea about the rural hospitals just had to pan out.

PREPARING TO RUN OUT TO VISIT PD, Billy Jo grabbed her keys and the grocery list she had written out. "Dory, I'm leaving for PD's place. What are you doing?"

"I'm going to take True to the vet to see if I can get a clean bill of health for her. Dr. Marsh, the child psychiatrist from the hospital, thought my idea of letting Teddy play with the dog could help unlock his speech. She's going to be my partner on a clandestine mission tonight. We're smuggling True into the pediatric playroom where we will be meeting Teddy Chase Lovell." Dory's eyes were dancing.

"So, you'll finally be able to see the little guy in person. That's great. I sure hope it works and that Teddy loves True."

"Well, who doesn't," Dory said grinning. "Little Runt is just irresistible."

"Did we hear back from any of the rural hospitals yet?" Billy Jo asked.

Dory's smile faded. "Nothing yet. If I'm right and the woman is dead, it's going to practically kill Wayne." The two women looked at each other in silence. Behind her back, Billy Jo superstitiously crossed her fingers for luck.

TWENTY

SHERIFF BEN BRADLEY WAS SITTING IN HIS CONFERENCE ROOM with his former Chief Detective Wayne Nichols and Deputy George. They were surveying the dusty box on the table. Wayne was looking pretty rough. He smelled of cigarettes. Ben was surprised, thinking he had given up smoking years ago. Mrs. Coffin, wearing her usual masks, gloves, and face shield, was cleaning the conference table and chairs with bleach wipes until Ben asked her if they could have the room. She departed, but not before squirting all three men's hands with sanitizer and making sure Wayne's mask was positioned property.

"Go ahead and get everything out of the box, George," Ben said.

George removed the purse, the cell phone and the leather-bound book from the box. He opened the purse and tipped out its contents, spilling them forward onto the table. It was all pretty routine stuff—a checkbook, a lipstick, comb, a mirrored-compact, a plastic folder containing credit cards, several packages of wet wipes, and a little bottle of hand sanitizer. At the bottom of the purse, however, was a sealed legal-sized envelope with the words "Final Instructions" written on the outside.

"Shall I open this?" George asked. Ben nodded. George unfolded the letter and laid it on the table.

They leaned forward to read the following: "Edward James Lovell and Pansy Jane Delaney, biological parents to Theodore Chase Lovell, their son, hereby inform all legal authorities that we wish Theodore Chase Lovell to be raised by Poppy Ann Delaney, (sister of Pansy Jane and Aunt to Theodore Chase) in the event of our deaths or disability that would make it impossible for us to raise him.

"A codicil to our most recent will specifies sufficient funds to support both Poppy Ann and Theodore Chase for two decades. If either parent is unable to raise Theodore, the monies are to go to whoever serves as his legal guardian. The remainder of the estate is to be split equally between Lexie Lovell and Theodore Lovell. Lexie Lovell shall receive her inheritance at the age of twenty-one. Teddy's guardian may access his funds as soon as need be." The letter had been signed by Pansy Jane Delaney and Edward James Lovell. It was notarized.

"What was the name of the guy who was the attorney for Edward Lovell?" the sheriff asked.

"Bradley Carver, but I'm wondering if they used a different attorney for this. Carver didn't mention anything about this codicil when we discussed the estate. It's also possible there's a second will," Wayne said. His voice turned cool when he added, "Now that we have Pansy's phone, I'll have Mark Schneider do more work on her cell phone data. It won't hurt him one little bit to have to work hard for a change," Wayne said. His tone spoke volumes.

"I thought you liked Mark. Don't you?" Ben asked, frowning in confusion.

"He's okay," Wayne said shortly.

Sheriff Bradley opened the leather book and ran his finger down what looked like a list of extremely expensive items. There were several pages worth.

"What are you going to do with the book, Sheriff?" Wayne asked. Had he been in his former role as Chief Detective, he would have made some suggestions, but it wasn't his place now.

"I'm going to call the Assistant DA and see what she suggests," Ben said.

"Have you started looking into Bradley Carver and whether he could have caused Ed Lovell's death?" Wayne asked.

"I have Detective Rob on it. You were right that Lovell was cremated. That eliminates the body, which usually provides the most clues. We'll see what Rob comes up with."

"It's just so spooky," George said, his pudgy forehead was wrinkled up in deep thought.

"What did you say, George?" Wayne asked.

"It's like they could see the future, Mr. Lovell and Miss Delaney, I mean. Why appoint a guardian for your son when they were both relatively young and healthy? But as it turns out, they must have been psychic. Mr. Lovell is already dead and I guess Miss Delaney is presumed dead at this point."

Ben cast a blazing "shut up" look at George, but it was too late.

"Not yet, Goddammit," Wayne said, clenching his teeth as discouragement poured down into his soul.

BILLY JO DROVE INTO THE CIRCULAR DRIVE for PD's cabin in the late afternoon. He told her he might be sleeping and to come in. His key was hidden under a decoy duck sitting on the front porch.

"The man was in law enforcement for decades and still leaves his house key under a duck on the front porch," Billy Jo said, shaking her head.

Letting herself inside, she was dismayed to find the place a complete disaster. Unwashed dishes were piled in the sink. A stale smell permeated the room. Newspapers had been thrown on the floor by PD's chair. Dirty clothes were slung over the couch and pizza boxes had been tossed on the carpet. Straightening her shoulders, Billy Jo adjusted her mask, used her hand sanitizer, pulled out the broom, and got to work. She cleaned the kitchen first and stocked the refrigerator with the groceries she'd purchased. PD woke up, greeted her sleepily, and said he was going to take a shower. She stripped his bed and put the bedding in the recently-installed washer/dryer.

"Thank God I won that battle," she murmured. By the time she had mopped the floor in the living room and kitchen, the sheets were clean and dry. She made the bed. The last thing she did was to open all the windows. It was a warm balmy afternoon and the bright breeze would dissipate the remnants of the stale smell. She was in the kitchen when PD emerged.

"Thanks for coming out, Billy Jo, and for bringing groceries. Reimburse yourself from my wallet. I was taking a nap because I walked the whole perimeter of my property today. Being out in nature helps me think, but I stepped into an animal's burrow and fell. Think I sprained my ankle. I taped it up, that's about the only thing you can do with sprains."

"Let me take a look." When PD pulled up his pant leg she could see bruising forming above and below the self-adherent wrapping tape. "Do you want me to take you to Urgent Care?"

"No. I've had sprained ankles before. Took some painkillers. They make me sleepy but certainly haven't taken away my appetite," he grinned.

"Are you hinting for me to cook something?" Billy Jo asked.

PD nodded and limped over to sit on the couch. Billy Jo made a grilled cheese sandwich and warmed some chicken noodle soup, but carrying the lunch on a tray toward the couch she heard the distinctive sound of snoring. Her adopted grandfather was once again sound asleep. The pain pills had knocked him out.

She took the tray with the food on it out on the deck thinking it would be silly to waste the sandwich. Looking down at the small lake below the cabin, she sat down to enjoy the early evening light. As the fireflies appeared and the sun went down, she texted Dory and Wayne, *"PD sprained his ankle. We need to make a plan. Can you come out?"*

"Nope. 1st stage of the covert mission," Dory texted back.

Wayne texted back a bit later saying, *"Nothing found on CCTV. I'm coming out."*

An hour later Billy Jo heard Wayne's truck drive in. The screen door slammed behind him, making its distinctive sound. She was sitting on the back deck. The cabin had spotlights on the eaves that lit up the ravine. Having found a pair of binoculars earlier, she was watching a vixen fox followed by two skinny kits with their tiny black legs. The mother was putting them into her den at the base of the gully.

Both men joined her on the deck. PD was limping.

"There's a mother fox, a vixen, down there with two kits," she said, handing the binoculars to Wayne.

"Beautiful," he said, passing the binoculars to PD who nodded.

"What have you found about the case, PD?" Wayne asked after they took their seats.

"I've been calling all my old cronies, retired Detectives for the most part, and confidential informants, asking about any connection between Lovell and the mob. So far, there's no evidence. I told Billy Jo earlier I think this case is all about money, either stolen, embezzled, or possibly laundered. Should have some results soon from the feelers I've put out."

"Interesting. Let us know what you learn. Billy Jo says you're feeling pretty isolated out here," Wayne said and PD nodded.

"I've had an idea to help with that," Billy Jo said. "I'll come to the office for a few hours every day, but I'm spending nights here for the rest of PD's quarantine. That way you and Dory won't be worried about me at night. I was hoping the two of you could come out occasionally during the week and on Friday afternoons we could have a staff meeting here on the big deck. How does that sound?" she asked.

"Like an excellent plan," Wayne said as PD nodded.

Later, after PD limped off to bed, Wayne and Billy Jo sat in silence listening to the low sounds of water lapping at the shore of the little lake as the moon rose.

"Do you think you will ever find Pansy Delaney, Wayne?" Billy Jo asked. "It's been six days since Teddy was found and you began the search."

"I will find her," he said, adding under his breath, "or die trying." But the thought of finding Pansy's dead body caused him to shudder.

DORY DESCENDED ON HER SMALL WHITE DOG, True, with towels and shampoo. Alarm showed in the dog's eyes as she was scooped up in warm brown arms and carried into the bathroom. Realizing her fate, the dog began to struggle valiantly, but it was too late.

"It's just a bath, Runt. You got a clean bill of health from the vet, who was very understanding about you trying to *bite* her, by the way," Dory said, as she lowered a wildly pugnacious animal into the bathtub filled with soap bubbles. True tried scrabbling up the side of the tub and Dory pushed her back down.

"Stop that fighting now. It's not that bad." Dory grabbed a plastic glass and poured bathwater over the dog's head and back. Furious and wet, True turned betrayed eyes on her owner. The whole time in the tub, she struggled furiously. Once clean she was lifted out.

"See, it's all over. That wasn't that bad now, was it?"

True gave her a scorching glare and shook herself ferociously, sending water all over Dory.

"That does it, Runt. I was going to let you air dry, but not now," Dory said as she pulled her hairdryer from under the bathroom counter. True ran behind the toilet, squealing. Dory was unmoved.

Late that evening, Dory and True left for Rosedale General hospital. Dr. Marsh, the child psychiatrist, had texted her saying she managed to get the keys to the pediatric playroom. If they got caught, she would lose her hospital privileges, but desperate times called for desperate measures. They were going in.

TWENTY-ONE

WAITING IN THE PARKING LOT for her comrade in arms, Dory stuffed True into her tote bag and covered the opening with a towel. The dog growled quietly. "You just hush. We are saving lives here tonight." True began to struggle and Dory wondered whether she should have given her the sedative which the vet offered. At the time, she thought it would be better to have the dog be her usual exuberant self—not perhaps the wisest decision.

Dr. Marsh pulled into the parking lot behind them, got out of the car, and held a ring of keys triumphantly aloft.

"You got them!" Dory called out happily through her car's open window.

"Shhh . . . yes, I did, but needless to say, I didn't inform hospital administration. I talked with Teddy's nurse in Peds. She's been a friend of mine for over twenty years and thinks this is worth a try. She's going to bring Teddy to the playroom and then leave. If asked whether she allowed a dog to be brought into the unit, she will be able to honestly say she didn't. I see you dressed in black," Juanita said. She had tied her ash-blond hair back in a French twist and wore a surgical hat with navy blue scrubs.

"This is my surveillance outfit," Dory said.

"Are high-heeled boots normally worn for surveillance?" Dr. Marsh asked. When Dory looked slightly guilty, she said, "Never mind. Put on your mask. We best get moving."

The two women walked briskly across the parking lot. It was getting dark and most of the lot was empty of cars although some late employees were still leaving. The main entrance to the hospital was well-lighted and guarded by a uniformed security officer sitting at a table with a clipboard.

"How are we going to get past that guy with this dog?" Dory asked.

"We're not. Follow me," Dr. Marsh said, and the twosome walked around the corner of the building to where a flat door with no handle barred their entrance.

"Hope these are the right keys," Juanita said and began trying them one by one. The fourth key worked and they walked in, finding themselves in front of a service elevator. A sign listed the names of all the departments. Pediatrics was on the third floor. They entered the elevator and pushed the button. When the doors opened, they saw a woman wearing a nurse's uniform coming toward them. She was leading a little boy by the hand. Only about half the overhead lights were on in the corridor, making it hard to see her or the child.

"Stay here a minute," Dr. Marsh whispered to Dory who ducked back into the elevator. Juanita walked out to greet and thank her friend who departed quickly, looking from left to right as she did so. As soon as the woman disappeared, Juanita pushed the elevator button and the doors opened. "She's given us twenty minutes before she comes back. Come on."

THE PEDIATRIC PLAYROOM HAD MULTIPLE BOOKCASES placed around the room creating miniature book-walled rooms that were dedicated to reading, doing puzzles, or playing video games. A large mural had been hand-painted on the back wall. It depicted a fairytale castle complete with a drawbridge, knights on horseback, and a princess with long golden hair. The floor was made of vinyl. Brightly colored images of flowers and leaves had been cut out and inserted into the base material. It was a welcoming, attractive space and Dory imagined little kids would enjoy their playtime there.

As they entered the room, Teddy pulled his hand from Dr. Marsh's and dashed to an Indian-patterned teepee that stood in a corner. He crawled inside and disappeared from view.

"Should I release True?" Dory asked.

"Let's just wait a bit. Once he gets used to his surroundings, maybe he'll crawl out."

They waited, talking quietly, but the wiggling tote bag kept getting heavier. Dory finally set it down on the shining floor. True immediately escaped, cast Dory a furious backward glare, and headed for the teepee. She started to grab for the dog's leash but Dr. Marsh stopped her. "Let's see what happens," she said.

True sat down just outside the slice in the teepee that served as the door. A tiny hand pushed the fabric aside and the dog's little white bottom with its curly tail disappeared inside. They could hear tussling sounds and then a tiny shriek. Dory took a step toward the corner, but Juanita grabbed by the arm saying, "Hang on."

"I'm afraid Teddy will be scared," Dory said.

"No worries. That, my friend, was a delighted shriek."

Her assumption was reinforced a few minutes later when they could hear Teddy start to giggle. Dory sent a fervent prayer to the heavens that the little boy would say something. Anything at all. The teepee was positively thrashing around by then when suddenly it fell, trapping both child and dog inside. True barked wildly.

Both women ran over and lifted up the teepee, revealing a toddler with blonde hair and a beaming smile. He had a tight grip on True who was in his arms, not even attempting to escape. Dory knelt beside them. She reached over and touched the little boy's curls gently, feeling a lessening of remorse for not honoring Wayne's intuition and finding the child earlier. Teddy looked healthy and happy.

"Hello, Teddy. This is True. She seems to like you. Can you say her name?"

Teddy opened his dark blue eyes wide but didn't say a word.

Shortly thereafter, there was a quick tap on the door to the room and the face of Juanita's friend, the pediatric nurse, appeared in the window glass. The psychologist took Teddy by the hand and led him over to her. Dory grabbed True and stuffed her back in the tote bag. Just before the door closed, the voiceless little boy looked back at the dog. He hadn't said a word, but he was waving.

THE NEXT MORNING, HAVING MADE PD SOME SCRAMBLED EGGS and settled him in front of the TV with his taped ankle elevated, the remote in his hand, and his phone on the end table, Billy Jo left for the office. It was still early and driving down the dirt two-track, she opened her car windows to smell the fresh air. Bird song greeted the morning and a rabbit dashed into the underbrush. It was going to be another beautiful day, but she needed to think. And for that, she needed opera.

Although operas were in Italian for the most part, and she didn't understand a word of the language, the music often helped her solve a problem she'd been wrestling with. Putting Mozart's *Magic Flute* opera into the tape player, she listened to the aria sung by the Queen of the Night. The brilliant cascading notes spilled over themselves. She had reached the village of Rosedale before she had the answer to the problem. "If I'm going to ever convince Lexie to care about her little brother, it's going to take more than pleading. It's going to take evidence," she said.

When Billy Jo got to Rosedale Investigations, she went immediately upstairs to take a shower and change her clothes. As she stepped into the spray, Billy Jo hesitated. Was that the sound of the tinkling bell on the front door? Oh well, no matter, only Wayne, Dory, and PD had keys. She was lathering her hair and humming a Harry Styles song when the shower curtain was swept abruptly aside. Billy Jo screamed her head off—until she saw it was Mark.

"Oh my God, you idiot. You scared me to death." She covered her breasts with her hands.

"Nothing I haven't seen already," he grinned. "Want some company in the shower?" He started to pull his t-shirt over his head.

"No, I don't! Go away!" Billy Jo said. "And stop leering. Just let me rinse my hair and I'll come and talk to you. How the hell did you get in? Never mind, I'll be out in a minute." Closing the shower curtain forcefully, she returned to her ablutions.

TEN MINUTES LATER, MARK AND BILLY Jo were seated at the conference room table.

"Damn you, Mark Schneider, you know I got shot at a few weeks ago. That guy is still out there somewhere. If you found a key to the building lying around somewhere, I want it right now. Hand it over."

Shamefaced, Mark pulled the key from his pants pocket and gave it to her. "I'm so sorry, Billy Jo, I should have realized you would be scared. This is a copy of Dory's key. She left it on the conference room table last time I was here. I nabbed it, made a quick copy, and put the original back."

"So, on top of being a peeping Tom, my boyfriend is a thief," Billy Jo frowned at him.

"Boyfriend? Am I your boyfriend?" Mark asked with raised eyebrows and a little grin.

"Possibly, although not this morning," Billy Jo said firmly.

"We hadn't seen each other since the night Detective Nichols caught us necking, and I wanted to see you. I have his report on Pansy's cell phone by the way."

Billy Jo was feeling mollified by then. Mark looked so sweetly sorry for trying to join her in the shower. "Okay. I forgive you, Nutcase, but never and I mean *never*, sneak up on me like that again," she patted his arm and continued, "Wayne texted me saying he had gotten more CCTV tapes from the night Pansy Delaney disappeared. He's coming over to watch the video here."

Mark looked a bit uneasy. "Maybe I should leave my report and get going."

"Oh no, you don't, Mark Schneider. Grow a pair. The man isn't going to shoot you."

At that moment, they heard the sound of heavy footsteps and Wayne's voice saying, "Hello? Anybody here?" Mark started to stand up, but Billy Jo grabbed his arm and pulled him back down into his chair.

"We're in the conference room. Coffee's in the kitchen." Mark gave her a desperate "please save me" look, which she ignored.

Wayne opened the door carrying his coffee mug. Seeing Billy Jo and Mark at the table, he frowned. "I thought you and Dory were in here," he said.

Billy Jo poked Mark in the ribs and he stood up. "Good Morning, Detective Nichols," he said. He still looked guilty, but manfully stuck his hand out to shake. Wayne declined to shake.

"I've got the report from Pansy Delaney's cell phone," Mark said.

"What did you find?"

"On the last day any calls were made from her phone, Pansy dialed three numbers. One was to the Women's Prison in Nashville. She also made a call to Mr. Brad Carver, Lovell's attorney, and her last call was to Lucinda Wells."

Wayne grimaced. "Did you check the cell towers? Where was the phone when she called those numbers?"

"Yes, sir. I did. The cell pinged on the tower in the little town of Appleton. That's the closest tower to the old Delaney farm. Does this help?" Mark asked, looking hopefully at the Detective.

"Not really," Wayne said, feeling the hungry wolves of failure circling. *It was day seven since Pansy Delaney went missing.* So far, they had found nothing on the CCTV. If Pansy was still alive, it could only be because someone had taken her to receive medical care. He clung to that hope but knew it was a long shot.

"Did you get the rest of the CCTV footage from the Nashville post, Wayne?" Billy Jo asked.

"Yes. I did. Going to watch it now."

"Could you use some help, sir?" Mark asked and Wayne's expression lightened a bit.

"I'll help too," Billy Jo said. "It will go faster with all three of us."

"Thank you, guys," Wayne said and they hunkered down to the worst job in the world, watching hours of grainy black and white footage from the cameras installed on the streets near the buildings that served the physically and mentally ill.

TWENTY-TWO

BILLY JO WAS FIELDING CALLS from prospective clients and responding to insistent messages from PD. He'd called her cell for the fourth time when the office phone rang.

"Sorry, PD, that's the land line. Have to go," she said, trying not to sound relieved at the chance to fob him off. "Rosedale Investigations," she said, picking up the phone.

"Is this Miss Bradley?" the caller asked.

"Yes, it is. How can I help you?"

"This is the DNA Diagnostics Lab. We have the results on the bone fragments you sent."

"That's great," she said, before realizing that getting DNA from a dead person was not something that would normally be greeted with such enthusiasm. "I mean, thank you for doing the test. Can you give me the results verbally?"

"Slow down, Miss. I understand you wanted to see if the DNA from the bones matched that of Charles Carson, the person you believe this to be."

"That's right. Did it match?"

"Well, obviously, to do a match, we have to have something containing Mr. Carson's DNA. *Duh.*"

"Oh, right," Billy Jo said, feeling like an idiot. "The next step would be for me to bring you something to compare it to, I assume. Can I ask what kinds of things work best?"

"A toothbrush of the person's works well."

"The problem is that he had false teeth," she said.

"In that case, see if you can find a hairbrush or comb with fine bristles, one that nobody used except the person you want to identify, or a piece of worn clothing, like a t-shirt that hasn't been washed. The first test took us longer because we had to extract the marrow, find a viable bit of tissue, and sequence the code. We can have the comparison sample done more quickly."

"Thank you for letting me know. I'll try to get a hairbrush or a comb to you today," she said and hung up. She dialed Mrs. Roberts' phone number. Nobody answered. She left a message that she would be stopping by later to get an item of her grandfather's to use for the DNA comparison.

She then checked her incoming messages, seeing another call from PD and a text from Wayne. Ignoring PD's call, she read Wayne's text. He was headed to the Sheriff's Office. They had a lead on a suspect who might be Snake Wrist. He said he'd see her tonight. They all planned to meet at PD's house around 8:00.

Dory breezed in half an hour later. She was dressed in her best finery, a long purple and gold embroidered tunic over a silk blouse and loose pale lavender trousers. "Morning, Billy Jo," she called out joyfully.

"Hi, Dory. How did the clandestine mission go last night?"

"Come into the kitchen and I'll tell you all about it. I brought blueberry donuts (Dory expected everyone to be as enthusiastic as she was about them, nobody else was), some fresh peaches from the fruit stand, and two lattes."

Billy Jo silenced the wringers on both her cell phone and the landline and joined her in the kitchen. "So, how did it go? Did Teddy say anything?"

"Nothing yet," Dory said. "I can see from your expression that you are disappointed. I was too, but Juanita, the child psychiatrist, said our visit was a very encouraging first step. Up to now, Teddy has been completely mute, not a laugh, not a sound. He hasn't even *cried* since he's been in the hospital. And last night, he gave a happy shriek when True crawled into the Indian teepee with him. Then they romped around until the teepee collapsed and during that tussle, I heard a giggle. When Juanita and I lifted it off them, Teddy was holding my dog in his lap. When the nurse came to take him back to his room, Teddy turned and waved!" Dory raised her arms over her head in a V for victory gesture and twirled around in a circle. She looked as jubilant as Billy Jo had ever seen her.

"I'm so happy for you, Dory. That's a great result. A little more time and Teddy will start talking again, I bet. Changing the subject, I have a question. Have you stopped blaming yourself for not going back to the Delaney place when Wayne wanted you to?"

Dory's expression fell. For a moment, she was silent, and then she said, "Not yet. After I get Poppy out of jail and Teddy starts to talk, maybe then . . . I can forgive myself."

Billy Jo patted her on the arm and said, "Hand me one of those peaches, will you? Can you stay in the office for a bit? I have to go over to the Roberts' house and get something that belonged to her grandfather for the DNA comparison."

"I've got plenty of work to do to get Miss Poppy Delaney's case before the Parole Board."

As Billy Jo left the business, she could hear Dory singing, "I am a Poor Wayfaring Stranger." She had a fine contralto and the anthem quality of the song came through powerfully. It was a song of intense longing and in her voice, Billy Jo could clearly hear Dory's remorse about the soundless Teddy Lovell.

WHEN BILLY JO ARRIVED AT PD'S EARLY THAT EVENING, she had two large pizzas, two bottles of wine, and a twelve-pack of beer. "Hi PD, I'm here," she called out, setting the food down on the kitchen counter and pouring a glass of wine for herself.

"I'm on the back deck," he responded.

She was pleased to see he was dressed, although he looked tired and his ankle was still badly bruised. "Is the ankle any better?"

"It is. Even managed to drag four lawn chairs out here. Please note that they are six feet apart," he said. "Tell me what's happening at the office."

Billy Jo took a seat in the red plastic Adirondack chair. "I don't know if Wayne told you, but he made me lead on the Missing Grandfather case."

PD nodded.

"It was a challenge to find the old guy's ashes. He died in Minnesota and was cremated there. They told me his ashes were sent to Rosedale. It should have been a slam dunk, but the ashes went to Rosedale, *Texas*, not Rosedale, *Tennessee*. I tracked them down and had them sent here. So far, so good, but when I called Mrs. Roberts, the man's granddaughter, to see if she wanted the ashes delivered to the cemetery, she balked." Billy Jo took a long look at PD. He was gazing off into the distance, down toward the cattail-fringed Round Lake below the cabin. "Are you listening, PD?"

"Yup."

"Okay. Mrs. Roberts wanted proof that the ashes were her grandfather's. I had a private lab do a DNA test. They needed a comparison sample which I ran over there today. I asked them to do the test ASAP. On my drive out here, the technician texted me that the ashes were a match to Mr. Charlie Carter. I called Mrs. Roberts. She was sufficiently pleased that I took it upon myself to *double* her bill." She grinned winsomely at PD, hoping he would say something like 'good work' or even that she deserved to be a partner in the firm.

"Take a look down there, Billy Jo," PD pointed to the valley below the ridge and handing her the binoculars. "It's the fox family."

"I know. I've been watching them. The vixen is a good mother. Did you hear me say I doubled our bill?"

PD nodded and Billy Jo sighed and took a sip of her wine.

DORY AND WAYNE JOINED THEM as the sun was going down. Billy Jo passed out re-heated pizza slices and beverages. They took them out to the deck. The mist was rising from the ravine and the sounds of cicadas and small birds could be heard, twittering in the native shrubs around the cabin.

"What's happening with Poppy Delaney, Dory?" PD asked.

"I called in every favor in the book, and Poppy is going to come before the Parole Board soon. Legal Aid is providing representation to help her with her presentation. The problem isn't the solicitation, prostitution is a minor crime, and most girls only get 30 days, but Poppy had a knife and cut the guy she was with and took his money. He had beaten her. Her face was bruised in her intake photo, so she will be alleging self-defense. I'm hopeful they will release her."

"Dory is also working on getting Teddy Lovell to talk," Billy Jo said. Neither she nor Dory wanted PD to ask Wayne how his search for Teddy's mother was going.

"How is that going?" PD asked.

"Did you know I took my dog, True, into the hospital to see Teddy?" PD shook his head.

"Well it was a risk, but we got in and the little guy gave a shriek and a giggle. No talking yet, but any sound is good. Plus Teddy waved goodbye to the dog when we left. Juanita, the child psychiatrist, said it was a great first step."

"Anything happening about the guy who shot at Billy Jo?" PD asked. He waited for a bit. "Wayne, I'm speaking to you."

Hearing his name, Wayne was roused from his thoughts. "Sheriff Bradley talked to one of his CI's who gave him a name. He's put an all-points bulletin out on him."

"Since we brought the bullets and shell casings to Sheriff Bradley after the incident, he should be able to get a warrant and obtain his gun for comparison analysis," PD said. He and Wayne talked a bit more about rifling and ballistics (boring Dory to tears) before she said she was going to take off.

Billy Jo walked her to her car.

"Nice work on the Missing Grandfather case. And also on distracting PD from asking Wayne about the search for Teddy's mom. I wish he would give it up. I just know in my heart that Teddy's mother is not ever coming back," Dory said, shaking her head sadly.

TWO HOURS LATER, ONLY WAYNE AND BILLY JO were seated on the deck. She had helped PD get into bed before pouring herself the last of the wine. It was completely dark by then, the only illumination was the glowing tip of Wayne's cigarette. He said he would quit again when he found Pansy Delaney. Remembering Dory's premonition, Billy Jo felt a heavy band of sorrow wrap around her heart.

"Do you hear that?" Wayne asked her, standing up suddenly.

"Nothing but the night sounds," she said.

"No. Just listen. There's a car coming."

Billy Jo felt a chill. She could hear it now.

"Go into the house," Wayne said, his voice was preemptory and dark.

Watching from the kitchen window, Billy Jo saw the dim outlines of a car pull up by the cabin. Wayne was standing on the porch by one of the columns, virtually invisible in the shadows. He had drawn his weapon. The overhead dome light in the car came on when the driver opened the door. Billy Jo heaved a sigh of relief. It was Mark.

Wayne holstered his gun and walked out to the car. "How the hell did you find us?" he asked.

"I got the directions from Dory," Mark said.

"Hi Mark," Billy Jo called from the open kitchen window. "Come on out to the deck. We're catching up and having drinks. Would you like a beer?" She glanced at Wayne who seemed irked at Mark's arrival.

"I have some news for you," Mark said.

They got seated and Mark took a swig of the beer Billy Jo handed him. "I found your lady, Detective," he said with a slow triumphant smile.

"OMG, that's great! Isn't that great, Wayne?" Billy Jo said, wanting him to say something appreciative to Mark.

"Are you sure it's her? Where did you find her?" Wayne asked.

"At Summit Medical's ER," Mark said. "It's a rural hospital located several hours east of Nashville."

"What makes you think it's Pansy?" Wayne said, his voice challenging.

"I have a friend who is in medical school. He's doing a rural medicine rotation at Summit and shadows a doctor in the ER several nights a week. I contacted him after Billy Jo told me that Dr. Lucy thought we should look at the rural hospitals. He was there the night a nurse picked up a Jane Doe off Route 37. That's the road that runs past the Delaney farm. Her speech was garbled and she had no identification, but my friend gave me her hair and eye color. It's her all right."

"That's just awesome. We owe you a huge one, Mark. Thanks so much," Billy Jo said, giving Wayne a glare.

"What did they do for her in the ER?" Wayne asked.

"They examined her and did the routine things they do for a person who's not making sense, namely a screen for drugs and several labs. They also did a CT scan, but my friend was starting to get concerned about confidentiality by then and backed off. He wouldn't tell me anything else, just that the woman was admitted."

"I'll try to get in to see her tomorrow or at least talk with her doctors. I must make sure it's her," Wayne said. "I was about to leave. I'll walk you out to the car, Mark."

Billy Jo cast him an exasperated glance. "Come here, Mark," she said and kissed him goodbye.

The two men walked out to their cars. They talked for a while in the driveway before both cars drove off. A few minutes later, Billy Jo's cell rang. It was Wayne.

"Wayne Nichols, I can't believe you didn't even *thank* Mark for finding Pansy. What is *wrong* with you? You should be jumping up and down with joy. She's alive for God's sakes and you were being a total jerk," Billy Jo said.

"You're right. I should have been more appreciative about Mark's finding her," he said, but the relief he expected to feel hadn't come. Although the hunt for Pansy Delaney was over, only when he saw her and told her Teddy was safe, would he feel at peace.

"You certainly should have been nicer to Mark. And what were the two of you talking about before you drove off?"

"I asked him if he was serious about you," Wayne said.

"OMG, you didn't!"

"He admitted he was crazy about you. He told me it was because you smell like strawberries. I get it now. You see, Lucy's hair smells like lemons."

"I will never understand men," Billy Jo said, and hung up the phone, but climbing up the ladder to her loft bed at PD's cottage, she found herself smiling. Strawberries and lemons danced in her dreams all night.

TWENTY-THREE

W AYNE LAY AWAKE ALL NIGHT, tossing and turning beside Lucy. He knew Billy Jo was right. He had been a jackass to Mark. This missing person's case was one of the hardest ones for him. He searched his heart for something he could still do for the woman he had tried so hard to find for seven long hard days. Hours later it came to him—Pansy had to wake from coma so he could tell her about Teddy being found. When the sun came up, he called Billy Jo's cell phone.

"Where are you?" he asked.

"I gather you've forgotten your manners, Detective. What happened to a good morning or even hello?"

Wayne made an irritated sound.

"Never mind, in answer to your question, I'm driving into Rosedale. I left PD sound asleep. I'm meeting Mark for breakfast at Sunshine Café," she said.

"Cancel it," Wayne said abruptly. "I called Summit Medical and confirmed the physical description of the woman Mark thought was Pansy Delaney. Sounds like he's right. We need to decide on our next steps."

"What about PD?" Billy Jo asked. "If the grumpy old curmudgeon had internet we could meet on Zoom, but his cabin is too far out in the country and the driveway is a mile long. I've called the cable company so many times, I think they are blocking my calls. Plus his computer is so old, it's only good for playing solitaire."

"Tell him to wear a mask, but he has to come in," Wayne said.

Half an hour later everyone began arriving. Billy Jo had made a full pot of coffee and handed out cups of the fragrant beverage to the partners when they appeared.

"What's up?" Dory asked taking the coffee from Billy Jo. Despite the hour, she was wearing a nicely tailored periwinkle blue suit, blouse, and heels. She glanced at her young associate who had managed jeans, a T-shirt and flip-flops.

"Mark found Pansy Delaney last night and came out to the cabin to tell us. Wayne wants a group decision on our next steps."

"Wow. That's great! Wonderful news. Now we can concentrate on Teddy and maybe Wayne will chill out a bit," Dory said.

PD limped in the back door only minutes later.

"Morning, PD. How's the ankle," Dory asked.

"Better. Wayne left me a message saying Mark found Pansy Delaney and that we had to meet in person. Hurt my ankle a bit to drive, but I was glad for an excuse to get into the office and out of the cabin. When we're done with Wayne's urgent issue, I've like an update from everyone."

When Wayne arrived they all trooped into the conference room.

While PD looked like he was feeling better, Wayne looked like crap, Billy Jo thought. He had lost more weight, had a two-day stubble, there were nicotine stains on his fingers, and his hair was sticking up in patches. He tended to run his fingers through it when he was concentrating.

"Okay, Wayne, let's have it," PD said. "Why the urgent meeting? We all know by now that Pansy Delaney is at the rural hospital. Everybody's relieved by that info. She's getting good care, I assume?"

"Well, that's the problem. Lucy knows the administration at Summit and called them this morning. It's a good rural hospital, apparently, but they don't have the psych and neuro sub-specialists that will be needed to bring Pansy back to full consciousness."

Silence greeted his words as Dory, PD, and Billy Jo exchanged confused looks.

"What is it that you think we could possibly do to help?" Dory asked.

"You know all the big-wigs in Nashville, PD, and Dory you know practically everyone in Rosedale. We have to find someone who can put enough pressure on Summit to get Pansy transferred to Nashville. That's the only way she can get the specialists she needs to come out of the coma and be a mom to little Teddy again," his voice cracked.

"Isn't Lucy the best person to do this?" PD asked.

"She's doing all she can," Wayne said, taking a shaky breath.

To Dory, he looked like a desperate fox cornered by a pack of hounds. After a few silent moments, she laid a gentle hand on Wayne's arm and said, "I understand your concerns, Partner, but if Dr. Lucy can't get her transferred from Summit, with her medical expertise and connections, we certainly can't. I'm sorry."

"What's really going on here, Wayne?" PD asked, frowning. "I'm not getting this. I don't see that we have any input at all in this matter. Is there something that I'm missing?"

"Shall I tell him?" Dory asked and Wayne nodded. "When Wayne was about Teddy's age, his mother left the family. A traveling evangelist had visited the reservation the night before, and Wayne's mother attended the services. She got caught up in the movement and left to follow the Jesus road. That's what it's called by the First Nations people when a convert follows a charismatic Christian pastor to proselytize others." Dory stopped and looked at Wayne before continuing, "As I understand it, Wayne, your mother didn't abandon you. She called your grandfather and left him a message to come and collect you. Unfortunately, the old man didn't get the message for several days."

Wayne nodded. His normally ruddy complexion was drained of color and he was breathing unevenly. His memories of that day in his life had taken over.

In the silence that followed, Billy Jo got up from her seat and walked over to stand by Wayne's chair. "I understand now," she said gently, patting him on the shoulder. There were tears in her eyes.

Wayne patted her arm and Billy Jo sat down beside him.

"I'm sure Dr. Lucy will do all she can to help get Pansy transferred to the best care available, but I think that's all we can do for the moment. Nobody is going to listen to a couple of retired Detectives, or an Investigator, even with all our combined street cred. This is a serious medical matter and has to be left to professionals. We'll just have to cross our fingers and hope for the best. Sorry, Buddy," PD said.

Billy Jo glanced quickly at Dory, remembering her premonition that Pansy was never going to be in a position to be a mother to Teddy again.

"Pansy just *has* to come out of her coma and soon," Wayne said. "The longer a person is comatose, the less likely they will come out of it and Teddy needs his mother," Wayne said and all the people sitting around the table knew what he was really saying, that as a small boy he had needed his mother and she had left him behind.

"We all will keep Pansy in our prayers and hope Dr. Lucy can get her transferred soon. Are you okay with moving to other business now?" Dory asked.

Wayne took a deep breath and nodded. Some of the color had come back to his face.

"Okay, let's bring PD up to date on our other cases. I'll go first. We've collected several old past-due bills, as well as what Carver told me was half of the sum from the Lovell case."

"Why only half?" PD asked.

"Since the inheritance was split in half, we get half our fee from Lexie's money and half from Teddy's share. There have been no decisions about where he's going to live once he's discharged from the hospital, so we won't get the rest of our bill paid until a guardian is assigned. We also received a nice bit of change from Billy Jo's handling of the Missing Grandfather case. At present, we're okay," Dory told him.

"Good work," PD said, looking at Dory, and Billy Jo felt a nip of resentment. He hadn't said 'good work' to her when she doubled the Missing Grandfather money. "How are you coming on Poppy Delaney's release?"

"Meeting with all the principals today to help prepare her for her appearance before the Parole Board. If all goes well she will be released. It won't be right away, she'll owe a fine, and probably some community service time, but I'm hopeful that she will be a free agent soon. I'm meeting with Hayley Drummond, Dr. Juanita Marsh, and the legal aid attorney whose name is Robby Willoughby. We are all having a Zoom meeting with Poppy."

"Can't the legal person, Willoughby, make the presentation?" Billy Jo asked.

"Nope. That's not how it works. It must be the convicted individual him or herself. They have to write a letter to the Parole Board requesting release. Here's the tough part for Poppy. She has to express remorse, and I get the feeling that she's not in the least regretful about stabbing the pimp. She feels he deserved it. Our meeting is taking place at Hayley's office at Community Mental Health."

"Unfortunately, I can't stick around after this meeting either," Billy Jo said. "Sheriff Bradley has arranged for me to view a line-up of five guys who have snakes tattooed on their wrists. I doubt I will be able to help him at all. It was very dark that night."

As the team started picking up coffee cups and preparing to leave, PD asked Wayne if Dr. Lucy was at work or at home.

"At home. She's not on duty until this afternoon," Wayne said.

"Then let's run out to your place. It will give us some more time to talk and I'd appreciate Lucy taking a look at my ankle. Maybe she would tape it again."

Wayne nodded and the men left the office.

Billy Jo looked at Dory and said, "That was the most emotional meeting we have ever had. I hope it helped Wayne. Do you think he's okay?"

"Probably good to have all that out in the air and for him and PD to spend a bit more time together," Dory said. "Having Dr. Lucy re-tape the ankle was just an excuse, you know. He had taped it up just fine. PD often comes across as gruff and irritable, but he can be very supportive. Good luck with identifying Snake Wrist. I'm off to my meeting."

WHEN HAYLEY OPENED HER DOOR to a quiet knock, she saw a tall skinny kid with brown curly hair, glasses, and a wide smile. It was Robby Willoughby, Poppy's legal aid attorney. She introduced him to Dory and Juanita who were seated at the round table in her office.

"Thanks for coming, Robby," Hayley said. "We have about ten minutes before the Zoom meeting starts. Did you get the case file on Poppy Delaney?"

"I did, but have some questions. Is that okay?"

"Fire away," Dory said.

"I haven't advised a client coming before the Parole Board yet, so this is new. I get that we are going to try to help her write her letter of appeal, but she has to go before the Board in person, right?"

"Yes, that's right. She is allowed only one advocate in the room with her, and that will be you, Robby. You will be seated behind her, the Board Members don't allow the prisoner to make eye contact with their advocates."

Robby looked slightly startled at that prohibition. "Okay. Second question. I saw in the file that Poppy is an aunt to a child in the hospital. I gather the parents want her to take over with the boy. Where are the parents?"

"His father is dead and his mother is in a coma," Dory said softly.

"Oh, that's too bad. If Poppy is released where will she live? How can she support herself and the child?"

"We are discussing those questions today," Hayley said. "I talked with her on the phone a couple of days ago and told her that her sister's alive, but in a coma. She was willing to become Teddy's guardian, although there are some steps to go through to become a foster parent. She said if she had the money from Teddy's father's estate, she would never go back on the streets. I believe she's being truthful with me, but she didn't have good answers when I asked her what kind of job she wanted or where she wanted to live."

"That's the sound announcing the Zoom meeting," Dory said as Hayley tapped the computer's keys and the face of Poppy Delaney appeared on the monitor.

"Hi, Poppy. I want to introduce your legal advocate, Robby Willoughby and Dr. Juanita Marsh. Robby will be with you when you go before the Parole Board. Dr. Marsh is a child psychiatrist. Investigator Dory Clarkson is also present. When we talked last time, I asked you to get started on your letter requesting release. Do you have that?" Hayley asked.

"Yes, I do, it's here. Just a minute," Poppy pulled out a wrinkled piece of paper and laid it down on the table.

"Can you read it to us?" Dory asked and Poppy began.

"Dear Honorable Members of the Nashville, Tennessee Parole Board: My name is Poppy Anne Delaney. I am in jail because I stabbed a man with a knife and took some of his money. I should be released because I only did it in self-defense. It wasn't even my knife. I never wanted to be a prostitute. I was forced into it to support myself after my parents died.

My twin sister has a little boy named Teddy. She is in a coma and may not come around. The child's father is dead. I would be so proud to be a real aunt to Teddy. I would take such good care of him. I am a good cook and would make nutritious meals. When he is old enough, I will take him to school. I regret what I did because it means I can't be a mom to Teddy when he needs me.

My parents owned a farm where Teddy and I can live. Once he starts school, I want to become a lunch lady or a secretary at the school. My family went to church regularly and I will start going again as soon as I am free. The Minister is going to arrange counselling for me. Thank you for reading my letter." Poppy raised her eyes to the screen hopefully.

"It's a good letter, Poppy. I'll get it typed up on letterhead and have it forwarded to the Board. Dory and I are going to write character reference letters for you. It would be helpful if the Minister for your church would write one too. I suggest you ask him," Hayley said.

"We will be waiting outside the room the day of your hearing. I have a good feeling about this. Good-bye, Poppy," Dory said.

Hayley clicked off the Zoom meeting and turned to the other people in the room. "What do you think her chances are, Dory? You have had the most experience with this sort of thing."

"My partner, Detective Nichols, has had more experience. He got the Parole Board to release his foster mother, and she was in for murder. As far as Poppy's chances, I think they are about 50:50. My concern is that the Board may believe she will slide back into 'the life' and will re-offend. A lonely woman on a deserted farm with a little kid isn't a good scenario. She won't have any kind of social support, outside of the church."

"I agree that it's not optimum. Are we certain there is no other family? Hayley asked.

"You know, you just gave me an idea," Dory said and her eyes twinkled.

BILLY JO HAD TO FORCE HERSELF to drive to the Sheriff's Office to see the line-up of men who might be Snake Wrist. Reaching the parking lot, she realized she was trembling, too scared to get out of the car. It was already ten minutes past the time she was supposed to arrive. She scolded herself saying, "Stop being such a wuss. You know perfectly well in a line-up they can't see you. It's a one-way mirror."

Straightening her shoulders and taking a deep breath, she forced herself to open the car door. A vehicle drove in behind her and she whirled around to see who it was, terrified it was the perp who shot at her. It wasn't. It was Mark. "I am so glad to see you," she said feeling a wave of relief.

"You told me you were worried about this. Figured you could use a little moral support," Mark smiled at her and they walked into the Sheriff's Office hand-in-hand.

TWENTY-FOUR

W HEN DR. LUCY LEARNED THAT PANSY'S STATUS had changed from being 'confused' to becoming 'deeply lethargic', she called the attending physician once again. Her multiple insistent phone conversations finally paid off when the exasperated attending doctor at Summit Medical agreed to have Pansy moved by ambulance to Nashville. She called Wayne with the good news.

"I got her transferred, Wayne. At first, I was patient, then I was irritable and finally downright obnoxious, but it's happening."

"Thanks, Lucy. I am so appreciative," he said. Hanging up the call, Wayne envisioned Pansy . . . lying in her hospital bed . . . wearing a white hospital gown . . . sleeping beneath cool white sheets . . . in a white-walled room. How he wished he could talk to her and tell her Teddy was okay. But talking to Pansy in person wasn't going to happen, no one but the patient or occasionally a family member was allowed inside a hospital. In despair, he searched his mind for something else he could do for her. Remembering the signed and notarized letter stating Teddy's parents wanted Poppy to care for him in the event of their deaths or disability, and feeling pretty sure the attorney who prepared the document wasn't Carver, Wayne decided to locate the new lawyer. Before he set off on the hunt, though, he needed a cigarette to settle his nerves.

It was late afternoon and the air was humid. He hated high humidity and thought he'd find an air-conditioned bar that served food. Driving in behind Paul Revere's Tavern, he parked his truck. Reaching for the pack of cigarettes he kept for emergencies in the glove box of his truck, he stashed it in his shirt pocket and approached the back door of the drinking establishment. At one time, Wayne had had problems with alcohol and although he drank now, it was only occasionally.

When he opened the back door to the bar, the scent of tobacco, alcohol, bacon frying and old drunks hit him in his core. It disgusted him that he used to live like that. Turning around and walking back to his car, he passed a trash can. Taking a deep breath, he tossed his last pack of cigarettes down deep inside. The bar was in an area of Rosedale near the townhouse complex where Lucinda Wells lived. Since it was a Saturday, she might be home and know who Pansy and Edward used for their new attorney. Wayne knew it was protocol to inform Bradley Carver of his intentions, as the attorney who prepared Lovell's initial will. He dialed his office.

"Bradley Carver," the man answered.

"Hello. Detective Nichols calling. Do you have a minute to talk?"

"Um-hum," he said, but sounded wary. Wayne was used to it. Perfectly innocent people came over all funny when contacted by the cops. He wasn't on the force now, but the word Detective did the same thing.

"I don't know if anyone told you, but Pansy Delaney has been found. She's in the hospital. Unfortunately, she's only minimally conscious so I'm calling to ask you some questions."

"What hospital is Pansy in?" Carver asked and Wayne heard both the relief and the urgency in his voice. The man knew a lot more than he was saying about both Ed Lovell and Pansy. He wondered how Detective Rob was coming along in his investigation and whether Carver had been involved in Lovell's death.

"Are you aware of any provisions Mr. Lovell or Ms. Delaney made for their son, in the event they weren't able to raise him?"

"Beyond leaving half his estate to the boy, I'm not aware of any," Carver said. He was sounded a tad more confident, although still guarded.

"That's interesting," Wayne paused. "Because we found a notarized document in Pansy's purse about the child. You didn't prepare it?" he asked.

"I did not."

"Then they must have contacted another attorney. Do you have any idea who they would have used?"

"Sorry, Detective, I can't help you." He knew Carver was about to hang up and wanted to keep him talking.

"Well, perhaps you should think about this some more, Carver. I'm certain as a *lawyer*, you will want to be cooperative with the authorities, especially now that Sheriff Bradley is investigating Ed Lovell's death," Wayne said in an ominous tone.

"Of course," the attorney said as he hastily clicked off the call.

WAYNE PULLED INTO A PARKING SPACE across the street from Lucinda's townhouse and waited. God, he wished he had kept a single cigarette, but Lucy had been adamant. She wasn't living with a smoker. Smoking was terrible for his health and hers. He could go and stay with PD if he was going to smoke, although even there he would only be able to smoke outside. He promised her he'd stop. He'd snuck outside several times for a smoke since—always while Lucy was at work. The woman had the nose of a bloodhound though, and he worried she'd smell it, even hours later. He thought he'd be able to quit when he found Pansy Delaney, but he still struggled with cravings. Hopefully, ditching the last pack of cigarettes was the end of it.

Lucinda's car pulled into her spot in the carport half an hour later. Wayne got out of his truck and walked over.

"Hello, Lucinda," he said and she dropped the sack she was carrying to the ground.

"Goodness, Detective Nichols, you startled me," she said. Her hazel eyes went wide and cautious.

"I'm sorry. Let me help you pick this up," he said and together they assembled her shopping. "Do you mind answering some more questions?"

"I don't have a lot of time, but you can come in for a few minutes," she said with a "*what choice do I have*" expression.

They walked in and she offered him an iced tea. He accepted and thanked her. "I wanted to tell you that Pansy Delaney has been found."

Lucinda closed her eyes in relief and took a shaky breath. "Thank God," she said.

"However, she's in a coma," Wayne said, looking carefully at the girl. "I know you took them out to the old farm, Lucinda. I compared your tire tracks to those in the yard by the farmhouse. I'd appreciate your telling me the truth from now on."

"I will," she said, looking incredibly guilty. "I promise, Detective."

"We found a notarized document in Pansy's purse. It stated she wanted her sister to raise Teddy if something happened to her or the child's father. I'm wondering if you know who she used as an attorney to prepare that document."

Lucinda started to say she didn't know but Wayne stopped her. "Tell me who it is, Miss Wells or I will have you brought in to the Sheriff's office and they will charge you with wasting police time."

She took a shaky breath before saying, "I can't recall her name, Detective, but it's something French. She has a family law practice in Rosedale."

"Now that wasn't so hard, was it," Wayne said, almost smiling. He understood the young woman now. She hated bowing to authority. It was one of his character traits too. "Let me give you some advice, Lucinda. You are going to be a teacher. In that environment, you are going to have to take orders from the administration. If you want to succeed, you'll accept their authority and won't ever lie."

"Already figured that one out," she said and smiled. "If Pansy wakes up from the coma, will you call me? Or if Poppy gets out of jail? I want to help both the twins and Teddy."

"I will."

DORY WAS DRIVING OUT TO THE LITTLE COUNTRY CHURCH in Appleton that Poppy Delaney said they had attended. It was very warm and her air conditioning was operating intermittently. Despite being a brand-new car, the dealership said it might need the air conditioning compressor replaced. The cost would be fully covered, of course, but Dory realized she was no longer in love with her little red convertible. Having been the cause of her failure to find Teddy, she suddenly found all sorts of things she didn't like about it.

She located the church and walked inside. Some houses of worship were locked on weekdays, but this one was open, peaceful, and empty. It was a traditional white clapboard-sided church with a steeple and stained glass windows on both sides. Above the altar at the rear of the sanctuary, there was a circular rose window. Bright sunlight splashed through the stained glass, painting the stone aisle in brilliant shards of color. The tranquil atmosphere in the place gave Dory hope that her brainstorm would pan out. She slid into a pew, bent her head, and prayed to the Lord for forgiveness for her failure to find Teddy.

Later, she heard quiet footsteps and raised her head, seeing a pastor dressed in black with a white ministerial collar. To her surprise, he was African American.

"I didn't mean to interrupt you," he said.

"You didn't. I'm here to see you."

"Then let me introduce myself. I'm Pastor Fred Warren. I'd shake hands with you but am being careful about COVID."

"I'm Dory Clarkson, an Investigator with Rosedale Investigations."

"I often have some lemonade at this time. Would you care to join me?" he asked.

"That would be lovely," Dory said.

The pastor's housekeeper had set a small table on the back porch of the parsonage. She was leaving but quickly added a glass and plate for Dory. She'd put some Snickerdoodle cookies out on hand-painted china. The cookies had just come out of the oven and the cinnamon aroma filled the air. A vase of bright pink wildflowers graced the table's white linen tablecloth.

"How can I help you?" Pastor Warren asked after they got seated. "Anything you tell me is confidential, you know."

There was something very comforting about his voice and, although trained to keep virtually all details of cases secret, Dory found herself telling Pastor Warren everything. She talked about the Delaney twins, (one a prostitute, one in a coma), her failure to go back with Wayne to find little Teddy at the farmhouse, and her fears that the mob might be involved in the Lovell case. She told him about Billy Jo being shot at and even her worries that her boyfriend, Al, had been talking quite a lot about a woman he met in the Caribbean. She asked the Pastor if he had written a letter attesting to Poppy's good character for the Parole Board. He said he had. Having shared everything, Dory gave a big sigh of relief.

"It seems like it was good to get all that off your chest," Pastor Warren said, smiling.

"It was. Thank you. The reason I'm here though is I'd like to take a look through your Parrish records and see if there are any relatives of the Delaney family left. They lived in this area for decades and attended church here. As I think you know, we are hoping Poppy can come back to the old family farm and raise Teddy. Sadly, it looks like the boy's mother is unlikely to emerge from her confused state. If Poppy is going to live at the farm, she'll need a lot of support. It's an isolated place way out in the country without any social life. Not much fun for a young woman. As a kid, I spent all my summers with my paternal grandparents down in Mississippi on their farm. Remembering those wonderful childhood years got me to wondering if there could be a grandmother or an aunt still living. What do you think?"

"Come with me," Pastor Warren said.

Parish records had been carefully kept for a half-century in a huge leather-bound book. Each birth, death, and all new members of the congregation were recorded in the beautiful cursive script all children were taught in former years. Looking through the years Pastor Warren thought would be relevant, they found notations that Mr. & Mrs. Delaney were both dead. Mr. Delaney had died of cancer, Mrs. Delaney died a year later of complications after lung cancer surgery. No other relatives were listed.

"I'm sorry to leave you, Miss Clarkson, but I have a parish call I need to make. One of my parishioners is very ill and has asked me to come. But, one other thing occurred to me. My predecessor told me when I started here that the Lovells had been members of this church at one time. I never met them because they moved away shortly after I took this position. You could look for them."

"It's certainly worth a try, Pastor. Thank you very much," Dory said and bent to the task.

Two hours later, Dory raised her head from the old ledger. She snapped a picture of the entry with her cell phone and took her leave of the small peaceful parsonage. Driving home as the sun went down, Dory felt it had been a very productive day.

PD RETURNED TO THE OFFICE AFTER SEEING DR. LUCY, who re-wrapped his ankle, to answer phones as the rest of the team disbursed. He was looking tired and frazzled when Billy Jo and Mark returned to Rosedale Investigations after looking at the line-up of potential Snake Wrist men.

"It's about time you two showed up," PD said irritably. Covering phones was his least favorite task. "Hi, Mark."

"Phones been ringing off the hook, have they?" Billy Jo asked.

"Yes, they have. Tell me what happened. Were you able to identify anyone in the line-up?"

"The Sheriff found four men with snake tattoos on their wrists. He had them walk right up to the window and show their wrists to me. At first, I had trouble looking at them. It was scary but one guy's tattoo looked like the one I saw that night at Edward Lovell's mansion."

"Did you tell the Sheriff?" PD asked.

"She did, and then the sheriff had a brainstorm," Mark said.

"What was it?" PD asked.

"He decided to do a voice ID. Each of the men had to call out the words, 'Who's there?'"

"That's what the guy yelled at me the night I was trying to escape by dashing across the lawn," Billy Jo said.

"And?" PD asked, raising his eyebrows.

"And she identified the same guy whose tattoo she picked earlier," Mark said.

"Good work, little partner," PD said.

"Partner?" Billy Jo asked hopefully.

"Well, not yet," PD said. "What happens now?"

"The Sheriff is holding the man Billy Jo identified on suspicion of felonious assault. He's getting a warrant this afternoon and having his deputy search the perp's place. With any luck, he will find the guy's gun and once ballistics compares the striations on the bullets to the rifling in the gun barrel, he'll have him dead to rights," Mark said.

"It's such a relief that Snake wrist is in custody," Billy Jo said. "I won't have to have a guard any longer. Although, I just might enjoy one," she said smiling sweetly at Mark who leaned forward as if to kiss her.

"God, will you two get a room," PD said. "Billy Jo, you're on phones for the rest of the day. I'm going home." He stomped off, limping a little, leaving the couple laughing and clearly not obeying the social distancing rules.

TWENTY-FIVE

Dory Clarkson, Hayley Drummond, and Dr. Juanita Marsh were standing in the hall outside the room in the courthouse where Poppy Ann Delaney was in front of the Parole Board. Her Legal Aid attorney, Robby Willoughby, had gone into the room with her. Half an hour had elapsed. The waiting was driving Dory out of her mind.

"She should be out by now. Poppy was only the third prisoner they were to see this morning. I can't understand why it's taking so long."

"Calm down, Dory. Stop pacing. The waiting is hard for all of us. Tell you what, maybe I can distract you with a dream I had about Poppy last night," Hayley said.

"What happened in the dream?" Dr. Marsh asked. "I am one of the few people in my profession that likes to do dream interpretation."

"Poppy and I were walking down a dusty country road. Dark clouds were rumbling in the sky and a flock of geese flew overhead. We looked up at them and . . ."

At that moment the door to the room opened and Poppy and Robby Willoughby came out together.

"What happened?" Dory asked, grabbing the girl by her arm.

"They asked us to leave," Poppy said and Dory trembled. The one other time she had assisted with a Parole Board Appeal, the woman had been asked to leave the room. When called back in, she was told she had another five years.

"Start at the beginning and tell us the whole thing," Dr. Marsh said.

"There were so many of them, all dressed in black robes and wearing white surgical face masks. I was terrified," Poppy said.

"But she read her letter aloud and I could see one of the judges nodding," Robbie said.

"Go on," Dr. Marsh said.

"When I got to the part in my letter where I said the knife wasn't mine, one of the probation judges wrote something down on his pad of paper. He asked if the man had cut me with a knife. I told him he did and showed him the scar on my arm. He then asked how I got the knife away from him and I said since he was lying on top of me, I was able to knee him hard in the crotch and grab the knife when he dropped it."

"They are speaking right now with Officer Joel Rutherford who was present for the hearing. He's a vice cop who has been looking into a big prostitution ring," Robby said.

"That sounds like normal procedure," Dory said, just as the door to the room opened and the Bailiff called for Miss Delaney and her advocate to go back in.

As the door closed behind them, Dory asked the young social worker to continue her story. "Go on about your dream, Hayley. It's helping pass the time."

"Okay. There was a stream that ran beside the road. It wasn't frozen and the geese came racketing down out of the sky. The wind whistled through their feathers and they landed in a group, splashing around and honking. That was about all there was, except for one thing." Hayley looked a smidge embarrassed.

"What was that?" Dr. Juanita asked.

"Poppy and I were both naked in the dream," Hayley told her.

"Interesting dream, Hayley. Let me think a bit."

Five anxious minutes later, the door opened again. This time there was a smile on Robby's face. Poppy wasn't with him.

"What happened, Robby?" Dory asked.

"Officer Rutherford informed the judges that Poppy's fingerprints on the handle of the knife were *on top of* the client's fingerprints. That finding corroborated Poppy saying the knife wasn't hers. Then the officer went further. He had looked into the guy's police record and discovered he had been questioned previously about reports he used a knife on other prostitutes. That did it. The Bailiff took Poppy back to her cell, but she's to be released by the end of the week."

"You are the MAN! God, I wish I could hug you," Dory said holding out her arms.

"Me too," Hayley said and Dr. Marsh nodded, all of them were smiling at the abashed young lawyer.

WALKING OUT TO THE PARKING LOT LATER, Hayley asked Juanita if she had any thoughts about what her dream meant.

"I think it was a subconscious way of presenting the worry you felt about what would happen today. The geese probably represent the Parole Board judges and were the symbol of your fears that she wouldn't be released. The stream not being frozen was likely representative of your hope that she would be freed," she smiled at the girl.

"What about us being naked?" Hayley said, coloring.

"Normally that means the person is feeling exposed and defenseless. I have a question for you, though. I don't mean to embarrass you, but appearing naked in a dream can also mean the dreamer wishes for an intimate relationship. Do you have a boyfriend at the moment, Hayley?"

"No. I'm not dating anyone right now," she said.

"I wonder if our Robby is single," Dr. Marsh said. "He's pretty cute, don't you think, Hayley?"

She nodded, still blushing.

WHEN LUCINDA TOLD WAYNE the name of Edward Lovell's attorney was French, he knew immediately who it was. It was Evangeline Bon Temps, J.D. She had been a consultant to the Sheriff's Office many times. When he called, Evangeline said she could see him after lunch.

She opened the door when he knocked, saying her secretary was working from home due to the epidemic. As usual, she was professionally dressed in a rose-colored suit which complimented her bronzed complexion and dark hair. She had helped Wayne professionally during the time he was working to get his foster mother released from prison, and he had the utmost respect for her.

"It's good to see you, Wayne. Come on in. Please have a seat." Evangeline was born in New Orleans and still had the soft accent of her Creole ancestry. "I ate at my desk today and am just finishing up. There's a food truck just down the street with really good Po Boy sandwiches. It's the taste of my childhood." Evangeline swept the detritus of paper wrappings and small packets of hot sauce into her wastebasket. Swabbing her hands with antiseptic gel she passed the bottle to Wayne and asked, "How can I help you?"

"I am here on behalf of Edward Lovell and his fiancé Pansy Jane Delaney. Are you their attorney?" Wayne asked.

"Yes, I did new wills and instructions regarding their young son, Teddy," she said. "If you're looking to read the will though, I have to disappoint you. You know I don't share confidential client information, not even with old friends," Evangeline smiled sweetly.

"I understand. Did you know that Mr. Lovell died about a year ago?"

"Yes, I read it in the paper. It was a surprise. When he was here, he looked healthy."

"I agree and now Pansy is in the hospital with mental confusion that isn't dissipating."

"Oh dear, I'm so sorry. That's so sad. What I can tell you is that I prepared a separate notarized document that specified her twin sister, Poppy, was to raise their son in the event something happened to them. They made a point of telling me the information about their son was not confidential. Can't her sister help?"

"She's in jail," Wayne said, but at Evangeline's stricken expression added, "She's going before the Parole Board today and we hope she will be set free."

"I will say a prayer for her at church and for the little boy. His name is Teddy, isn't it?"

"Yes. I may need to see the will if Pansy doesn't come out of the coma."

"If you want to see their wills, I will need death certificates for both parties or, if Pansy survives, but remains permanently lethargic, you must bring a subpoena or you won't see anything at all," she said firmly.

There was something about Evangeline's steely determination combined with her feminine sensibility that reminded Wayne of Lucy. Thinking of the hoops he'd have to jump through to obtain a subpoena, Wayne patted his shirt pocket and sighed, remembering throwing away his final packet of cigarettes.

PD HAD LEFT A VOICE MAIL for Billy Jo to call him. It was late afternoon when she had time to return his call.

"What's up, PD? Want me to come out this evening and cook you some dinner," Billy Jo said.

"That would be great. I'd like to see the whole team tonight if possible. I've got an announcement."

"I'll check with Wayne and Dory and I'll bring food."

"Thanks, Kiddo," he said and rang off.

Billy Jo was finishing washing the dishes at the cabin after dinner when she heard cars pulling up. "They're here, PD," she called. Dory and Wayne came into the cabin and set down the beer, wine, and snacks they brought. "PD has some big announcement he wants to make. He'll be out shortly. Let's grab our drinks and retire to the deck."

They walked out into a cooling evening and took their usual seats. Wayne always sat in the blue Adirondack chair, Dory chose the purple. Billy Jo sat in the red one, leaving the green chair for PD. Little Round Lake had turned a shining pink with the descending sun's rays when Billy Jo picked up the binoculars and checked the ravine below the cabin for the fox family. There was no sign of them.

"Hello all," PD said as he joined them. "What has everyone been up to?"

"Dory has the big news. She should start," Wayne said.

"It's good news, PD, the Parole Board agreed to release Poppy. She has some papers to sign, a fine to pay, and a bit of community service, but she'll be out by the end of the week." Applause greeted Dory's news and she smiled widely.

"Is she going to be there for Teddy?" Wayne asked bluntly.

"There are steps in that process as well, but she wants to be. It was the part of her letter to the Parole Board that I found most moving. She loves the little guy and is looking forward to serving as his foster mom."

Wayne, who had been so committed to his foster mom that he managed to get her released from prison where she was serving a life sentence, smiled a little sadly. She had died of cancer only weeks after her release. He worried that history was going to repeat itself. Had Lucy gotten Pansy transferred only to have her die without hearing Wayne's reassurances about her son? He sighed as despair settled on his heart.

"Billy Jo?" PD asked.

"Everyone knows my news by now. I was able to identify Snake Wrist and he's being questioned at the Sheriff's Office."

"We are all relieved by that decision," PD said. "Wayne, do you want to tell us what you've been up to?"

He took a deep breath and said, "I found Pansy's purse and there was a Notarized letter in the bottom that stated their wishes that Poppy raise Teddy in case they could not. The document was not prepared by Bradley Carver but I found the lawyer who did their subsequent wills and the Notarized letter. It was Evangeline Bon Temps. She won't tell me what's in the will without a subpoena, though," Wayne's voice trailed off.

"You know Evangeline, she is a consummate professional," Dory said. "What did you want to tell us, PD?"

"As you know, I gave you all a week to find Pansy. She's been found, transferred to Nashville, and her care is now a medical matter and none of our business. Her son's placement is being handled by the social worker. Other than the normal urge we all have to tie things up at the end of a case, can any of you convince me that there's anything else that needs to be done? Dory?"

"I went out to the church in Appleton the Delaney's attended and met with the Pastor. He wrote a character reference letter for Poppy's appeal, and more to the point, he let me look at the Parrish records. The twins' parents have passed away, but the pastor told me that Edward Lovell's parents attended the same church years ago. If Poppy ends up with Teddy on that lonely old farm, it would be a blessing to have some family there for her. It's a lead I'd like to pursue."

PD frowned and said, "As you are well aware, Dory, we are not social services. Rosedale Investigations is a business and we all need to get back to it."

"You're right, PD, but what I want to do will only take a day or two. Okay?"

PD nodded, a bit reluctantly. "What about you Billy Jo?"

"Since Snake Wrist is in custody, I'm good," she said. But remembering her intention at the beginning of the case to convince Lexie Lovell to have a relationship with her brother, Billy Jo knew she still had work to do. "I don't know if everyone is aware, but Bradley Carver has still not released all our money. His most recent excuse is that Lexie has to sign a paper acknowledging her brother. Once she signs that paper, he'll have no more excuses. I have to say, I'm finding his stalling more and more questionable."

"Please note, everyone, that Billy Jo here is focused on making income for the business," PD said. "What about you, Wayne?"

"This has been a hard case for me, but I agree that it's time to move on," Wayne said, but the polite phrase was a lie. He knew he wasn't done. It would take Pansy waking up from the coma before he would be able to step away from the case. In the meantime, there was one more service he wanted to perform for Pansy Delaney.

"What have you been doing, PD?" Dory asked.

"As you know, I've thought all along that this case is predominately about money. One of my CI's who works at the bank Lovell used discovered that Carver has a suspiciously large balance and has been making regular withdrawals from Lovell's account, supposedly to pay bills. I have an appointment tomorrow with the Assistant DA in Nashville to discuss what I've found. And now I'm off to bed."

As PD walked into the house, the threesome looked at each other. "Quite the dark horse, our PD," Dory said. "What do you think, Wayne?"

"I think our leader is about the shine some light into the darkness of the Blind Split case," he said, looking off in the distance.

Fireflies, like miniature candles, flashed in the evening light. The mist was rising from the ravine. Soon its cool white tendrils would reach the deck. An owl hooted and Wayne recalled the Native American superstition—if you heard an owl call your name, it meant someone nearby was going to die. Envisioning Pansy Delaney in her hospital bed, he inhaled shakily.

TWENTY-SIX

K NOWING SHE ONLY HAD A FEW DAYS to locate the Lovell family, if they were still living, Dory got right down to business. All she had to start with was their names. In church records, Betsy Lovell's occupation was listed as a homemaker. Her husband Verne was a carpenter and his last place of employment, twenty years earlier, was the lumber yard in Appleton. She called the Chamber of Commerce.

"Appleton Chamber of Commerce," the receptionist said.

"Good morning. I'm wondering if Appleton has a lumber yard business."

"Not any longer. The old lumber yard closed down years ago. We couldn't compete with the big box stores. It was a shame. That place had been in business for a close to a century."

"By chance do you know the name of the owner?" Dory asked. "I'd like to talk to him for some . . . local history I'm gathering for a newspaper article."

"Yes, his name is Willy Sharp. He lives in the Appleton Nursing Home over on Orchard Street."

"Thank you very much, ma'am," Dory said and hung up. She quickly texted the team that she was going to search for Teddy's grandparents and would be in later that afternoon.

Setting off for the Appleton Nursing Home, Dory turned on the radio. It was the usual report on the COVID-19 epidemic but was focused on the staggering number of deaths in old folk's homes. She realized, even with her recent negative test, they might not let her in. And if they did admit her, a seemingly innocuous interview with an old man could be more dangerous than dealing with an armed perpetrator. Talking with

Willy Sharp could carry a death sentence. Dory frowned and reached for her mask and gloves.

Arriving at the facility, Dory saw a nurse seated at a table on the porch. She walked up and said she was there to see a resident. The nurse scanned Dory's forehead. She had a normal temperature and was able to show the woman her recent negative test results.

"Who are you here to see?"

"Mr. Willy Sharp," she said.

"The policy of the Home is that residents may leave to visit with friends and family for short periods, but nobody but medical staff can enter. I can call Mr. Sharp's room and see if he will come out to talk with you. What's your relationship with him?"

"I'm trying to locate a man named Verne Lovell who used to work for Mr. Sharp at the lumber yard," Dory said.

The nurse's eyes looked dubious. "Willy Sharp has been retired for decades and has intermittent dementia. I doubt he'll be able to help you. Why do you need to find this man?"

Dory thought fast. "He's the grandfather to a child in the hospital. The boy hasn't got any other family and he's about to have surgery on his heart." Looking at the nurse, she didn't think she believed her for a moment. There was something about the nurse that reminded Dory of her mother—who had eyes in the back of her head.

"Hmm. Well, as I said, Mr. Sharp is only intermittently aware of his surroundings, but I'll ask him if he'll see you. What's your name again?"

"Dory Clarkson. Tell him I am a long-time friend of the Lovell family." That might have been one fib too many, she thought, but luckily the woman picked up the phone.

The facility had a long porch with multiple white rocking chairs carefully positioned six feet apart. If Mr. Sharp was willing to come out, she could talk with him on the porch. It would be safer by far than going inside. Ten minutes later, an elderly man in a wheelchair pushed by a male attendant, came through the sliding glass doors.

ONCE THE MALE NURSE MOVED MR. SHARP from his wheelchair into a rocking chair on the porch of the Appleton Nursing home, Dory walked up to introduce herself. "Hello Mr. Sharp," she said loudly, knowing old people were often hard of hearing.

Willy Sharp looked off in the distance and Dory's heart sank. He

wasn't going to be able to help her. Too far gone into the mists of dementia, she feared, but then his eyes cleared. "Who are you?" he asked.

"My name's Dory and I'm looking for a man who used to work for you
a long time ago. His name was Verne Lovell. Do you remember him?"

Mr. Sharp looked like he was trying hard to remember. "He ran the
plane," he finally said, and Dory's heart sank thinking she had lost him
again.

"No. Mr. Lovell wasn't a pilot. He had nothing to do with planes."

"Nobody knows anything these days," Mr. Sharp said irritably. "Lovell
ran the plane at the Yard. It's the tool that makes the wood smooth."

"Do you know where they went when they left town, he and his wife,
Betsy?" she asked and for the first time, Willy Sharp met her gaze and
looked alert.

"Betsy and I were high school sweethearts. Even after they were married, she wrote letters to me. Always told her she was making a mistake
marrying that loser."

"If you tell me where they moved, I'll try to find her and bring her
to see you," Dory said, hoping to capitalize on Mr. Sharp's failed hopes.

"Don't remember," he said in a dreamy tone and she could tell she
was losing him again. Then he rallied and his rheumy blue eyes turned
sharp. "Kept her letters though. Have a hard time reading now. My old
eyes aren't good."

Those letters could still be in their envelopes and have return addresses,
Dory thought. "If her love letters are in your room, I could read them to
you," she said.

It took a fair bit of negotiating with the staff, who had to take Willy
inside to get the letters and then bring him out again, but two hours later
Dory had what she needed—an address in Brooksville, Mississippi for
Mr. & Mrs. Verne Lovell.

Billy Jo had picked up the legal documents from Bradley Carver that
were supposed to release the rest of Rosedale Investigations' fee for finding Teddy Lovell. Carver had cited all kinds of lame excuses for holding
off on paying them. She wondered why he'd been such a jerk about it.
Driving away from the attorney's office, she called Lexie Lovell.

"Hello, Lexie. It's Billy Jo Bradley from Rosedale Investigations."

"I'm too busy to talk to you, Billy Jo. My wedding is only weeks away
and I have tons left to do. Sorry." She sounded sleepy.

"This will only take a few minutes. As you know, we located your little brother, and finding him allowed you to receive your inheritance—which you probably needed to pay for your wedding, right?"

Lexie sighed. "What do you want now?"

"Rosedale Investigations' fee is being held up. There's a legal document you need to sign saying that you have identified and acknowledged Teddy before we can be paid. I know you haven't seen him. He's been hospitalized since we located him."

"You know I won't be allowed to see him in the hospital because of the COVID-19. I just can't deal with this right now. You woke me up by the way."

"Could you use some coffee? I'm driving through Starbucks. What's your favorite brew? I'll bring it over."

BILLY JO ARRIVED AT LEXIE'S MOTHER'S HOUSE shortly thereafter with cappuccinos and muffins. She rang the bell, juggling the drinks holder with the coffees, a bag full of cranberry muffins, and the legal document. Lexie came to the door, still dressed in pajamas and looking none too happy to see her.

"Come in," she said brusquely and led her into their kitchen.

Billy Jo set the coffees and muffins down on the counter and pulled her cell phone from her pocket. "I brought some photos taken of your little brother, Teddy. Did I mention that his mother is in the hospital in a coma and that his aunt is in jail? Take a look at the pictures, you just have to scroll from left to right to see them all." She passed her phone to Lexie who looked at the photos carefully for a surprisingly long time.

"Let me see the document," she said, handing the phone back, and Billy Jo passed it to her.

"This says I need to identify and acknowledge him."

"That's right."

"I don't think I sign this," she said.

"Why not?"

"A picture of a little boy in a hospital gown doesn't prove we're related," she said firmly. "And you said my inheritance has all been released. I've only received ten thousand dollars. I'm pretty sure there's more," she frowned.

"That's interesting. He's only paid part of our fee as well. He told us you got *all* your money."

"At first he said I had my share, but then he wavered and admitted there was a little more. He told me that Rosedale Investigations was paid in full," Lexie said.

The young women looked at each other and Billy Jo had the first inkling that she and Lexie might be connecting.

"As to proving you're related to Teddy, we could do a DNA swab on both of you. I remember earlier in this case, you told us you wanted to have a DNA test done. I just had the lab do a test for me on another case, we could probably get it done pretty quickly."

"What would I have to do?" Lexie asked. "This is a real pain right now."

"Go to the lab and have a Q-tip run around in your mouth. I could take you over there now. Could be worth it financially for both of us," *And it might be the key to having Lexie finally start bonding to her little brother*, she thought, recalling her hopes that Lexie would learn to love Teddy, and for just a moment she heard the lilting, tumbling notes of *The Magic Flute*.

While Lexie went upstairs to change, Billy Jo turned her thoughts to Bradley Carver. He seemed so slippery. Why had he told Rosedale Investigations that Lexie got all her money? And why had he told Lexie that Rosedale Investigations had been fully paid? An image rose in her mind—black silhouettes of people standing around a bonfire. Was Carver there that night? She had a feeling he had been there with Snake Wrist and Lexie Lovell's mother.

WHEN PD TOLD ALL OF THEM HE WAS GOING TO MEET with the Assistant DA the previous evening, Wayne felt frustrated and even a bit hurt that PD hadn't included him. He and PD were the only ex-cops on the team. Although Dory was his partner, she had never attended the police academy. Sheriff Bradley had conferred the honorary title of Investigator on her as a tribute to her many years of service to the office. If he and PD discussed the situation, perhaps they could help the DA. Although it hurt his pride, he decided to call PD and ask if he could accompany him to the meeting. He dialed PD's cell, but there was no answer. He left a message for him to call back before he met with the DA. He said he was pretty sure there was something criminal going on between Lovell and Carver.

Disgruntled and irked with himself for sulking, Wayne decided to go home. Lucy was off at 4:00, although if the ER was particularly busy she would often stay for another hour or two. Still, she'd likely be home by six. He would cook dinner for the two of them as a thank you for the help she'd given him on the case. Standing at the meat counter at the grocery store, he had selected a pork tenderloin when his phone rang.

"Hi Lucy, I'm at the grocery store, planning to cook tonight," Wayne said

"Put the groceries back, Wayne. I just talked to Pansy Delaney's doctor. He has approved us seeing her."

"That's great!"

"Not really. She's failing, Wayne. We don't have much time. Come get me now," Lucy said and hung up.

TWENTY-SEVEN

WAYNE WAS SPEEDING DOWN MAIN STREET to pick Lucy up when he heard a siren coming from behind him. He glanced in his rearview mirror seeing a Sheriff's Office patrol car. He pulled over to the side of the road and stopped. Getting out of the police car, was Deputy George.

"Sorry, George, was I speeding?"

"You were about ten over, Detective." George took out his ticket pad. He had an intensely concentrated look on his face. Wayne knew how slow he was at writing tickets. He didn't have time to wait.

"I need your help, George. It's an emergency. I have to get to Rosedale General ASAP." George hesitated and Wayne mentally counted to ten. "You can lead and turn on your siren."

"Really? Cool," George said, put away his ticket pad, and got back in the patrol car.

They pulled into the ER entrance to Rosedale General a few minutes later. Lucy was already outside. She was wearing her white coat and her shiny hair was swept back from her forehead by the wind. Wayne parked his truck and thanked George, telling him to send him the ticket in the mail.

The Deputy was driving off when Wayne heard Lucy honk the horn. To his dismay, his determined girlfriend was already in the driver's seat of her vehicle. Lucy was a terrible driver. Half an hour later, they reached the hospital in Nashville. They both put on their masks and walked up to the entrance where the security guard and a nurse were stationed.

"Hello. I'm Dr. Lucy Ingram. Dr. Flannigan has a patient in the ICU he wants me to see. It's a criminal case. This is Detective Nichols who is investigating the matter."

They were screened and had a thermometer run over their foreheads before the security guard called the ICU and got permission for them to go up. Wayne was once again impressed, and a trifle concerned, truth be told, at the creative license his girlfriend was willing to employ to get her way.

Riding up in the elevator, he said, "You are a shockingly good liar, Dr. Ingram. How did you accomplish this visit exactly?"

"I know how many times you've tried to see Pansy, so I called Dr. Flannigan and pulled a few doctor strings."

"May I ask how you know this Flannigan guy?"

"We have history," she said. "We dated a long time ago." At Wayne's raised eyebrows she added, "Just drop it."

He dropped it.

Getting off the elevator, she said, "Wait here while I talk to the nursing staff." Lucy returned a few minutes later and said, "We need to wash our hands for a full five minutes and change into scrubs. The changing areas for men and women are down this hall."

Wayne changed into a green shirt, draw-string pants, and boot covers. Once his surgical mask was on, he looked at himself in the mirror. He felt like an imposter, someone imitating a surgeon about to operate on a potentially fatal case. His anxiety rose. How would he feel when he finally saw Pansy Delaney, the woman he had failed to find in time to save her? His conscience stabbed him.

Lucy opened the door to the men's dressing room a crack and said, "Come on. I have her room number. There isn't much time."

THE DOOR TO THE PATIENT'S ROOM swished silently open and they walked in. Although he had never seen Pansy Delaney before, Wayne knew her instantly. Her red hair was distinctive and even in a coma, she was the mirror image of her twin. Her face was as white as carved marble. She lay flat on her back with arms stretched out to either side, like an effigy. For a few moments, she didn't move and Wayne looked at Lucy. She was reading the panel above the bed with its measurements of oxygen, blood pressure, the rate and flow of the I.V. liquids, and more.

None of that made sense to Wayne, but even he could see that Pansy was hardly breathing. She inhaled shakily and then would pause. He found himself counting, waiting for the exhale. Then she began to thrash back and forth on the bed and he noticed what he should have seen before, she was restrained. Her wrists were tied down to the side of the bed. She began to cry out, no words were spoken, but her anguished wail hit Wayne right in his solar plexus. The woman was suffering horribly.

"Can she hear my voice, Lucy?" he asked and she nodded.

This was it, the final service he would perform for Pansy Delaney. Wayne bent down close to her ear and began the monologue he had mentally rehearsed a hundred times. "Pansy, my name is Wayne. I have been out to the old Delaney farm." Her thrashing slowed slightly and he thought he'd gotten through. "I found Teddy. He did what you told him. He hid, but I found his hiding place. I took him to the hospital. Your son is safe and well."

Pansy had stopped any movement by then. She lay completely still and Wayne looked at her face. A little color appeared in her cheeks. Her mouth opened as if she would speak, but no sound emerged. Wayne heard only the soft noises her hands made as they batted helplessly against the restraints.

"Tell her about her sister," Lucy whispered.

"Your sister, Poppy, has been released from prison. We are going to take Teddy to her. They will be living together. I promise you that your wishes will be followed," Wayne paused and looked desperately at Lucy. His last sentences hadn't seemed to help. She was still panting and thrashing. Then she stopped moving at all. Her chest barely rose and fell with her minimal breathing.

"Tell her she can leave us, Wayne," Lucy said looking intently at him.

"What?"

"Tell her it's all right to let go. Teddy is safe. She can stop fighting." Tears rose suddenly in Lucy's eyes and she brushed them away.

Wayne tried desperately to think of a way to phrase what he wanted to say. He envisioned the long bramble-clad lane leading to the farmhouse and deliberately slowed his breathing. In a low voice, he said, "The blackberry bushes are in bloom now, Pansy. They hang in long curving arches on either side of your folks' driveway. The flowers smell like violets. Poppy and Teddy are walking down the sandy road in a cloud of scented air. Hand in hand they walk to your parents' old farmhouse, and they are singing. The terrible pain you are in is almost over. When you are ready, you can stop fighting and let go."

Lucy placed a hand on Wayne's upper arm and he stopped talking. She took his hand and led him from the room just as a nurse came in.

Lucy said a few things to the nurse who nodded. Wayne didn't even bother to listen. He was struggling to control his emotions, knowing he had given Pansy permission to die. The owl he had heard the night before had been prophetic. She would be gone before morning.

Descending in the elevator, Lucy said, "I'm glad we came today. She only has a short time left, probably just a few days. You were good with her, Wayne."

He shook his head. They walked outside and Wayne looked up into a misty falling rain. "She will leave us tonight," he said and the rain fell like tears on his face and shoulders.

Lucy looked at him in bewilderment, but he didn't add another word.

DORY WAS AT HER DESK AT ROSEDALE INVESTIGATIONS when the phone rang. Picking up the receiver, she heard Poppy Delaney's quavering voice say "Hello?" It was obvious she was struggling to control her emotions. "What is it, Poppy? Are you okay?" Dory asked.

There was a long pause before her choking voice said, "She's dying. My sister is dying. It will be soon." Then the phone went dead.

Dory sat quietly for a few minutes wondering if she should call her back but doubted it would help. Poppy, who originally denied an empathic connection to her twin, now seemed certain her sister's life was coming to an end. She wondered if she should call Wayne but superstitiously decided not to. Even if there was a slight chance Pansy would make it, Dory didn't want to somehow seal her fate by telling Wayne about the prediction. Tearing her mind away from the all-too-likely end to Pansy Delaney's life, Dory dialed the phone number she found for the home of Mr. & Mrs. Verne Lovell. It rang for a long time and she was about to give up when an old woman's high quavering voice answered.

"Hello."

"Hello, is this Mrs. Lovell?"

"Yes, it is," she said.

"I'm Dory Clarkson and I'm calling from Rosedale, Tennessee."

"Rosedale, Tennessee. Now that's a town I haven't heard of in a long time. My son lives there," she sounded sad and her voice trailed off.

"Edward Lovell is your son? I'm sorry to tell you that he passed away," Dory asked.

"He's dead? No, no, God no," she wailed. "He was my only child. A child should not die before his mother."

Dory felt for the woman and waited while she cried. After some time, hearing the sobbing fade away, she said, "I'm so sorry for your loss, Mrs. Lovell. I thought you would have been informed."

"Did Edward have a family?" Dory could still hear the tears in her voice.

"He married," she said, feeling like it was the oddest conversation she had ever had. The woman must not have been in touch with her son for decades. "And he had two children," she added.

"I have grandchildren?"

Dory heard the note of hope in her voice. "You certainly do, and I'm calling because they need you. Were you and your son estranged?"

"There was a terrible fight between my son and his father when we left Appleton. It was decades ago. It was about some lawyer Edward was working with who my husband said was a crook. After the fight, my husband cut off all contact and forbade me from speaking to my boy. Edward has been all-but-dead to me for over twenty years."

"Are you and your husband together?" Dory asked, knowing if they were, this wasn't likely to work.

"He passed away a few months ago and if I have grandchildren, I want to know them." Her little voice suddenly rang with determination. "I'm sorry, Miss Clarkson, but hearing all this has made me feel a bit faint. If you don't mind, I'm going to get a drink of water, and then I want to hear all about them."

And it will be my privilege to tell you, Dory thought and felt her spirits rise.

BILLY JO BRADLEY AND LEXIE WERE ON THEIR WAY to the laboratory that did DNA tests for private citizens. There was a prominent sign outside the building saying, "You must wear a mask, gloves, and shoe covers to enter this facility." Billy Jo and Lexie slipped on their masks. There was a dispenser for gloves which they accessed.

They entered the unremarkable brick structure through a revolving door and walked down a corridor to the back of the building. There was an interior door to the area with a window that said "DNA Testing." Billy Jo knocked. A person, dressed from head to toe in a white Hazmat suit, including a white mask, gloves, and shoe covers, answered the door. Billy Jo explained that Lexie wanted to have her DNA profile done in order to have it matched with a child who might be her sibling.

"A familial match, no problem, but only the person being tested may enter. You need to put on these shoe covers," the attendant said, handing a pair to Lexie. She then pulled out a thermometer and checked Lexie's temperature. After noting that her temperature was normal, the attendant led her into an adjacent glass-walled room where Billy Jo could see her donning a Hazmat suit. Then a second white-clad attendant entered the room, ran a Q-tip around in Lexie's mouth and put it in a labeled tube.

"I'll take care of providing something from the little boy for comparison later today," Billy Jo told the attendant when she brought Lexie back.

Walking to the parking lot, she said, "While you were in there, Lexie, I've been thinking. I believe we've both been getting the runaround from Bradley Carver. How much of your father's estate have you received so far?"

"About $10,000 which the lawyer said was half what my father left me."

"That's the amount we received as well." She thought for a while before adding, "I'm beginning to think Carver is a crook and is trying to keep your money. I work with two detectives. I'm going to talk with them about this. The police may need to be involved."

"If Carver is hanging onto my money, as well as yours, I am happy to have the police involved," Lexie said firmly.

"Do you mind if I ask you a personal question, Lexie?"

"Go ahead," she said.

"Why were you so adamant about not sharing your father's estate with your brother?"

Lexie sighed before saying, "At first, I was so angry with Dad for having a relationship with this Delaney woman and even having a child with her," two little spots of red appeared on Lexie's cheeks and she clenched her teeth. "Then my mother told me that she and my dad were never divorced and all his money should belong to us. Later, she confessed she had lied. They were divorced many years ago and she got a big settlement at that time."

"I remember you bringing us a picture of your brother with a teddy bear that was identical to the one you had as a child. Seeing that photo must have been hard for you," Billy Jo said. She was finding it easier to be sympathetic.

"It was awful. I was so disappointed in my dad."

"If the DNA tests confirm that Teddy is your brother, will that change matters?"

"Possibly. Over the last year, I've been furious, sad, unbelieving, and depressed. My fiancé has been more positive. He says that since I'm an only child, maybe the time will come when I'd enjoy having a little brother."

"Little Teddy has been through so much—abandoned in an old farm-house, terrified and traumatized—I think it would help him to know he has a big sister," Billy Jo said. "Did I tell you he can't even talk because of the trauma he experienced? And that he has a heart murmur?"

Lexie shook her head and for the first time, her face showed some sympathy for Teddy.

When they got in the car and drove toward Lexie's house, Billy Jo recalled the metaphor she had selected for this case—the Blind Split. If she could convince Lexie to meet her little brother, perhaps the blind split between them would begin to heal.

TWENTY-EIGHT

W AYNE WOKE TO LUCY ANSWERING HER PAGER. He could tell by her body language that it was bad news.

"I appreciate the call, Nick. We were afraid this would happen. Thanks for arranging the visit. I presume she never regained consciousness? That's what I expected." Lucy clicked off the call and looked at Wayne. "You were right," she said. "Pansy expired late last night."

He nodded. Taking a deep breath, he realized he was feeling somewhat better. Pansy Delaney had gone on to the world that lies beyond the one they knew. Her suffering had come to an end. He had performed the final service by telling her Teddy would be with her sister. Now he could focus on the murder of Ed Lovell—the man Pansy had loved with all her heart.

"What are you going to do now?" Lucy asked.

"I need to tell the team about Pansy passing away and confer with PD. He and I need to put our heads together and figure out what the two men, Bradley Carver and Edward Lovell, were up to. If you don't have to go to work right away, I'll grab a shower first, okay?"

"That's fine. I'm working the late shift today. I'll get some breakfast going. And, Wayne, I'm very sorry about Pansy. I found out a bit more about her case from Dr. Flannigan. They did an initial CT scan on Pansy when she was brought into Summit's ER. Once she was admitted and spent time on the medical ward with no resolution of her confusion, as you know I pushed to have her transferred to Nashville where she was placed on a psych ward. She deteriorated, was moved to the ICU & given another CT scan. It was positive for a brain bleed. Her death was accidental and I know you feel guilty that you didn't find her on the farm. But, even if you had found her immediately after she fell and hit her head, the outcome would have been the same. I checked her films, the bleed in her brain was just too extensive." She leaned across and kissed him.

Wayne walked into the bathroom. Lucy saying Pansy's death had been inevitable had helped. He felt immensely relieved he'd been able to say goodbye and tell her that her sister, Poppy, and Teddy would be together. Now, he needed to confer with PD. Hopefully, they would be able to pinpoint what Bradley Carver and Edward Lovell had been up to. He would also check with Sheriff Bradley to see what Detective Rob had discovered about Carver and his potential role in Lovell's convenient demise. It was time to return to the role he had filled for so long. He was ready to solve a murder.

AFTER BREAKFAST, HE GOT IN HIS TRUCK and headed for the office. He'd texted PD to ask if he would meet him there. PD called back as he was driving.

"Good morning," PD said.

"Morning, PD."

"After I got your call yesterday, I canceled my appointment with the Assistant DA. You're right, we need to spend more time figuring out how this whole puzzle fits together before we meet with the authorities."

"I'm at the office. Can you come over?"

"Yup," PD said and hung up the phone.

Since it was before business hours, Wayne rang the doorbell instead of using his key and Billy Jo came to answer the door. She was still in her pajamas.

"You didn't bring me any coffee," she said, sounding disappointed.

"Sorry. I have some bad news. Come into the kitchen." Billy Jo did so as Wayne made a pot of coffee. "Lucy and I saw Pansy Delaney yesterday. I was able to tell her that her twin sister and Teddy would be together. We were just in time," he said.

"She's gone then?" Billy Jo asked softly.

"Yes. I knew it would happen. I heard the owl call her name in the dark at PD's."

"I'm so sorry, Wayne," she said. "Let's take the coffees into the conference room. I have some news too, better news."

They sat at the conference room table and sipped their coffees. Wayne told her that PD was on his way and said he would tell him about Pansy's death. "What's your news?"

"Dory found Teddy's grandmother yesterday and she thinks Gramma Lovell will agree to come here and live with Poppy and Teddy."

"That's excellent, really wonderful. Anything else?" Wayne asked.

"Yes. I met with Lexie yesterday and got her DNA tested to determine whether she and Teddy are related. The hospital agreed to provide a sample of Teddy's blood for the familial test. Here's my concern. Both Lexie and I think Carver is giving us the run-around. It turns out that Carver has only given Lexie $10,000. That's the amount he released to us as well. Do you think he is trying to keep the rest of the money for himself?"

"I wouldn't be one bit surprised. PD has said all along that money is the primary motive in this case. He's working that angle. Now that Pansy has passed away," he paused before adding, "I'm focused on whether Carver caused Lovell's death."

They heard the front doorbell ring and Billy Jo got up to let PD in. They returned together.

"I have some sad news, PD. Pansy passed away last night," Wayne said.

"Guess it was expected, but that's a shame, poor woman. So young and with a small child. I'm glad you got to say good-bye."

The sun came out and shone through the windows, it was going to be a hot day. Nobody said anything for a bit. The news about the death of Pansy Delaney was hard for all of them.

After a while, Wayne said, "Billy Jo thinks Carver is hanging on to our money and Lexie's too. What do you think this is about, PD?"

"Having heard back from all my old detective pals and confidential informants, I think Carver and Lovell were working together to get their hands on a large pot of money. Lovell was probably planning to leave the country with Pansy and Teddy. They were going to Greece and he must have needed the money to start a new life."

"And then he died," Wayne said thoughtfully. "And Carver was the only person in his hospital room when that happened."

"Lovell's death left Bradley Carver the last man standing. He could release as little of Lovell's money as possible to his children and to Rosedale Investigations. He intended to keep the rest," PD said.

"If Lexie and Teddy were to die, he would have it all . . ." Billy Jo's voice trailed off.

"I think that's unlikely. Even the mob doesn't usually kill kids. Teddy is too young to be any kind of a threat, Lexie doesn't seem to know anything pertinent, and anyway I doubt the mob is involved," PD said.

"I agree, I don't think it's the mob either, but if it isn't, where is all this money coming from?" Wayne asked.

They all were silent for a few minutes until they heard the front door open. It was Dory.

"Good morning all," Dory said. She was clearly in an excellent mood. She was wearing a mid-calf length purple flowered dress, silver stilettos, and bright amethyst combs in her hair.

"What's happening?" she asked cheerfully, before noticing their serious faces.

"Pansy Delaney died last night," Billy Jo said.

"Oh dear. I'm so sorry," Dory said, recalling her sixth sense that Pansy would never be able to be Teddy's mother. Sadly, she had been right. "Poppy called me before you and Lucy went to the hospital, Wayne. She knew Pansy was dying. I felt so sad for her. We will have to let Poppy know that her sister is gone."

"We all wish Pansy had survived," PD said and everyone nodded.

"Wayne was able to tell Pansy that her wishes about her son would be honored. That's thanks to you, Dory. You got Poppy out of jail and also found Lexie and Teddy's grandmother," Billy Jo said.

"Given that Teddy's mother is gone, I think having Poppy and Mrs. Lovell taking care of him is the best outcome we could achieve. You two look like you're leaving," Dory said to PD and Wayne who were gathering up keys and cups.

"We're going to see the Sheriff. We have some questions to ask Snake Wrist, whose real name, by the way, is Jonesy Patterson," PD said.

"And we want to find out what Detective Rob has learned about Carver's possible involvement in Lovell's death," Wayne said, and the two men departed.

"Let's turn the office answering machine on, Billy Jo. I'm running out to the Delaney farm this morning and I could use your help. I've already arranged for the woman who cleans for me to meet us out there. And what are you doing down here in your pajamas?" Dory frowned as a barefoot Billy Jo skipped up the stairs.

THE TWO WOMEN DROVE SLOWLY DOWN THE LANE between the blossoming blackberry canes and pulled in at the old farmhouse. There were already several cars parked by the house. A young man was mowing the lawn and a window company was replacing the broken window in the back bedroom.

"What's all this?" Billy Jo asked.

"The place needed fixing up. I've ordered new mattresses for both the beds and we had to have a crib for Teddy. I bought one of those convertible ones that become twin beds when the child is old enough. I am also having that large dumpster removed. Poppy doesn't need to be reminded of how her twin died every time she looks out the window."

"Good idea. I see the power company is here as well."

"Yes, there wasn't any air conditioning in the place."

"Dory, are you sure Teddy's money is going to be enough to cover all this?"

"You'll recall that we tried to get Lovell's account information when Lexie first contacted us, but they wouldn't tell us anything. Yesterday, PD talked Lexie into going to the bank and signing documents giving the bank permission to release account information to us. It turns out Lovell has over three million dollars in his account."

"Wow, that's good news for Lexie and Teddy," Billy Jo said.

"Lovell had been receiving large monthly deposits for decades but so far the bank won't tell us the source of that money. I presented the bank officials with the contract Lexie signed with us for five percent of her father's money. They are going to pay what remains of our bill and it's going to be around six figures."

"Nice work," Billy Jo said.

The women walked inside the farmhouse and Dory greeted her cleaning woman, Ruby. The place was already looking much more welcoming. Ruby had made a list of items that were needed to make the place livable for Poppy and Teddy.

"We need new sets of sheets, blankets, pillowcases, and quilts. There are two full-sized beds and don't forget to get a package of crib sheets. You also need to buy towels for the bathroom and small rugs for the kitchen sink and the bathroom," Ruby said.

"Give me your list. I'm going to order new furniture for the living room too," Dory said.

"Don't forget groceries," Ruby reminded them as the two women headed out the door.

"We'll be back this afternoon. Make it sparkle, Ruby, we'll be bringing Poppy Delaney out later."

By the end of the day, Billy Jo was exhausted. Dory had been a shopping maniac. They had two cars full of household goods when they returned to the Delaney farm with Poppy. Billy Jo had to drive her car out as well. There was too much stuff to fit into one car.

Dory looked like Mrs. Santa Claus as she escorted Poppy Delaney in the front door. The soon-to-be foster mom to Teddy was stunned and speechless. She just kept saying, "Oh my God," over and over again.

Billy Jo helped out for an hour before leaving Dory and Poppy to put the rest of the things away. "I checked the answering machine remotely and PD wants me to come out tonight. I should get going," she said.

"Right you are. I'm picking Gramma Lovell up from the train station later this evening. I'll check in with you tomorrow. Ciao," she said merrily. Poppy just looked overcome.

WHEN BILLY JO GOT BACK TO THE OFFICE, she noticed the answering machine was blinking. PD had left another message. He said the sheriff's office was close to finding the evidence they needed to place Bradley Carver under arrest. She walked upstairs, assembled her nightclothes and toiletries. There wasn't much food left at PD's so she stopped by the grocery store and got some frozen dinners, eggs, bacon, coffee, and orange juice. The sun was going down when she entered the mile-long dirt track to PD's cabin. The light clouds were rendered rose-colored by the setting sun.

Surprised not to find PD's car parked by the cabin, Billy Jo pulled in and turned off her car. She grabbed the two plastic sacks of food and her overnight bag. As she walked toward the front door, she stopped, feeling apprehensive. *What was that on the porch? It looked small and furry, but it wasn't moving.* Dread made her spine tingle.

Billy Jo reached the porch and looked down at the small furry creature. It was the baby fox. His mouth was open and a yellow substance was leaking out between his lips. Somebody had poisoned him. Under his lifeless head, there was a note. It read, "Stop looking into the Lovell case, or the girl will be next."

The world spun and picking the baby fox up in her hands, Billy Jo sobbed as if she would never stop.

TWENTY-NINE

DORY STOOD ON THE TRAIN STATION PLATFORM waiting for the arrival of Edward Lovell's mother. It was sundown. She could hear the train approaching and its loud distinctive whistle as it slid into the station. The hiss of escaping steam, the whistle, and the announcement of the train from 'All Points South,' were evocative of an earlier era. She watched the passengers as they stepped down, often directly into the arms of family and friends. Nobody was being very careful about social distancing.

Betsy Lovell was one of the last to exit the train car. She had short brown hair, wore a boxy Chanel-type suit and flat heels. The suit was good quality but had been out of style for decades. She had tied a bright red scarf around her neck, the item she and Dory discussed which would identify her. Dory knew she was close to sixty-five but looked a decade younger, a good sign if the woman was going to be taking care of an active little toddler. She walked over to meet the woman.

"Mrs. Lovell, I'm Dory."

"Thank you so much for meeting me. It's a long ride from Mississippi."

"I'm sure you're tired. Let's stop and get you something to eat. If you can bring your suitcases to the front door, I'll get my car out of the lot. I have a little red convertible."

Mrs. Lovell nodded and Dory walked across the road to the short-term parking lot. She was exiting the lot, having paid for the time her car was parked, when the phone rang. The caller at the other end was screaming and Dory held her phone away from her ear as she circled back to the front of the station. It was Billy Jo and she was sounding terrified. It reminded her of the night the girl arrived at her house in the middle of a crashing rainstorm having escaped a gunman.

"Billy Jo, slow down a minute. I can't understand you. What's happened?" The girl was crying. She kept saying something that sounded like "the little b . . . b . . . box" and "dead."

"Honey, you need to call PD or Wayne or the sheriff. I'm at the train station picking up Mrs. Lovell."

"He's going to get me next!" Billy Jo cried and Dory felt a shiver of fear run down her spine.

"Honey, you need to call the Sheriff's Office. Go inside the house and lock the doors. Do it now. I will call Wayne and PD." She hung up, frowning.

As the porter put Mrs. Lovell's two suitcases in the trunk of her convertible, Dory took a moment to text Wayne and PD saying Billy Jo needed help. She had called saying something about a dead box and that somebody had threatened her.

Betsy Lovell got into the car and they drove off. "What sounds good to you in the way of food and drink?" Dory asked.

"Could we just go to a drive-thru?" she asked.

"We could, Betsy if that's what you prefer, but if you are short of money this is my treat. How about I take you to Southern Comfort? It's near here and has marvelous fried chicken, mashed potatoes, green beans, and sweet tea. They have removed half of their tables so we will be separated from other diners."

"That sounds perfect."

"After dinner, we're going to see your house, where you and little Teddy will be living."

All the fatigue left Betsy's face and she looked like a child on Christmas morning. "God bless you for finding me, Miss Dory. Your phone call was an answer to my prayers."

"You are most welcome. I'm the one who is grateful that you dropped everything and were willing to come and help with your grandchildren. Are you really able to move to Tennessee at this point?"

"I am. I listed my house as a furnished rental. Someday, when they are grown, I may want to return to Mississippi and show the place to both my grandchildren."

"The farmhouse where you will be living with Poppy Delaney and your grandson is being fixed up at the moment and is probably still a bit of a mess, so you are going to be my guest tonight."

"I can't thank you enough, Miss Dory. I will always be grateful that you tracked me down and for everything you have done for Teddy. There's a granddaughter, too, you said? Tell me about her, please."

"Yes. Her name is Lexie, she's twenty-one and engaged. Her wedding is coming up in just a few weeks. We are arranging for you to meet." When they stopped at a red light, Dory said, "Excuse me a minute, Mrs. Lovell, I just need to send a quick text to my colleagues." She sent a joint message to Wayne and PD saying, "*call me ASAP about Billy Jo.*"

Then, knowing her partners would do all they could to protect their youngest colleague, Dory deliberately set aside her fears. As she and Mrs. Lovell headed for Southern Comfort, with the convertible top open and the warm evening wind in her hair, she felt her guilt about Teddy slowly but surely blowing away. With an aunt and a grandmother to love him, Teddy Lovell was going to be just fine.

WAYNE AND PD WERE LEAVING THE SHERIFF'S OFFICE when they got Dory's text about Billy Jo needing help. Wayne checked the location of Billy Jo's phone. "Billy Jo's out at your place," he said. "I think we should both go."

"On the way, how about I summarize what we learned just now from Sheriff Bradley," PD said. "We now know that Carver employs Snake Wrist, aka Jonesy Patterson, to do his dirty work. Both Snake Wrist and Carver were at the red stone mansion the night Billy Jo was copying the Lovell emails. Snake Wrist didn't confess to the attack on Billy Jo but said they were burning files that would have tied Edward Lovell to an *embezzlement scheme*. That was important information. According to Snake Wrist, Lovell and Carver were planning to split a big pot of money."

"What was the ex's motivation for burning files do you think? Since she and Edward Lovell were divorced, she was unlikely to be trying to save his reputation."

"Agreed. I think Lovell's ex wanted to get rid of any evidence that would slow down her daughter's receiving her inheritance. The big problem is that we don't know whose money was being embezzled. Do you think it was mob money, Wayne?"

"No. I'm thinking there's another source. It has to be the person who was depositing money all those years into Lovell's account. Changing the subject, we both know Billy Jo doesn't usually push the panic button unless there's a real threat. We need to get out to your place."

The two men looked apprehensively at each other as PD pushed down hard on his accelerator.

PD REACHED HIS TURNOFF, bordered in shivering poplars, in record time. He looked for tracks in the dusty road ahead of him, seeing only Billy Jo's tire prints.

"Only one set of tire tracks," PD said.

"They're Billy Jo's," Wayne said.

"Yes, but it poured down rain last night, so any prior tire tracks would have been washed away," PD said.

Pulling up in front of the cabin, they saw Billy Jo's car but didn't see her. Wayne jumped out of the car heading in the direction of the deck. PD's heartbeat raced and his breathing became irregular. He got out of the car with some difficulty, trying not to reinjure his ankle, and visually scanned the area around the cabin.

"Billy Jo, where are you?" PD called and thought he heard a noise. It was coming from down in the ravine. He limped to the far edge of the deck that jutted out over the hill. Grabbing the binoculars hanging on the back of his deck chair, he brought the image into focus. At the bottom of the gully, he could see a small bent-over figure. He dropped the binoculars and began to run. Wayne was already crashing downhill through the brush. The sun was going down. They had to find her before it got completely dark.

Reaching the base of the gorge, PD saw her. She raised her head at his approach and pointed a gun at him. Her eyes were narrowed in determination. The weapon was heavy and her skinny arms wobbled. PD recognized his father's old service revolver. Old guns could backfire if bullets were stuck in the barrel.

"Billy Jo! Put that gun down. Now," PD yelled. As he emerged fully from the thicket, she recognized him and laid the revolver on the ground. Her face was filthy and tears had left tracks on her dirty cheeks. She was shaking all over.

Wayne had reached her by then. "What are you doing?" he asked.

Billy Jo didn't answer and they could tell from the shocked look on her face that she wasn't going to be able to tell them much. She had dug a hole. At the bottom of the hole was a white pillowcase. The pillowcase was lumpy, something was inside it. Billy Jo had been sprinkling wildflowers into a shallow grave. PD pulled her to her feet.

"Oh, PD," she said, as her voice caught.

"What happened here? Are you burying something?" he asked.

"It's one of the baby foxes. It's so awful. He's dead."

"Lots of young animals die, Billy Jo. It's sad, but not uncommon." He patted her back.

"My beautiful baby was poisoned, PD," she said in a flat discouraged tone and pulled a note from her pocket.

Wayne took the note from her hand, realizing as he did so that Billy Jo had touched it and now he had touched it. Getting fingerprints would be a long shot. There was only a single sentence but the message was unambiguously threatening. If they kept looking into the Lovell case, Billy Jo would be next. "You need to come up to the cabin now," he said firmly.

"No. I have to finish this."

"You can come back another time, but right now we need to talk," Wayne said, and taking her by the hand, led her through the dense undergrowth up the hill. PD followed, pulling himself up by hanging on to tree saplings. They reached the deck and went into the cabin.

"Go and wash up. I'll get you a glass of wine," PD said. Walking up the steep hill had just about done him in. "Is she okay do you think, Wayne?"

"She's so upset about the baby fox, I don't think she's even registered that the note says if we don't stop looking into the Lovell case, she will be next," Wayne's face darkened.

"From now on, she's going to be with one of us at all times, and we are going to be armed," PD said.

DORY HAD DRIVEN MRS. LOVELL OUT TO SEE the Delaney farmhouse. They were sitting in her car in front of the house which was already almost unrecognizable. The wood exterior that had originally been a silver-gray patina, was now a pale buttery yellow. Navy blue shutters were being attached to the windows on the front. The front door had been painted to match the shutters. The last of the workmen were leaving.

"As I mentioned earlier, Betsy, the house still might need some work, but let's go inside so you can see where you will be living." Dory got the house keys out of her purse and handed them to Mrs. Lovell just as her phone rang. "Sorry, I need to get this. You go on in."

She watched the woman walk up to the porch as she answered the phone. "PD, what's up? Have you found Billy Jo?"

"Yes. Somebody poisoned one of the baby foxes we've been watching and left a note threatening Billy Jo. It said if we didn't stop looking into the source of the Lovell money she would be next. I want you to come out. She needs you."

"I can't right now, PD. You and Wayne will just have to cope. Sometimes I just hate people. How could a person threaten a young girl's life and poison an innocent baby animal? It's disgusting," she said fiercely. "As far as Billy Jo goes, promise me you won't let her out of your sight."

"We won't. Wayne wants to talk to you about what we learned about Snake Wrist," PD said, handing him the phone.

"Hi, Dory. We got a fair bit of information from Jonesy Patterson, the creep we've been calling Snake Wrist. He was singing like a canary to the sheriff. This whole thing is about an embezzlement scheme, but we are still trying to figure out where the money was coming from. Why can't you come out?"

"I'm at the Delaney farm with Mrs. Lovell. You saw how decrepit the place was. It needed fixing up."

"Dory, what have you done?" Wayne said in an accusatory tone.

"Just spruced the place up a bit," she said, feeling guilty.

"With what money?" he asked.

"Um . . . well I used the Rosedale Investigation's credit card, but we can get it reimbursed once Lovell's money is released."

"Damn it, woman. Has it not occurred to you that if Carver's money comes from proceeds of a crime, we won't get paid? And if it is mob money, although we now think that's unlikely, the FBI will take it all."

"Oh, dear," Dory gulped. "And you and PD think this is all about embezzlement?"

"Looks to be, and I think Carver and Lovell were in it together."

"Whose money was being embezzled?" Dory asked.

"That is what we have to figure out."

"While you're doing that, Detective Nichols, just keep our girl safe," Dory said

"I will. I promise," Wayne said and clicked off the call.

THIRTY

D ORY GOT OUT OF THE CAR and joined Mrs. Lovell in the kitchen, delighted with how it looked. All the cupboards had been scrubbed and the doors painted. New handles had been added. Dory opened the refrigerator. It was fully stocked with the juice, milk, vegetables, and fruit she and Billy Jo had bought earlier. The freezer was filled with microwavable dinners. The kitchen table was covered with a red and white gingham-checked oilcloth and someone had found a clear glass jelly jar to use as a vase for the white wildflowers that grew in abundance in the fallow fields around the house.

"Do you think you will be comfortable living here, Betsy?" Dory asked as they walked into the living room. The room had a fresh coat of paint and the wooden floor had been mopped and polished, but there was no furniture in the room. The old living room furniture had been hauled away. Unless she canceled the delivery, (another five thousand dollars for a couch, chairs, coffee tables, and end tables as well as lamps and paintings) it would arrive the following day. *In for a penny, in for a pound*, she thought, praying Wayne was wrong and that the charges she'd incurred could eventually be repaid from the Lovell estate.

"I have always wanted to live out in the country," Betsy Lovell said in a nostalgic tone. "When we lived here before, we lived in Appleton. And I've never had such a nice place as this."

"You are a treasure," Dory said and they proceeded down the hall to see the bedrooms. Ruby had dusted and mopped the floors. The beds with their new mattresses had been made up with the blankets, pillows, and quilts she and Billy Jo had selected. Even the bathroom, although tiny, was immaculate. New towels were hung on the towel racks.

They walked into the nursery. It had received a fresh coat of pale blue paint. A chest of drawers occupied one side of the room and the new crib occupied the opposite wall. The windows were open and a gentle night breeze came inside, lifting the new eyelet curtains.

"When can I meet my grandchildren and Poppy?" Betsy asked.

"Poppy will be able to come out here in a couple of days. Hayley, the social worker, and Juanita, the child psychiatrist, are bringing Teddy out here that same day. Lexie will come that day, too. There's one problem though. I'm sorry to tell you this," Dory hesitated, "But since my partner found him, Teddy hasn't spoken at all." She had been reluctant to tell Betsy about it, fearing it might put her off.

Betsy Lovell tipped her head to one side. "Once when Edward was a little boy, he had a high fever and what the doctor called febrile seizures. He couldn't talk for weeks after that. I'm not worried. My grandson is just like his father. He will talk when he is ready," she smiled calmly at Dory.

Dory sent a little prayer of thanksgiving to the universe for giving her the miracle that was Gramma Lovell.

CAREFUL NOT TO MENTION THE LETHAL THREAT in the note, PD and Wayne were recapping what they had learned about Snake Wrist for Billy Jo. She was slowly retreating from the baby fox's death and becoming interested in the case again until they mentioned that Snake Wrist did the dirty work for Carver.

"I assume this means that Snake Wrist was the person who *murdered* my baby fox," she said darkly.

"We think so, but we have no actual evidence of that," Wayne said. He noticed that the fox had gone from being one of a family of foxes they all enjoyed watching and had become *her baby fox* and that he hadn't be poisoned but *murdered*.

"Although it was a horrible thing to have done, killing a fox is not a crime in Tennessee. Chicken farmers are allowed to shoot any foxes who take their eggs or chickens. Foxes aren't endangered, Billy Jo, and are classified as vermin," PD said.

"Vermin!" Billy Jo almost spat out the word in shock.

"I don't like it either, but to prove that Carver committed a crime, we have to show that embezzlement took place and determine whether or not Lovell was murdered."

"Which brings us right back to where the money was coming from," Wayne said. "We're all getting tired, let's just pick this up in the morning. I presume you're staying here tonight, Billy Jo?" he asked.

She nodded, looking small and vulnerable, wrapped in a fuzzy blanket sitting on the couch.

"I'm thinking I should stay over, too, PD. We could take shifts on guard, in case the creep tries something else," Wayne said.

Because of his sprained ankle, PD swallowed before saying. "Where do you want to be stationed? I've got to be somewhere I can sit down."

"I was thinking of parking my truck behind those trees at the top of the hill and watching from there," Wayne said. Hearing a scuffling noise, he turned to see Billy Jo. She was headed toward the door leading to the deck, carrying the blanket from the couch, and holding PD's revolver. "Just where do you think you're going?" he asked.

"You two unenlightened chauvinists might not consider the murder of a baby fox a crime, but I do! If you aren't going to guard the fox family tonight, I will sleep at the bottom of the ravine by my little fox's grave, and I'm taking the gun with me."

"Oh no, you aren't," PD said, pulling the gun from her hands. "We'll take turns watching the fox family from the deck, won't we, Wayne?"

"We will indeed. I'll take the first shift," he said, thinking he might not even wake PD up for the second shift. He looked so pale.

Leaving PD and Billy Jo inside, Wayne walked out onto the deck and looked down at the small lake. It had turned silver by then, reflecting the light of the full moon. He gazed across the water to the other side. He hadn't noticed previously that a country road ran right along the far side of the lake. It would be possible to bring a canoe across the water in silence and get to the ravine, kill the fox, and leave the note without leaving any tracks. He sat there thinking about the case as the fireflies rose into the night skies and the cicadas sang.

DORY CALLED WAYNE EARLY THE FOLLOWING MORNING, waking him from his uncomfortable position on PD's couch. She couldn't talk long, she said, just wanted him to know that she'd gotten the bank to reveal the source of the monthly deposits that had been made into Edward Lovell's account. The money came from an account belonging to a woman named Eloise Embry.

"You'll have to take it from here, Partner. I'm showing Betsy Lovell around Rosedale today and we've still got some work to do on the house. Keep Billy Jo with you at all times. I'll check in later."

Setting his phone down, Wayne heard the sounds of PD emerging from the bedroom. It had been a long night on guard and he worried it had been too much for him. He stood up and went into the kitchen. After starting the coffee, he looked up the name Eloise Embry on his phone. There were dozens in the U.S., but only one in middle Tennessee. There was a picture of her at some festive get-together wearing a long black gown. The woman had to be ninety if she was a day. Further digging got him nowhere. He needed Billy Jo.

PD emerged from the bedroom. His face was nearly gray with fatigue. "Morning," he said.

"How is the ankle today? I held off on waking you until about four this morning," Wayne said.

"I appreciated that. I presume you saw absolutely nothing?"

"Right, but I talked to Dory this morning and she's found the person our perps were embezzling from. It's a wealthy old lady by the name of Eloise Embry."

"Embry, Embry," PD said and then snapped his fingers. "That's a name I recognize. I think Embry had a mob connection." He called up the ladder to the open loft, "Billy Jo, wake up."

"Not yet," she said, plaintively.

"Yes, come on down. Wayne made coffee."

Grumbling noises emerged from the loft, but ultimately they saw bare feet descending the ladder. Wayne handed her a cup of coffee to forestall further complaints.

"We need you to do a background on a woman named Eloise Embry. She's local," PD said.

"I need food," Billy Jo said.

"I'll make us some scrambled eggs and bacon while you do your magic," Wayne said.

THE MEN WERE OUT ON THE DECK WATCHING the fox family through binoculars when Billy Jo joined them. "You have *got* to get a better computer and a printer out here, PD. The office can buy you a new computer and printer and I'll get Mark to help set it up. He's looking into some satellite thing so you can have internet. Now, I have found some background, but all I can do is summarize what I found because I can't *print it out* for you to read." She frowned.

"I know, I know," he said. It was a sore point between them. "Talk to us, Girl."

"Eloise Embry is the widow of one Raymond Embry. He died about twenty years ago, leaving her very well off."

"How much is she worth?" Wayne asked.

"I'm not a miracle worker you know, Wayne," she frowned at him. "Even I can't check the amount of money a husband wills to his wife, and despite your touching faith in me, I can't get into private bank accounts," she looked severely at the men. "However, I can tell you it's a very large estate. I've seen pictures of her at fancy charitable affairs and of her property online."

"Where did her husband's money come from?" PD asked.

"Now that is where I'm pulling theories out of the air, but there's a ten-year gap in Raymond's life, and I suspect he could have spent that decade in prison. I can't access the database of felons from here, but I could from my workstation in town. If I'm right, once Raymond got out of prison, it looks like he went straight."

"You say you aren't a miracle worker, but between you and Dory, we have identified the source of the money Lovell and Carver were embezzling, and even the connection with the mob," Wayne said, feeling elated and energized. Stifling the urge to hug her (she was still cranky about being awakened early and there was that pesky six-foot distance rule), he restricted himself to saying, "Really good work."

"And we have some more news for you, Billy Jo. The fox family is alive and well at their den at the bottom of the ravine," PD said and a relieved smile appeared on Billy Jo's face.

THIRTY-ONE

WAYNE WAS DRIVING TO THE SHERIFF'S OFFICE with Billy Jo's background on Eloise and Raymond Embry tucked in his pocket. They had gone by Rosedale Investigations so their little computer maven could do some further digging and print out her report. In addition to what she had found about Eloise Embry, she discovered that Raymond Embry had been convicted of racketeering in a big RICO sting run by the feds in the 1980s. PD was staying at the office to protect Billy Jo.

Getting out of his truck at the Sheriff's Office, Wayne almost shut the door before he remembered to grab his mask. No use irritating Mrs. Coffin when he might need her help.

"Good Morning, Detective," she greeted him in a muffled tone of voice from behind multiple layers of masks and a Plexiglas screen.

"Is Ben in?"

"He's in a meeting with some very official-looking men in dark suits. They are in the conference room with Detective Rob and the deputies. Shall I buzz Ben and tell him you are here?"

"Yes, please do," Wayne said. Official-looking men in dark suits sounded like the FBI to him. Sheriff Bradley and Detective Rob had been busy. He wondered if Carver had been picked up yet and whether Snake Wrist was still in custody.

"Ben said for you to wait. He's just about done. He's going to bring you up to date when they leave. He also said to remind you that . . ."

"I know. I'm not in law enforcement anymore," Wayne said. He thanked her and walked down the hall past his old office that now belonged to Detective Rob Fuller. He was so pleased with how things were going, he didn't even wince seeing Rob's nameplate on his old desk.

He was finally adjusting to his new role.

Sheriff Ben Bradley showed his visitors to the door a few minutes later. Once he and Wayne were seated in his office, Ben said, "Tell me what you know. I have to be careful what I reveal since men in suits are involved."

"I understand. What we know is that Ed Lovell was being paid for his services by Eloise Embry, the widow of a former mob guy, Raymond Embry, who served time for racketeering about forty years ago. The old gal is still alive and kicking. I assume those guys who just left are FBI?"

Ben didn't verbally confirm Wayne's assumption and instead asked, "What else did you guys dig up?"

"In addition to being partners in crime, Bradley Carver was Ed Lovell's attorney. I've had my suspicions all along that he was complicit in Lovell's death. Carver was the only person in the hospital room just before Lovell died. Has Rob found anything?"

"He is making progress. What else did you find?" Ben asked.

"Since Carver was the Executor for Lovell's estate, once Lovell was dead he had an opportunity to get all the money, both Ed's and Mrs. Embry's. You already know that Carver employed Snake Wrist to do his dirty work for them, including attacking Billy Jo. I assume he's still here on remand?"

"Damn it, Wayne, I'm sorry, I forgot to tell you," Ben said, looking frustrated. "Our local sleaze bag lawyer, Ramsey Tremaine, got Snake Wrist before a new and inexperienced Judge who tossed out the bullets and shell-casing evidence you provided, saying it couldn't be included since it had been provided by a civilian. He's been released until his court date. I'm sorry, Buddy."

Wayne shook his head. If only he had known, he might have saved the little fox's life and prevented the threat to Billy Jo. "I believe Snake Wrist has been out at PD's. He killed a young fox and left a note. It's serious, Ben. He's threatened Billy Jo's life. Maybe you can get a handwriting expert to determine if it's his handwriting," he said, handing the sheriff the note he'd put in a plastic evidence envelope.

"If it's his writing, it will definitely get him a longer sentence," Ben said. "I'll see to it that this is considered. And I'll upgrade the case from felonious assault to attempted murder. The note shows clear evidence that there's a continuing threat to Billy Jo. I'll have him picked up this morning, and this time the bastard's staying in jail. Where is Billy Jo now?"

"PD's with her at the office. We're not letting her out of our sight," Wayne said grimly. "Has Carver been arrested?"

"We questioned him before, and he's being brought back in today."

"I'm just thinking out loud here. The men in suits obviously can't charge Ed Lovell, since he's dead, but is his money at risk? I ask because Dory has jumped the gun by using Rosedale Investigations' credit card to fix up a house for Poppy Delaney, Teddy Lovell, and Teddy's grandmother. She assumed that the Lovell money would reimburse us."

"That woman is just ridiculously lucky because it might not be a problem. I don't know why, but my visitors seemed singularly unconcerned with Ed Lovell's estate," Ben said.

"They must know something we don't know," Wayne said. He was thinking he might know what it was.

"I assume so," the Sheriff said.

"Is there any reason I couldn't speak with Eloise Embry?" Wayne asked. In his theory of the crime, she could provide the missing piece.

"I probably shouldn't tell you this, but if you get to her right away, you could. The men who just left aren't meeting with her until late this afternoon. I'm not going to ask you why you want to talk to her and needless to say, I trust you will deny that we ever discussed this," the Sheriff said.

"Needless to say," Wayne said and grinned. Even with Ben's careful observation of confidentiality, he'd managed to confirm everything Wayne suspected. It was like old times, having the Sheriff trust him again. "Call me when Detective Rob is ready to tell us what he's found."

Walking out of the Sheriff's Office, Wayne hoped he could get one of his colleagues from Rosedale Investigations to go with him to visit Mrs. Embry, but Dory was still busy arranging things at the Delaney farm as well as getting Poppy legally appointed as Teddy's guardian. PD was guarding Billy Jo who was busy scheduling new cases and catching up on reports. He gave a brief thought to asking Lucy if she would accompany him to meet the elderly woman, but she was at work and he'd already asked her for a lot of help on the case. He would have to go alone. Billy Jo had given him a phone number for Mrs. Embry and he dialed it.

"Hello?" It was an old woman's voice, high and breathy.

"Mrs. Embry, my name is Wayne Nichols. I'm a private investigator and I wonder if I might come out to speak with you this morning."

"Goodness, I'm popular today. I assume this has to do with the appointment I have this afternoon with those men who were so secretive. I suspected they were international spies," she chuckled and Wayne decided not to disabuse her of the notion that he was connected with the feds. "Come on ahead, young man. I assume you know the address," she said.

"I do. I'll be there in about half an hour. Is there anything you would like me to bring? Coffee perhaps?"

"If you could bring me the secret of youth that would be good," she chuckled. "Otherwise just bring yourself."

THE MANOR HOUSE HAD BEEN CONSTRUCTED of huge blocks of gray granite and was three stories tall. Wayne knew, in days gone by, the household staff of maids, footmen, and cooks usually slept on the top floors. The second floor held the bedrooms for the owners. The rooms on the main floor were living rooms, parlors, or libraries. The kitchens were often in the basement. The property was large and the house was set back from the road, fronted by an immense, manicured lawn. As he approached the estate, he saw a fence with arched wrought-iron gates. He wondered if there would be a guardhouse, but as he drove up the gates opened silently. When he rang the bell to the front door, an old man with white hair in a suit and tie greeted him.

"You must be Mr. Nichols. I'm Hughes. I'll buzz Mrs. Embry and let her know you're here. She is meeting you in the library."

"Thank you, Hughes," Wayne said. He wondered if the man could be a butler. Eloise Embry seemed wealthy enough to be able to afford such a service.

He followed Hughes into an oval room with curved glass windows looking out on expansive gardens. The old white hydrangeas were in full bloom. Behind the house, the lawn stretched back until it reached a forest. Between the windows stood floor-to-ceiling bookcases. They were filled with books that looked so old they could be first editions. There was one section of the wall without a bookcase. That wall showcased a full-sized portrait of a man standing in front of a forest.

"I'll bring Mrs. Embry in now," Hughes said. Only moments later, he ushered her into the room.

The woman entered the room walking slowly. She used a cane, but her posture was faultless. She was wearing a pink beaded dress and carrying an armful of cut flowers. Her curly white hair framed her softly-wrinkled face with its rosy cheeks and bright blue eyes. Hughes came forward and took the flowers. She gave him some instructions before gingerly taking her seat in a small upholstered chair. Wayne was committing every detail to memory, Dory would expect a full report.

"You must be Mr. Nichols who called earlier, I'm Eloise Embry," she said. "You may be seated." She waved a hand graciously.

"Thank you so much for seeing me, Mrs. Embry. I have some questions for you but first, if it's okay I'd like to tell you a story. It's a true story about a little boy named Teddy who I saved from a deserted farmhouse."

"Lovely," she said, smiling and folding her small hands with their shining pink nails in her lap. She turned to the butler and said, "Coffee for two please, Hughes," she said. "Go ahead, Mr. Nichols, I'm listening."

Wayne told her everything pertinent about the case, ending by saying that Teddy Lovell was going to be living at the Delaney farm with his aunt and grandmother. He was concerned that her mind might wander, as the attention of elderly people often did, but her concentration was absolute. She was bright-eyed and entranced. She stopped him only once when he mentioned the men in suits.

"These men I'm meeting with later today, I assume they will want to discuss the source of Raymond's money. Am I correct?"

The old lady was sharp as a tack. "You are. Do you mind telling me how your husband made a living?"

"As you probably know, Raymond worked for the mafia as a young man. He was sent to prison for that. It was all before he met me. When he got out, he was penniless because the law took the money he'd been paid working for them. That's when I learned that profit from crime is confiscated by the law. Raymond went straight from that day on. I told him right from the start that I wasn't going to allow a man to court me who couldn't earn an honest living."

"Good for you. Could I ask about your relationship with Edward Lovell?"

"Mr. Lovell was my financial guardian and managed my money for over twenty years. In addition to inheriting my husband's money, I also inherited my parents' estate, so the total was quite large. I paid Edward Lovell handsomely for his services and I liked him. He brought Miss Delaney to meet me when they fell in love and said they were going to have a child."

"What kind of business was your husband in?" Wayne asked. He felt a touch of apprehension as he asked that question. If Mr. Embry's business was legitimate, as Eloise believed, she was in the clear. If it wasn't, the old woman could lose everything.

"My husband owned and ran a commercial tree removal service during our entire married life. That's why I had his portrait painted in front of a forest on the wall there," She gestured to the painting. "Raymond's company removed large trees and cleared commercial land. In those years, the area was developing rapidly and vast tracks of land needed to be cleared rapidly. Taking the trees down was a dangerous business and therefore very well paid."

"One last question, if I might. What was the connection between Mr. Lovell and his attorney, Bradley Carver? At the outset, I thought they were working together."

"They weren't. Mr. Lovell told me he suspected Bradley Carver of planning to embezzle my money. He had been investigating the matter and was prepared to turn him in. I'm certain he would have, had he lived long enough."

"Have you engaged someone new to manage your money now?" Wayne asked.

"Yes, before he died Edward invested all my money in bonds and mutual funds. The brokerage I use at his suggestion provides sound financial guardianship." She smiled and rose from her chair. "I've enjoyed your story, Mr. Nichols, and I am very pleased to have Mr. Lovell's children enjoy the money I paid their father over the years. Hughes will show you out."

"Do you mind not mentioning my visit to the men you are meeting this afternoon?" Wayne asked quickly. "Visiting you has been a secret mission on behalf of Mr. Lovell's son."

"I'm very good at keeping secrets, Mr. Nichols," she said. "However, in return, I'd like a picture of the little Teddy."

"I'll see to it," Wayne said, and taking her tiny arthritic hand in his while feeling like a chivalrous Sir Lancelot, he went down on one knee and kissed it.

THIRTY-TWO

B ILLY JO FINISHED HER REPORTS ON the concluded cases and called Hayley Drummond's office. She'd finally gotten Lexie to agree to meet Teddy. With the COVID-19 epidemic still impacting the hospitals, getting in to see the boy would require the help of an employee. Thus the call to Hayley.

"Community Mental Health, Hayley Drummond speaking," she answered.

"Hello. I'm Billy Jo Bradley and I am working with Dory Clarkson on the Teddy Lovell case."

"Yes, Miss Clarkson has mentioned your name to me. How can I help you?"

"I'd like to be able to have Teddy meet his sister, Lexie. Is there any way that could be arranged?"

"Teddy has been moved into a house belonging to the hospital that's used for families who are from out of state or need housing."

With a little sliver of worry in her heart, Billy Jo said, "Please tell me he hasn't been living alone."

"Certainly not. It's called Sparrow House and is our version of the Ronald McDonald house. Teddy had recovered medically and the pediatric ward was full, so the doctors asked that he be moved. There's a housemother for the facility, a Mrs. Mary Anne Brooks. She's been taking care of him. I've visited him once since the move and so has Dr. Juanita Marsh."

"Do you think Teddy would be up to meeting his sister?"

"I think so. There's a lawn behind Sparrow House and it has a swing and a slippery slide. Mrs. Brooks has been taking Teddy out there to play for an hour or two each day. There's also a picnic table. If you and Lexie could get here by noon and bring something to eat, you could join us." she said.

"That would be perfect. One of my partners, Detective PD Pascoe will be with me. Thank you, Hayley," she said. Setting down the phone she called Dory to give her the news.

"Rats! You're getting to see Teddy and I haven't seen him since the one night with True."

"I only got in because Teddy has been moved out of the hospital to Sparrow House. Hayley's approved Lexie, PD, and me coming to the playground to eat lunch. Could you join us if she says it's okay?"

Dory sighed. "No, darn it. I can't. I'm still here at the Delaney house with Mrs. Lovell. I've hired a firm to lay a walkway from the garage to the house. Landscapers are putting in some shrubs. Even if they get all of that done in time, Gramma Lovell and I have to go by Fred's garage in Rosedale and get Pansy's car. We're bringing the repaired vehicle out here for her and Poppy to use. It just isn't going to work for me to see Teddy today." She sounded discouraged. "You're not going alone are you?"

"No, PD's with me. I'm sorry you can't come, Dory. I'll take pictures. The grand reunion where Teddy is going to join Poppy and Mrs. Lovell at the farm is happening soon. You will see him then and you can bring True."

"I know. It's just that the waiting has been hard. Hope it goes well with Lexie and Teddy," Dory said and bid her good-bye.

BILLY JO RANG THE DOORBELL at Lexie's mother's house an hour later. PD was waiting in the car. They had already picked up sandwiches and sodas. When Lexie came to the front door, dressed in jeans and an orange UT sweatshirt, she didn't exactly look welcoming.

"Hi Lexie, we've been permitted to . . ." She stopped speaking seeing Lexie scowling and shaking her head. "What's wrong?"

"I've changed my mind. I'm not going. I just heard that Mr. Carver has been brought in for interrogation and that my father made a second will. The new attorney, a Miss Bon Temps, called to say that my father made provision for Teddy and whoever raises him to be fully funded for twenty years. That took a third of the money. The rest is split between me and Teddy. I get my money now, and he gets his share when he becomes an adult. I'm only getting a third of the amount I should have gotten."

"I can see how that would be upsetting, Lexie, but it is still a large inheritance. Your father made his decision knowing Teddy was very young. He hoped Pansy would be alive and able to raise him. Most of the time, a wife or a fiancé gets *all* the money you know. In effect, he split his estate three ways, a third for whoever raised Teddy and two thirds for his two children." Billy Jo thought it was fair and struggled to feel any empathy for Lexie.

"I don't care. I'm still mad at him and I don't want to meet the kid," she stepped back preparing the close the door in Billy Jo's face. She quickly thrust her foot in the opening.

"I don't know if you have thought about what Teddy has gone through, Lexie. He has lost both his parents, was left alone in a deserted farmhouse where he would have starved to death had Detective Nichols not found him, and now he's lost his ability to speak."

Lexie looked down and Billy Jo could sense she was getting to her. She opened the door a bit wider which relieved some of the pressure on Billy Jo's foot. "He can't talk?" she asked.

"He hasn't said a word since Detective Nichols found him. He hasn't even *cried*. When the nurses come at him with the needles, he just silently endures the needle sticks. They have taken vials of blood from him and he had never made a sound. Sometimes he even faints. Teddy is alone in the world now, both his parents dead and his sister isn't even willing to *meet* him."

"The DNA lab called me with the results this morning and there's a familial match He's my brother," Lexie said in a resigned voice. She was quiet for a bit before saying, "It's an odd thing. I have this funny needle phobia. I faint when I got shots, too." Billy Jo waited silently until at last Lexie said, "I guess he does need me."

"And I believe your father would be very proud of you today," Billy Jo said.

IT WAS THE DAY BILLY JO CALLED, "The Mother and Child Reunion," an old song by Paul Simon, even though they all knew Teddy would never see his mother again. He would have his aunt, though, and being his mother's identical twin would help him enormously. In time, given that he was so young, the two could even blend to become one in his heart. And he would have a grandmother, as Gramma Lovell was already living in the Delaney farmhouse. Poppy had visited the place with Dory but hadn't moved in as yet. That would happen today. The day had dawned clear and blessedly cool, with a light wind blowing from the north.

Dory was driving her new car, a late model navy blue sedan. Wayne was in the rider's seat and Billy Jo was in the back with Lexie Lovell. PD had begged off, his ankle still hurt too much for him to join them. They promised to take lots of pictures to show him.

"What happened to your little red sports car?" Wayne asked Dory.

"Decided I didn't like it anymore," Dory said. "And a sedan is much better for hauling two old duffers like you and PD around." Lately, she found herself feeling sick to her stomach whenever she drove the car, remembering that the car was the reason she wouldn't go back to the Delaney farm to take a second look around for Teddy. Trading it in during the pandemic had been complicated, but she prevailed. Getting rid of her red convertible had been an important part of forgiving herself. All that remained now was to hear Teddy speak and see him living with Gramma Lovell and Poppy.

"Can you tell me what you've found out about the case recently, Wayne?" Billy Jo asked from the back seat.

"Sure thing. First off, Sheriff Bradley has Snake Wrist, aka Jonesy Patterson, in jail again and he's staying put this time. That should make you feel better, Billy Jo," Wayne said.

"It does," she said.

"In terms of the rest of the case, Brad Carver was Ed Lovell's attorney, but they were never partners in crime. Carver was only using Lovell to get to Mrs. Embry's money. Your father, Lexie, was Mrs. Embry's financial guardian, managed her money, and paid her bills. Luckily, Lovell figured out what Carver was up to before he died and arranged to have the rest of the old gal's money moved to a reputable brokerage. Carver embezzled almost a million dollars from Mrs. Embry before he was stopped. I also suspect Carver of being involved in your dad's death, but there's no proof of that, although it's being investigated."

"Those men in suits you mentioned, were they FBI?" Billy Jo asked.

"No, they were from the IRS. Carver bought some very expensive toys with the money he embezzled, including a yacht, a huge house on the ocean, and several pricey vehicles. Carver was dumb enough not to show an increase in his income or pay taxes on his ill-gotten gains. The Sheriff called the IRS based on the list of those items in the book we found in Pansy's purse."

"So all the property will be sold, the taxes paid, and the money will be returned to Mrs. Embry," Dory said. "Wayne took a framed photograph of Teddy out to her yesterday. She was pleased and mentioned something about wanting to contribute to Rosedale Investigations. By the way, Lexie, I assume the bank told you that your dad's estate came to more than three million dollars."

"Yes, they did," Lexie said.

"That must have been extremely good news, right?" Billy Jo asked.

"It was, but a funny thing has happened. I was so focused on getting all dad's estate at the beginning. Looking back, I guess I wanted dad's money as proof that he loved me more than Teddy, but the money doesn't seem as important now. I'm happy to share it with my brother. I do have one question for you, Detective Nichols. Did you ever find out if my father was involved with the mob?" Lexie asked.

"No, he wasn't. Mrs. Embry's husband was involved with them many years ago as a young man, but that was all. Your father was planning to turn Carver over to the law. In my view, your dad was the real hero of this story," Wayne said.

"I don't think so," Lexie said firmly. "The last few days I've been thinking about all of you and what you have done for me. I was a real brat at the beginning, but Billy Jo kept nudging me toward Teddy and because of her efforts, I now have a cherished little brother. Detective Nichols, you saved Teddy's life. And because of your work, Dory, I got a grandmother in the bargain. You three are the real heroes of the story in my book."

THEY PULLED INTO THE PARKING AREA at Motel 6 where Poppy had been living during the time needed for her to complete her community service obligation. She was waiting outside, having packed her minimal belongings in a single battered suitcase. She got into the back seat with Billy Jo and Lexie.

"I'm glad you are up to this today, Poppy. We are all sorry about the loss of your sister," Dory said, remembering her phone call about Pansy's life coming to an end.

Poppy thanked them with a sad little smile.

"We all hope you will be happy living here," Billy Jo said.

"I will always miss my sister, but I'm relieved to be free again and starting a new chapter in my life. Thank you for all you did, Dory," Poppy said.

"I couldn't believe how fantastic the house looked after all Dory's work on the place," Billy Jo said.

"It's quite something all right," Wayne said, giving Dory a seriously irritated look. His partner had spent a bundle fixing up the house and while it looked like the money could eventually be reimbursed from the substantial sum Rosedale Investigations would earn from the case, it had caused a definite rift.

"When will Teddy be coming to the house?" Poppy asked. "I can't wait to see him."

"The plan is for Hayley Drummond and Dr. Juanita Marsh to bring him from Sparrow House in about an hour. We are all to stay back and keep quiet. Dr. Marsh told him that he will be seeing his Aunt Poppy today. I thought perhaps he shouldn't be told and hoped he might mistake Poppy for his mother," Dory said. "But Dr. Marsh said children are always better off knowing the truth."

"So, only Gramma Lovell, Poppy, and of course you, Lexie, are going to greet Teddy today. We don't want him overwhelmed," Billy Jo said.

They reached the turn-off to the lane and Wayne darted a quick look at Dory. Her sedan was wider than the sports car and he wondered if she would be worried about scratching the paint. She didn't say a word, though, just smiled calmly as they headed down the pot-holed driveway through overgrown blackberry canes that scraped against the car.

"Look at the blackberry bushes, you guys. They were covered with white flowers just a couple of weeks ago. Now the blossoms are completely gone and there are already berries on the canes," Billy Jo said.

"They turn from red to a shiny patent leather black before they are ripe. I remember my mother making blackberry syrup for me and Pansy when we were little," Poppy said in a nostalgic voice.

They parked the car in front of the garage and the three principals from Rosedale Investigations got out and stood by the garage. Lexie and Poppy walked down the newly installed sidewalk to greet Gramma Lovell who was standing on the porch. She was drying her hands on a small ruffled apron and the scent of freshly baked bread came through the open kitchen window.

An hour later, they heard the sound of a car coming down the driveway.

"It's them," Dory said and clutched Billy Jo's hand tightly. "All I want today is for Teddy to say something, *anything*. Even if he just laughs, it will be perfect."

"Why didn't you bring your dog?" Billy Jo asked.

"Runt wanted to come, but with all five of us in the car, there wasn't room. Once they get settled, I'll bring her out to play with Teddy," Dory said. They watched in excited silence as the car pulled in. Dr. Juanita Marsh got out and lifted Teddy Lovell from his car seat. She set him down on the far end of the stone walkway. He was dressed in dungaree overalls and a blue and white striped shirt. He wore blue socks and white sneakers.

"I got him that outfit," Dory whispered.

Poppy, Lexie, and Gramma Lovell stepped off the porch and waited. Standing at the other end of the walkway, Teddy looked all around. At first, he looked panicky and Dory had to grab Wayne's arm to keep him from running over to pick the little boy up when suddenly Teddy saw Poppy. The sun lighted her red hair and Teddy began to walk, faster and faster until he was running flat out, his arms fully extended like an angel's wings. Poppy stepped forward and reached out her arms. And at that moment Teddy Lovell, who hadn't said a single word in weeks, gave a happy shriek. "Mommy!" he cried. Then, only moments later, Teddy looked at her more carefully and said, "Aunty Poppy," and smiled.

Lexie walked over to stand beside Poppy. "I'm your big sister, Teddy. My name is Lexie," she said, handing him her teddy bear from when she was a baby.

"Sissy," Teddy said happily.

Billy Jo hummed, "The Mother and Child Reunion." Dory, Hayley, and Juanita jumped up and down in jubilant screaming.

Wayne took a deep life-saving breath, as if he had been trapped too long underwater, and managed, at last, to burst through to air. Seeing Teddy smile contentedly in Poppy's arms even brought the old Detective to tears. There wasn't a dry eye in the bunch.

THIRTY-THREE

AN HOUR LATER, DORY AND WAYNE waved goodbye and got into the car. The ride back to Rosedale was companionable and quiet. They had agreed that Billy Jo could stay with the group at the farmhouse that night. Since both Carver and Snake Wrist were in custody, she would be safe. As they entered the city limits, Dory asked Wayne where he wanted to be dropped off.

"I need to go back to the office. There's one piece of this puzzle I still want to put in its place. Sheriff Bradley and Detective Rob are meeting me there. PD is joining us. They indicted Bradley Carver yesterday for murder, but I want to know what evidence Rob was able to find. You look worn out, so you can drop me off there and go home."

"I think you have briefly forgotten that we are *partners*," Dory said, giving him an oblique look.

"Never, but you look done-in after the last few days we've had," Wayne said.

"I am, but being your partner is far more important to me than sleep," she said. "I'm with you. Always."

Wayne nodded.

SHERIFF BRADLEY AND DETECTIVE ROB were in a squad car in the driveway of Rosedale Investigations when they pulled in. PD pulled in behind them. Everyone walked into the building together and got seated at the conference table.

"Congratulations on finishing up the Lovell case," Sheriff Bradley said. "I won't spend time on small talk, though, because I know what you want to hear. Just one thing before we begin. We were able to find the gun Snake Wrist used to shoot at Billy Jo. Believe it or not, the idiot was stupid enough to have kept it under his pillow and the bullet you found at the red manor house matched the gun. A new judge is now handling the case and the shell casings and bullets are back in evidence. Go ahead now, Rob. This is your success story."

Detective Rob nodded, pushed his silver-rimmed glasses back on his nose, and began. "This was my first murder case as a solo investigator without you, Wayne. You could hardly have handed me a tougher one. As you know, Mr. Lovell's body was cremated."

"Without a body, it's usually impossible. Where did you begin?" Dory asked.

"I interviewed Carver first because he was the only person in the room with Lovell before the resuscitation team started working on him. If anyone contributed to his death, we all knew it would be Carver. When I called to say I had some questions, he immediately lawyered up. I found that interesting since he's a lawyer himself."

"But not a criminal defense lawyer," Sheriff Bradley said.

"Please tell me it wasn't Ramsey Tremaine," Dory said. Tremaine had been Sheriff Bradley's opponent in the previous election. As a defense attorney, he was looked on with derision by the staff of the sheriff's office, all of whom spent hours gathering evidence for crimes, only to have criminals released and cases tossed out through Tremaine's efforts.

"It was Tremaine, all right," Rob said with a grimace. "At first, I got nowhere, except to confirm your suspicions with my own. By then we knew Carver had embezzled over a million dollars of Mrs. Embry's money. He was arrested for that crime, but since it was a non-violent white-collar case, the judge released him on his own recognizance. He was ordered to stay in town until the trial and he has to check in with the Sheriff's Office every morning."

"Sound to me like you were walking down a blind alley," Wayne said, glancing at Dory and PD who smiled, recalling Billy Jo's title for the case. "What did you do next?"

"I talked with the ER physician who did the intake on Ed Lovell. Lovell was having quite a bit of chest pain when he arrived. He was a smoker and had high blood pressure in addition to a family history of heart disease. His father died of a heart attack. Lovell told the doctor that he was extremely stressed, having discovered that his attorney was embezzling large amounts of money from a woman he worked for.

The doctor thought the stress added to his risk factors and decided to admit him."

"Heart issues run in his family. His son, Teddy, has a heart murmur," Dory said.

"Go on, Rob," Wayne said.

"After that, I interviewed the nurse administrator for Cardiology, Susan Wolfe-Campion. She had been suspicious from the start that something wasn't right and was very helpful. It was Director Campion who ultimately pointed me in the right direction. An internal medicine resident from Vanderbilt was on service the day Lovell died. She was doing a research project and it was her research that led to the evidence that put Carver away."

Everyone was fully attentive now, leaning forward, eyes fixed on Detective Rob.

"What was she researching?" Dory asked.

"The disposal of medical waste," Rob said. At their dubious expressions, he added, "I doubted it would lead to anything either, but the resident was tabulating the number of syringes disposed of daily and came upon an empty vial of insulin. It stood out from the rest." Rob paused.

"An anomaly," PD said. Wayne and Sheriff Bradley nodded. Anything that stood out as unusual in a murder investigation always put Detectives on high alert.

"It turns out Bradley Carver is what they call a brittle diabetic. It's a type of diabetes which is characterized by wide variations or "swings" in blood glucose in which levels can quickly move from too high to too low," Rob said.

"Which means he had to be ready at all times to give himself insulin," Dory said.

"You're correct, and insulin, as I have learned, can kill. Carver had been well-educated about his disease and knew insulin was critical to managing his blood sugar, but when it was given to the wrong person or in the wrong dosage, it can be dangerous. He also learned it is virtually undetectable after death."

"How does insulin work in the human body?" Wayne asked.

"I got the ER doc to explain it to me. Carver had what are called multi-dose vials of insulin for his condition. Usually, he just drew up one day's dosage from the vial, but that day he must have drawn up multiple dosages and when he and Lovell were alone in the hospital room, he injected Lovell with it. A large dose of insulin causes a rapid fall in glucose levels which triggers a massive release of adrenaline. Adrenaline can cause an electrical disturbance in the heart as well as a loss of consciousness. When the nurse noticed Lovell was barely conscious, she immediately called for assistance and a whole team came into the room to work on him. They did the entire array of life-saving techniques, but weren't able to get him breathing again."

"I assume when the team came into the room to try to save Lovell they asked Carver to leave?" Wayne said.

"Correct, and right outside in the hall there was a cart containing material used by the nursing staff, and on top of the cart was a box for the disposal of syringes. Carver put his insulin vial in the unit. When the resident was tabulating syringes that day for her research project and saw the multi-dose vial, she checked the patients on the unit and nobody on the floor required insulin. It troubled her and she gave the vial to Director Wolfe-Campion."

"When you questioned him, he couldn't have denied the vial was his because his fingerprints would have been on it," Wayne said, thinking aloud. "How did Director Wolfe-Campion connect Carver with the vial?"

"She didn't until we talked. However, even lacking an explanation for the insulin vial, she considered it odd enough that she hung on to it. When confronted, Carver admitted the vial was his, but couldn't give us a satisfactory answer for why he disposed of it in the container for used syringes in the hall outside Lovell's room," Detective Rob said.

"I'm surprised he didn't just put it in his pocket and leave the hospital," Dory said.

"But if he had left then, he wouldn't have known whether Lovell died. That was his primary goal," PD said grimly.

"Whatever his reasons for disposing of the murder weapon in the hospital, when confronted with the vial, he confessed," Rob said.

"Well, there was a little more to it than Mr. Modest here is saying," the sheriff said. "Rob suspected that Carver was motivated in part by greed, but also by jealousy of Ed Lovell. Ed had a beautiful woman he was going to marry and a young son."

"Carver asked about Ms. Delaney several times during our conversations," Wayne said. "I wondered why at the time. It seemed odd to me. Go on Sheriff."

"Lovell was independently wealthy, due to his decades-long working relationship with Mrs. Embry. Carver's legal practice never amounted to anything and he couldn't even get a woman to go out with him more than once. Rob suspected jealousy but he needed evidence—which he found when he went through Carver's desk. In a locked drawer, he found many photographs of Poppy."

"There must have been a thousand of them. It was a stalker's stash," Rob said. "I got a warrant to search his condo and his bedroom walls were papered with photos of Pansy."

"Finding those pictures gave Rob the cudgel he used in the interrogation. He just kept pounding away at how inadequate Carver must have felt, how much he must have wanted Lovell out of the way to have Poppy for himself. That did it. Carver fell apart and burst out saying how much he hated Lovell, that Poppy was too good for him. When Rob pushed him to admit he had killed Lovell, he broke down and confessed."

"We all know that fantastic moment when the perp caves and confesses," Dory said.

"He's in jail now and will come up for sentencing soon for both embezzlement and murder," Rob said grinning proudly at PD and Wayne.

Everyone applauded and Wayne slapped him on the back feeling an unexpected relief. Rob had been the right man to investigate the murder. The killer had been caught, and he had kept his promise to Lucy.

THIRTY-FOUR

SUMMER WAS ENDING IN TENNESSEE. The Middle South lacked the brilliant fall colors of the northeastern states, but it had subtle indica-tions that promised the seasons were changing. Crispy yellow and brown leaves decorated driveways and sidewalks. They crunched when stepped on. Summer temperatures, which were often in the high nineties, had declined into the eighties. In summer, the color of the sky most days was a bleached white. Now it had reverted to a clear and cloudless blue.

The caseload for Rosedale Investigations had been steady ever since the Blind Split case ended. Dory, as CFO for the business, told the team they had emerged in good shape from the months when business was slow owing to COVID-19, and they were now in the black. To her sur-prise and relief, the office credit card balance had been paid to zero. No one seemed to know exactly where the money had come from, although Wayne suspected the deft hand of Mrs. Eloise Embry. PD had fully recov-ered from his sprained ankle and had been meeting with some big wigs in town, drumming up business. Billy Jo was finishing up her reports on the cases she called the Lesbian Lover and the Illegitimate French Child (the case of the WWII soldier who had a child with the French woman during the war). She has also been able to purchase a new computer and printer for PD for his home and Mark got it set up and working.

It was Friday and Wayne had nothing whatsoever to do. Lucy's birth-day was coming up and he had promised himself he would propose on her birthday. He'd even selected a place to take her. It was a high natural sandstone arch called the Sewanee Natural Bridge. The Bridge spanned fifty feet and was created from a giant sinkhole that had eroded to form the bridge. It was located in a designated state natural area. Once there, they could walk the trail and across the bridge. He decided he would stop at the apex of the arch to propose. When he discussed the plan with Dory, she reminded him that he had to kneel. His knees hurt too much, he said, but she said kneeling was obligatory.

He and Lucy had been a couple for almost five years and had lived together for three, but he still found himself thinking uneasily about what he would say or do if she said "no." He had been bringing the ring box with him everywhere, transferring it from trousers pocket to trousers pocket at the end of each day.

At four o'clock, Wayne said, "I'm taking off, people. I'm going to be out of the office for the weekend. It's Lucy's birthday and I'm taking her to a park for a picnic."

"Can we call you if something comes up?" Billy Jo asked.

"No," Wayne said and left the building.

Hearing the front door slam, Dory walked over to Billy Jo's desk. "Do you think he's finally going to propose?"

"Man, I hope so. One of these days that ring box is going to fall right out of the hole in his pocket and down to the floor."

"Fingers crossed she says yes," Dory said. "Provided all goes well, I think we should plan a get-together for Rosedale Investigations. What do you think, Billy Jo?"

"I agree. We've all worked hard this year. It will be good to blow off some steam. The band shell in the park is going to host a folk singer and backup band on Saturday evening. I'll leave a message for PD and we can make a food and drinks list. Luckily, the Mayor has opened up outdoor musical gatherings although they are restricted to fewer attendees."

SATURDAY MORNING WAYNE AND LUCY SET OUT for South Cumberland State Park. The would-be groom had almost chickened out when he checked the weather. Showers were predicted for the afternoon, but Lucy said she wanted to get out of town and was up for a trek in the State Park.

"Where are we going specifically?" she asked while directing him to highway TN 56.

"It's this natural arched bridge. You can walk to the other side if you aren't afraid of heights. The bridge is about three wide but at the highest point it's twenty-five feet in the air."

"How did you find out about this place?" she asked.

"I googled natural beauty spots in Tennessee," he said with a note of pride. It hadn't been that long ago when he had no idea how to look up things on the internet.

They parked the truck in a mostly deserted parking lot. The predicted rain had scared most people away. Lucy pulled the picnic basket from truck's back seat and they found a nearby table that overlooked the river where they could hear the sounds of the water running through a rocky gorge. Wayne had given Dory his credit card and asked her to produce a truly amazing picnic lunch. From looking at the receipt, she'd done him proud.

"Wow, this is some picnic, Wayne. Caprese bread and salami sandwiches, sliced Romano cheese, tomatoes, mozzarella, and fresh basil. And a pasta salad with feta, herbs, and lemon. Plus Ferraro Roche chocolates. Goodness! Open that bottle, will you," Lucy said, handing Wayne the wine opener.

He duly opened the wine and poured it into two plastic wine glasses. Everything was going perfectly, he thought . . . until he heard the thunder rumble. They finished eating just in time.

"We can eat the dessert in the car," Lucy yelled over the crashing of thunder. They put away the food quickly and grabbed the candy and wine for the car, dodging the raindrops.

Sitting in the car, sharing wine and chocolates Wayne realized there was no need to trek over a fifty-foot high bridge, no doubt slippery in the rain, and kneel on rocks. As the rain crashed down around the truck leaving them safely cocooned inside, Wayne pulled the ring box from his pocket. Lucy had turned away from him and was looking out the window at the dark wall of clouds approaching.

She said, "We better stay put for a bit until it blows . . . Oh, Wayne," her voice trailed off when she turned and saw the ring.

"Lucy, will you do me . . ."

"Yes, my answer is yes. Of course, I will marry you, Wayne Nichols."

Driving home as the storm moved through, they saw a rainbow. They hadn't walked across the bridge as Wayne had planned, but holding Lucy's hand with her diamond sparkling on her finger, produced in him an overwhelming and unaccustomed humility. Gratitude for the love of Lucy filled his soul. The woman was a Godsend and he was the luckiest man on earth. Peace descended and wrapped her gentle arms around him.

All four members of the Rosedale Investigations team were in a staff meeting on Monday morning. Billy Jo had been calling everyone who had made initial inquiries that got shunted aside during the Lovell case and making appointments.

"What have you got for us, Billy Jo?" PD asked.

"Are you going to let her attend a staff meeting in her pajamas?" Dory asked PD irritably, pointing to their young colleague. She was dressed in a long floral printed cotton-knit dress, jewelry, and heels and her hair was braided in a Caribbean style. She was leaving shortly for vacation, a trip with Al to his condo.

"These are not pajamas, Dory! It's a fleece top and matching pants. And before you give me grief for it, note that I am wearing shoes, earrings, and a silver cuff bracelet," Billy Jo said, rotating her wrist.

"Having dispensed with Billy Jo's attire, can we return to what's on the docket?" PD asked.

"We can. I'm not sure any of you remember, but early in the Lovell case, a woman called saying she had a painting she wanted us to look into. She inherited it from a cousin and thinks it's an antique," Billy Jo said.

"What does she think we can do for her?" Wayne asked. He was hoping the case would give him something to do soon. Otherwise, he was committed to going with Lucy to register for gifts she wanted as wedding presents. He felt since they already had a home that was fully equipped, they should put "no gifts" on the invitations. Lucy disagreed, saying it was a once-in-a-lifetime chance to get new sheets, bedding, and towels. Hers were threadbare apparently. He hadn't noticed.

"The owner's name is Mrs. Walcott. She wants to know what it's worth and the provenance."

"Provenance?" PD asked with a frown.

"That's the history of ownership for the painting. If it's as old and valuable as she thinks it is, the provenance will help establish whether or not it was stolen."

"What's the subject matter?" Wayne asked.

"It's a painting of children at the seashore," Billy Jo said. "She sent us a picture." She passed around her phone.

"More coffee anyone?" Dory asked standing up. She glanced out the window and turned back to the group with a brilliant smile saying, "I believe Miss Poppy Delaney, Teddy, Lexie, and Gramma Lovell are coming up the sidewalk."

They heard the doorbell ring and Billy Jo dashed to the entry. "Come in, come in. We're all here in the conference room."

They greeted each other. Dory ran her hand over Teddy's short curls. She told him that she would be bringing her dog out to see him again soon.

"We wanted to come by to thank all of you for getting us together. And for the house, we're enjoying it," Gramma Lovell said.

"How's it going for you, Poppy?" Wayne asked. He looked carefully at her. She was wearing minimal make-up, jeans, and a white blouse. She looked like a fresh-faced country girl, as far from a painted prostitute as it was possible to imagine.

"I'm still in therapy and Teddy meets with Dr. Marsh every week. He's going to start nursery school soon at the church in Appleton."

"How's Teddy's speech coming along?" Dory asked.

Poppy turned to the little boy and said, "Remember what you were going to tell Detective Nichols?" He nodded.

The whole room turned completely quiet as Teddy swallowed and then said, "Thank you for giving me back my Aunt Poppy, Detective."

"And Teddy has something to say to you too, Dory," Poppy said.

"Thank you for letting me play with your dog," he said.

"You are most welcome, little man," Dory said. She leaned down and kissed him on the cheek.

"I have something else to announce. I'm starting a job next week. I'm going to be the Parrish secretary for the church in Appleton," Poppy said. She was beaming.

"And I have gifts." Gramma Lovell reached into her tote bag and pulled out four glass jars filled with a dark purple liquid. "It's blackberry syrup from the laneway," she said passing them around.

"I helped make it," Poppy said.

"Me too," Teddy piped.

"Thank you. This looked delicious," PD said.

Wayne also has an announcement to make," Dory was smiling at her partner.

"Um, well . . ."

Dory interrupted him saying, "My embarrassed partner is dithering because he's pretty old for this, but he's engaged to be married to the lovely Dr. Lucy. None of us can figure what she sees in him, but all of you will be invited to the wedding."

As the group erupted in congratulations, Wayne went back in his mind to the evening he returned to the Delaney farm in the darkness and found a little boy who fought him like a wildcat.

"The rip in the Blind Split has finally been mended," Billy Jo said.

He nodded, remembering the long arching canes of wild blackberry bushes, lush with white flowers that smelled like violets, and the promise he had made to Pansy Delaney. Envisioning Poppy and Teddy skipping down the sandy lane in a shimmering cloud of scent, he hoped she knew the words for "Old MacDonald Had a Farm."

Lyn Farrell is the penname of Lynda Farquhar, Ph.D., the co-author of the Mae December mystery series which she writes with her daughter, Lisa under the penname Lia Farrell. She also writes YA fantasy, is a master gardener, an art sleuth always on the lookout for her famous grandfather's paintings, and a "dog mom" for Dezi, a Cavalier King Charles Spaniel who is jealous of her cell phone and tries everything he can think of to distract her from writing. She has two biological daughters, six step-kids and twelve grandkids. She is a retired professor emerita from Michigan State University.

CPSIA information can be obtained
at www.ICGtesting.com
Printed in the USA
LVHW042140221221
706965LV00014B/896